The Proof

Rich Goldhaber

This is a work of fiction by the author. All of the names, places, characters, and other elements of this written material are the products of the author's imagination, are fictitious, and should not be considered as real or true. Any similarity to actual events, locations, organizations, or persons, living or dead is entirely coincidental.

All rights to this work are reserved. No part of this book may be used or reproduced in any manner whatsoever without the written permission of the author, except in the case of brief quotations as part of critical articles and reviews.

Copyright © 2015 Rich Goldhaber

ISBN- 13: 978-1508824398

ISBN- 10: 1508824398

Acknowledgements

As usual, the author would once again like to thank a wonderful group of friends who have helped to make this novel better in so many ways. The following individuals are deserving of special recognition.

Kathlene and Lu Wolf have helped with editing and a critical review of this work. Their feedback is always on point and greatly appreciated.

Miriam and Luis Blanco's thoughtful comments added to the accuracy of this novel

Don Tendick's inputs have also added greatly to the accuracy of this story.

And as usual, Jeanne, my wife and chief editor, has continued to live up to her reputation.

Also by Rich Goldhaber

The Lawson Novels

The 26th of June

Succession Plan

Vector

Stolen Treasure

Risky Behavior

The four Roses

Other Novels

The Cure

These novels can be purchased at Amazon.com or Barnesandnoble.com.

Visit Rich Goldhaber's website at richgoldhaber.com

List of Key Characters

Ancient Israel

King Zedekiah: king of Judah
General Baruch: Israeli military commander
Ezekiel: Trusted minister to the king
Nebuchadnezzar II: king of Babylonia
Seraiah: high priest of Israel
General Nebuzaradan: Babylonian military commander

Principal Characters

Dr. Lisa Green: American archeologist
Ari Waldstein: architect
Professor Yehuda Bornstein: archeologist
Detective Moshe Stern: detective
Dr. Dalia Herbst: lead investigator in the Antiquities Authority
Detective Eli Fischer: Moshe Stern's partner
Professor Andre Braverman: historian
Professor Eli Gold: historian
Rabbi Friedman: Israeli scholar
Carol Winslow: astronomer
Director Jacob Berger: head of the Antiquities Authority
Uri Shafer: Ari Weinstein's best friend
Rachel Goodman: Prof. Bornstein's assistant

Israeli Defense Forces (IDF)

General Simcus: head of IDF
General Chaim Yidlan: head of Yaman anti-terrorist unit
Lieutenant Davis: General Yidlan's aide
Colonel Morty Weiss: leader of anti-terrorist team

Sammy: anti-terrorist team member
Abe: anti-terrorist team member
Jacob: anti-terrorist team member
Simon: anti-terrorist team member
Josh: anti-terrorist team member
Captain Morgan: lead Black Hawk pilot
Lieutenant Goldman: Haifa base security
Lieutenant Joseph: Haifa base bomb squad

Waqf Characters

Sheikh Muhammad Hussein: head of Waqf
Jamal Hashem: catacomb monitor
Imam Farouk Wadi: Islam scholar
Hakeem Kassab: head of Waqf security
Samir Salib: leader of Waqf soldiers

Bedouins

Saladin Abdul-Hamid: Bedouin
Malik Abdul-Hamid: Saladin's brother
Aziz Abdul-Hamid: Saladin's cousin

Mossad
Simon Levy: head of Mossad
Ruvain Lieb: Mossad lead operative

The Proof

Prologue

The 8th Of Av, 425 BC

The walled city of Jerusalem

King Zedekiah, the son of Josiah and a distant cousin to King Solomon, stood atop the highest tower of the rampart protecting the old walled city of Jerusalem. Baruch, his military commander and defender of the city, along with Ezekiel, his most trusted minister, were at his side. Nebuchadnezzar II, the King of Babylon, had laid siege to the city for almost thirty months. It was late afternoon, and the Babylonian army was once again preparing to advance their siege engines toward the Western Gate.

Previous attempts to break through the city's main gate had severely damaged the massive wooden structure, and attempts to reinforce the gate had proven marginal at best. General Baruch knew a well-placed blow from a battering ram would surely fracture the damaged cedar timbers.

The general looked at the massive machines designed to breach the fortified wall and knew the city would probably fall the next day. Food within Jerusalem was almost nonexistent, and the stores of weapons had been depleted during the lengthy siege.

Baruch turned to his king. "Tomorrow they will probably enter the city. Our engineers have strengthened the gate, but it will eventually fail. It's only a matter of time before the gate breaks apart. Their forces are too formidable. You must flee with the royal family. Once the gate fails, our soldiers will be able to hold off the enemy within the city for no more than a few hours, but then it will be over."

Ezekiel spoke. "Seraiah and his priests are prepared to remove the Holy Ark and the ancient writings from the city. With your blessing, I will have him execute the plan tonight."

King Zedekiah silently surveyed the land beyond the wall. The city of David and Solomon, the beloved city of his ancestors, was about to fall. Only a fool could not see the obvious. He would become the last king of Judah. Nebuchadnezzar II had made his intentions to destroy the city and exile the people clear. In the distance, Zedekiah could see the colorful banners surrounding the tent of the Babylonian king. Zedekiah knew his reign of eleven years was about to come to an end. He had mistakenly thought his alliance with Egypt would protect his country from the wrath of the Babylonian king, but Egypt, even with constant pleadings from Jerusalem, never committed its troops to breaking the siege.

Zedekiah turned to his Minister with tears in his eyes and issued his orders. "Have Seraiah remove our sacred objects. Remind him to carry out the plan exactly as we have agreed. I will take one hundred soldiers with me to protect the royal family, and we will attempt to reach Egypt. Order the people to flee through the hidden gate beginning tonight under the cover of darkness. Have your soldiers protect them as they leave the city."

As the king left the tower to assemble his family, Ezekiel rushed to the temple to inform Seraiah of the King's decision. The High Priest was waiting by the entrance. His own staff had already informed him of the instruments of war nearing the Western Gate.

10 The Proof

"The King has ordered your priests to remove the sacred objects from the city. He reminds you to carry out the plan exactly as agreed."

Seraiah left Ezekiel and joined his priests within the temple. The Holiest of Holies, the Ark of the Covenant, had been placed in a beautiful cedar crate. Alongside the ark, hundreds of sacred objects had been wrapped in protective fine white linen and placed in wicker baskets. Behind the sacred objects, thirty-three clay urns were lined up. Inside the sealed containers, the priests had placed all of the ancient scrolls containing royal decrees and other historical documents, some even predating the time of David and Solomon.

One-hundred priests had been tasked with saving all of the religious and historical records of the Jewish people. At Seraiah's signal, they began lifting and carrying the sacred relics. The procession entered a secret underground tunnel leading from below the temple to a point several kilometers away from the Jordan River.

As the last priest entered the tunnel, Seraiah fell to his knees and prayed to Yahweh for the safe journey of his priests. The High Priest had one additional task to complete. He walked to the most sacred room in the temple, the place where the Ark of the Covenant had been kept since the completion of Solomon's temple. He looked at the now empty altar where the Ark had rested and cried at the shame of what had caused its removal. Within the room decorated in gold and bronze, one final object remained; a simple clay urn. Earlier in the day, Seraiah had placed an important scroll inside the vessel and sealed the lid with bee's wax. He lifted the small urn, and carried it down into the catacombs below the temple.

He found the small alcove already prepared by his most-trusted men and placed the small urn within the space. Priests, who had been waiting for his arrival, quickly arranged precut stones to completely hide the precious urn. When the alcove was completely hidden, Seraiah used blood from a freshly sacrificed lamb to scribe a six-sided star on the wall above the hidden alcove. He said a final prayer and led the priests back into the temple.

One hundred camels waited for the priests at the exit to the tunnel. Two caravans formed, one carrying the sacred ark and other religious objects; and the second held the written history of the Jewish people. They moved off in separate directions, both caravans guarded by the priests. The priests looked back at their beautiful city of Jerusalem knowing they would never see their beloved families and homes again.

*   *   *

As dawn broke, King Nebuchadnezzar II and his cohorts, all dressed in silver and gold, left the royal tent and mounted chariots bedecked in the royal colors. Twenty-six-thousand Babylonian troops had moved into position during the night. The rising sun reflecting off of the soldier's metal shields was directed at the top of the city's massive walls where Israeli soldiers were blinded by the glare.

Four beautiful black stallions pulled the king's chariot forward onto the battlefield. King Nebuchadnezzar II rode with his eldest son at the reins. The king held his golden ceremonial sword high in the air encouraging his troops as his son steered the chariot to the front of the assembled forces.

Then, with a shouted order from his son, the horses raced in front of his main battle line to the shouts of approval from his soldiers. Following the royal display, the king's chariot moved to a more secure position at the rear of his troops where his generals awaited his arrival.

12 The Proof

General Nebuzaradan had made many attempts to breach the city's walls but without success. A change in tactics was required, and months ago he had ordered a series of fortifications be built around the walls of Jerusalem. His spies had already confirmed the Northern Gate to the city was the weakest, and because of the difficult terrain, it was defended with only a small force. A large battering ram, the largest ever used by the Babylonian military, was secretly moved under the cover of darkness into position behind the protective fortification overlooking the Northern Gate.

After conferring with his king, General Nebuzaradan gave final instructions to his senior commanders, who then left to lead their men into battle. The general looked to his king who gave the signal for the battle to commence. The general nodded to a soldier standing nearby who blew on a gilded ram's horn to signal the start of the attack.

General Baruch stood at the top of the tall stone tower above the Western Gate. He watched closely as the Babylonian force advanced slowly forward. A battering ram positioned at the front of the battle line was being pushed forward by two-dozen soldiers. Behind the ram, formations of archers readied their bows in an attempt to protect the soldiers pushing the siege engine.

The Israelites best archers were stationed near the gate. The height of the city's wall gave the archers an advantage of range, and at a signal from General Baruch, the archers released their arrows toward the soldiers pushing the ram. Many found their mark, and as wounded Babylonian soldiers fell to the ground they were immediately replaced by others.

The ram and battle formation moved quickly forward, and as soon as they were in range, the Babylonian archers began directing their arrows at the archers manning the wall. Their efforts were rewarded as many Israeli soldiers fell to the ground.

General Baruch had massed his troops behind the Western Gate. If the gate was breached, the battle would be won or lost at this very spot. The battering ram, now advancing at full speed, struck the center of the Western Gate at its weakest point. The timbers shuttered but held.

As the Babylonians moved the ram back to prepare for another blow, General Nebuzaradan nodded to a soldier who sounded three long blasts on his horn. The shrill sound of the horn could easily be heard above the roar of the battle. Strategically stationed soldiers repeated the three note blast on their horns until the signal was heard by soldiers hidden behind the fortifications at the Northern Gate.

As the main Babylonian force continued their diversionary attack at the Western Gate, the massive ram was quickly moved out from behind the protective fortification and advanced to the Northern Gate of the city. Archers protected the four-dozen soldiers who accelerated the ram to maximum speed. As the battering ram smashed into the massive gate, the Babylonian soldiers let out terrifying screams. The ten-thousand pound ram moving at almost nine kilometers per hour developed over 11,000 Joules of energy, and its pointed metal tip, directed at the weakest point in the gate, easily fractured the entrance's massive cedar timbers.

Encouraged by the opening created by the ram, the soldiers pulled the metal-tipped weapon back from the wall and once again advanced the ram. The second blow completely destroyed the gate. A soldier sounded a horn, and three-thousand warriors hidden behind a hill near the gate rushed the breach.

14 The Proof

Baruch, upon hearing of the Northern Gate's failure, diverted his main force to the breached entrance to the city. A two-hour hand to hand bloody battle for control of the northern section of the city resulted in the defenders being slowly driven back by the overwhelming number of Babylonian soldiers, who had now arrived from the Western Gate.

Understanding the battle for the city was lost, Baruch's troops set up a defensive perimeter around the center of the city to protect the women and children fleeing from the battle. His soldiers faced certain death, but they were fighting to give their families time to safely leave the city.

Meanwhile, thousands of residents had already passed through a secret camouflaged entrance near a wooded area east of the walled city. Tens of thousands fled the city as their sons and fathers fought a hopeless delaying action against the brunt of Nebuchadnezzar's forces now massing in the center of the city.

When the Northern Gate was breached, King Zedekiah and the Royal Family, along with one-hundred of the Royal Guards, entered the same tunnel used earlier by the priests. The Royal Guards had assembled dozens of chariots and carts at the exit to the tunnel to transport the King and his family.

As the King and his entourage were leaving the tunnel, scouts from the Babylonian Army spotted the small band of soldiers and the royal family. They quickly sent a messenger back to General Nebuzaradan who dispatched one-thousand soldiers to capture the king. They intercepted the royal party on the plains of Jericho where the Royal Guard fought to the last man to protect their beloved king, but outnumbered ten to one, the Israeli force was quickly overcome. King Zedekiah was taken prisoner along with the other members of the Royal Family, all of whom faced certain death.

Meanwhile, the Israeli forces defending the city had been driven back to the eastern wall, leaving the sacred temple open to attack. Nebuzaradan's forces entered the temple and confronted Seraiah and the other senior priests, who were quickly put to death.

Late in the afternoon the city was secured. Under orders from King Nebuchadnezzar II, the holy temple was set ablaze. The fire could be seen from as far away as fifty kilometers, and the fleeing residents of the city wailed at the visible destruction of their most revered holy site. King Zedekiah's words from the previous day would prove prophetic. He would indeed be the last king of Judah.

The priests in the two caravans fleeing the Babylonians with their precious cargo noted the date, the ninth day of Av on the Hebrew calendar, the worst day in the history of the Jewish people, the date of the destruction of the First Temple.

Chapter 1

Present Day

Tel Arad, Israel

Doctor Lisa Green sat in the sand in the middle of the afternoon with the hot sun beating down on her head. She held a small mound of sand in her right hand and let it sift slowly through her fingers and fall back onto the ground. She wondered whether in the history of mankind another person had ever touched these ancient grains of silica. It was possible of course that another person tens of thousands of years ago had also let these very-same grains fall through their fingers, but it was highly unlikely.

She looked around Tel Arad. What had brought her to this unlikely spot in the Negev Desert? Perhaps it had all started when she was twelve years old. She had been helping her father fix a broken fence on their 140 acre dairy farm in central Wisconsin. The auger they were using to drill new fence post holes had brought broken pieces of pottery to the surface.

After repairing the fence, she had stayed behind, and after an hour's work, she had managed to unearth a variety of ancient artifacts. Lisa showed them to her mother and father, and they immediately called the local school's science teacher.

A weekend visit to the University Of Wisconsin Archeology Department allowed her to show the artifacts to one of the professors. He instantly became very interested in her find, and a week later Professor Wilson and three of his students arrived at the family farm and began excavating what turned out to be an ancient Indian burial mound from the Woodland Period, about 300 B.C.

From then on, Lisa was hooked on ancient history and archeology. She received a B.A. degree majoring in Archeology from the University Of Wisconsin in Madison and then went to UCLA on a full scholarship where she completed her PhD degree in Ancient History. Money was tight at the university, so she was offered a position as an Adjunct Professor, with the possibility of getting a permanent position on the UCLA faculty as soon as the budget-crunch was over.

She had met Professor Yehuda Bornstein from the Hebrew University in Jerusalem at an archeology conference in Las Vegas three years ago, and they had become good friends and colleagues. He told her she was like the daughter he never had. Then, just as her teaching assignments for the spring semester were winding down, he had called her out of the blue. He had insisted that she come to Israel for the summer and work at the Tel Arad site he was managing.

He explained the ancient site was located west of the Dead Sea in an area known as the Arad Plain. The site was divided into a lower city and an upper hill which held an ancient temple dating back to the time of King Solomon.

The lower area was first settled around 4000 BC by the Canaanites who remained there until 2650 BC. The site remained deserted for over 1500 years until it was settled by the Israelites. The new residents fortified the area, building a citadel in the lower area and a sanctuary on the hill overlooking the garrison.

18 The Proof

The citadel was destroyed by the Babylonians around 580 BC. Several new citadels were eventually built, one on top of the other, until the area was once again destroyed by the Romans. During the Islamic period, the citadel was rebuilt until it was finally abandoned for unknown reasons around 861 AD.

In short, the area was a classical archeological site with new settlements being built on top of previous buildings, creating discrete layers of history, each with their own unique artifacts and stories to tell.

Professor Bornstein had explained the history of the area and the potential of the new site he had recently discovered. He told Lisa it looked like an entirely new settlement, and that was certainly exciting.

Lisa was sold on the idea in a minute, and she decided to spend the summer helping the professor explore the new area. She immediately bought a Rosetta Stone Hebrew language teaching program for her computer and studied the foreign language until she became conversationally adequate. After arriving in Israel and taking up residence at a nearby town, she had been assigned a four-square meter section to explore.

With her long golden wheat-colored hair and bronzed athletic body, she might have been confused with a Valley Girl, but her off the charts high IQ and Midwestern work ethic had created a woman who was nothing like the stereotypical dumb blond from California.

Lisa stopped daydreaming and got back to business. She took out her whiskbroom and brushed away another half inch layer of sand from her assigned area. A glimmer of reflected sunlight from the late afternoon sun caught her attention. She carefully brushed away some more sand and uncovered what looked like a piece of bronze jewelry. She lay down in the hot sand with her face close to the find and slowly whisked away the last grains of sand holding the ancient artifact captive for thousands of years.

Just as Lisa was about to remove the last of the sand surrounding her latest find, a shadow suddenly blocked out the sun. She looked up to see her friend Ari Waldstein kneeling down by her side. "My, my, Lisa, what have you found?"

"It looks like a bronze necklace," she said.

With the last of the sand removed, she took several pictures with her i-phone to document her find and then carefully lifted the artifact up out of its sandy prison. She held it up to the light and examined the piece of ancient jewelry.

"It looks like Ishtar, a Babylonian fertility goddess," she said, "but I found it at the 800 BC level, clearly during the Israelite period. Why would a Babylonian fertility Goddess be in an Israelite town?"

Ari held up the neckless and examined it closely. "Her boobs are too big, and I don't think she's very cute for a goddess."

"Oh Ari, you're just like every guy, only focusing on her boobs. She's pregnant; she's supposed to have big boobs."

"Well Lisa, it seems you've got an archeologist's dilemma. How will you find out the answer about why this artifact is at the wrong level?"

Lisa smiled, "Why by doing some more digging around. The answer to my question is lying somewhere in this sand, and it will only be a matter of time before I solve the riddle."

Ari smiled at her. He was an architect who was taking a few weeks off to study ancient architecture. Bornstein had assigned Ari to the remains of an old building, and he was trying to identify the materials used in its construction and eventually, if he was lucky, use a graphic computer program to reconstruct the structure.

Lisa asked, "Anything new on your building?"

"I was just coming over to tell you; I found a decayed wooden plank. I think it's cedar, and I think it's a support timber for the roof."

"So what does that mean?"

"The clay tiles just above the timber are cleverly designed to capture rainwater and direct it to a small cistern, and I can tell the way the tiles are designed that they could easily fit on top of timbers placed one meter apart. So if we can find more wooden timbers to allow for one-meter spacing, then I think I have all the information I need to reconstruct the building."

Lisa clutched the artifact in her hand. "That's great news Ari. I think Bornstein is in Jerusalem at his lab today. I'll send him a picture of what I've found."

Lisa attached a picture of the necklace to a text message, *look what I found*, and sent the message off.

Ari looked at his watch. "Come on it's almost quitting time. Let's check your find in at the administrative desk and take the early bus back to the dorm."

Professor Bornstein had arranged for housing at the Ben-Gurion University in Be'er Sheva for all the volunteers working the dig. The school was almost empty during the summer recess, and the university was happy to get the extra money.

After checking in her artifact, Ari and Lisa boarded one of the Land Rover SUVs for the twenty minute ride back to civilization.

As the dirty Land Rover maneuvered its way over the sand to the closest road, Lisa quickly dosed off after a hard day's work. Ari couldn't resist staring at her. Why was he falling in love with this young American? Lisa certainly had that California look about her, at least the parts he could see. She had developed a taut muscular build from years of surfing and jogging, but it was her eyes that Ari adored, large brown penetrating eyes that seemed to be able to see beyond Ari's veneer and look directly into his heart. The sand and dust all over her clothes only added to her natural beauty. There was only one problem; Lisa would be going back to California in another month, and Ari wondered whether it was really worth getting more deeply involved, only to be heartbroken at the certain separation. He reached over and gently touched her arm. God, she was beautiful.

As the SUV pulled up to the university dorm, six dirty and tired workers headed into the building for much needed showers and a well-deserved weekend off.

Chapter 2

Lisa spent almost twenty minutes in her private room's tiny shower. She watched the sand and dust flow down the drain. Working the dig was a tough dirty job, but there were rewards: her latest find, the sense of discovery, gaining a better understanding of ancient history, and of course there was Ari.

He had arrived one day at the site, and immediately captured her heart with his smile and easygoing approach to life. He was six feet tall, and had a muscular build; not the type of muscles she had seen at Malibu beach, but the well-balanced body of a professional athlete. He kept his naturally curly black hair a little on the long side, but it only enhanced his looks.

Lisa at twenty-six was ready to settle down and get married. Unfortunately, she hadn't discovered mister right, at least not until she met Ari. Ari certainly fit the bill, but somehow she couldn't see his moving to California or her staying in Israel. Nonetheless, her heart skipped a beat every time she was near him. She'd just have to let things play out; what will be will be.

While drying off in her room, there was a knock on the door. She wrapped her hair in a towel and put on her terrycloth robe. She opened the door to see Ari.

"Hi, how about a nice romantic dinner at the pizza place over by Allenby Garden?"

Lisa thought about the offer for a microsecond and said, "Sounds good; what time?"

"As soon as you can. I've got the keys to the SUV. Knock on my door when you're ready."

Lisa liked the idea of a dinner alone with Ari. He was always fun to be with, and she wanted to spend as much time as possible exploring their relationship. She picked out a bright yellow flowery sundress. Ten minutes later she knocked on his door, and they headed out to the parking lot. It took them another twenty minutes to fight the Friday night traffic before they parked near the restaurant.

They found a nice table for two in the corner, and Ari moved his chair close to hers. He held her hand in his and kissed it. "I wanted to have a nice dinner with my California beach bum," he said.

Lisa's phone rang. It was Professor Bornstein. "Lisa, I just got back in town, and I saw your text. What a find. What do you make of it?"

"I found it at the 800 BC level. So the question is what's the fertility goddess Ishtar doing in an Israeli settlement?"

"Well, I'm sure you'll figure it out. Congratulations on the artifact. Actually I called about an opportunity that I think you'll find interesting. Can we talk?"

"I'm having dinner with Ari over by Allenby Garden."

"Well Ari would probably be interested as well. How about if I join you for dinner?"

24 The Proof

Lisa could hardly say no. She shrugged her shoulders at Ari who had been following the gist of the conversation. "Sure Professor, we're at the pizza place just on the southwest corner of the park."

"I know the restaurant. I'll see you in thirty minutes."

After disconnecting, Lisa turned to Ari, "I'm sorry, he said it was important, and you'll find it interesting too."

Ari looked disappointed but pulled an extra chair up to the table. They ordered a bottle of wine as they waited for the arrival of the professor. While they were waiting, Lisa asked, "Ari, I still can't understand why you decided to use your vacation time to work at the dig."

Ari answered, "You already know I'm focused on city planning. Take the Old City in Jerusalem. As new buildings go up, how do we make them blend in with the existing architecture? So many of them look out of place, just glass, steel, and concrete. It's become a hodgepodge of architectural design. We have a lot to learn from ancient architecture: the Dorian columns of Greece, the Ziggurat pyramids of Mesopotamia, the arches and viaducts of Rome, the relief facades of the Egyptian temples. They all can be blended into today's buildings. That's what I want to see happen. I want people to look at the city and really believe they are seeing it like the ancients.

"So to answer your question, I'm really trying to understand ancient construction techniques. We can learn a lot from understanding how they created their cities, and working this dig lets me better understand how they did it."

Lisa smiled, "So when do I get to see your sketches; all architects have sketches?"

Ari laughed, "You'll have to come up to my apartment in Jerusalem. That's where I do all my work."

Professor Bornstein arrived on time with little recognition that he was breaking up a romantic dinner for two. The professor, who was in his late sixties, was a little overweight, probably due to his many years of teaching and sitting at his desk. His full grey beard added another five years to his appearance. He immediately sat down at the empty chair and engaged them in conversation.

He held up an old rusted iron key and said, "This is the key to a great adventure. Today the Head Rabbi in Jerusalem gave me this. It's the key to a gate of one of the most important catacombs under the Temple Mount. I've been trying to look at it for the last few years, and I finally got the key; but I promised to give it back on Monday. I thought both of you would enjoy exploring the catacombs with me tomorrow."

Ari said, "I've already seen the catacombs."

Professor Bornstein looked disappointed. "Ari, I promise you, this catacomb is unlike any you've seen before. It's not open to the public because parts of it extend under the Dome of the Rock, and the Arabs don't want anyone exploring the catacombs beneath their sacred mosque."

"Why is that?" Lisa asked.

Ari answered, "Ah, that's a political question Lisa. First, let me give you a little bit of the history, and Professor, correct me if I get any of this wrong."

Bornstein smiled, "I await your understanding of our history. There's an old Jewish expression, *if you ask any two Jews about the history of the Jewish peo-*

ple, you'll get three answers. So, I will listen with great interest to your explanation."

Ari began, "It all starts with Jewish tradition. It is believed the Temple Mount is the place where God gathered dust to create Adam and where Abraham nearly sacrificed his son Isaac to prove his faith. The Bible states King Solomon built the First Temple there, only to have it destroyed by the Babylonian King Nebuchadnezzar II who sent the Jews into exile.

"Muslims believe it was on the Temple Mount that the Prophet Muhammad ascended to heaven on the back of a winged horse, and they commemorated the event by building the Dome of the Rock and other mosques on the site."

Lisa asked, "I know the history but you said it's a political question."

"I'm only giving you the history so you can understand the politics. Today, because of the history, both Israelis and Palestinians lay claim to the Temple Mount. Muslims deny Judaism's historical and religious ties to Jerusalem and the Temple Mount. After the 1967 War, Israel maintains security and legal control over the Temple Mount, and a Muslim organization called the Waqf has religious, economic, and administrative control."

Lisa asked, "Who's the head of the Waqf?"

Professor Bornstein answered, "That would be Sheikh Muhammad Hussein, the Grand Mufti of Jerusalem."

Ari continued, "So now Lisa, the story gets interesting. Every time peace talks have taken place, one of the main sticking points is who controls Jerusalem and specifically the Temple Mount. The Palestinian negotiators have always taken the position that they have the historical right to Jerusalem and the Temple Mount, and to make this argument they insist the First Temple built by Solomon never existed, and even if it did, it certainly was never built on the Temple Mount."

Bornstein interrupted, "Of course they never permit any archeologists to investigate the site because they know those excavations will uncover evidence of the existence of the First Temple. Every time the Israeli Government attempts to do any excavations near the Temple Mount, the Arabs riot and demand that the work be suspended."

Ari continued, "So peace between Arabs and Jews can never be made until the status of the Temple Mount is resolved, and I don't think that will ever happen, at least not in my lifetime."

Bornstein laughed, "Ari, I can't believe it, but I actually agree with you."

Lisa said, "So a trip to these catacombs sounds like an exciting adventure."

Ari said, "You've convinced me Professor. I'm up for the trip. What time do we leave for Jerusalem?"

Professor Bornstein said, "Let's leave early tomorrow at six o'clock. That way we'll have plenty of time to explore the underground tunnels."

Bornstein ordered another bottle of wine, and after a brief argument regarding the toppings for their pizza, Ari and the professor delighted Lisa with some of the old biblical stories of the history of the Temple Mount and the underground catacombs.

Chapter 3

Early the next morning Lisa dressed in comfortable beige cargo shorts and a white t-shirt. She added a windbreaker because Ari said the catacombs would be cool and damp. The trio left Be'er Sheva a little after six o'clock in Professor Bornstein's aging Jeep Wrangler. They avoided the direct route along Highway 60, because that road passed near Hebron in the West Bank, a hotbed of radical Arabs known for their desire to attack Israeli travelers. Instead, they took the Yitzhak Rabin Highway north toward Haifa and then turned east on Highway 1 leading directly into Jerusalem.

As they moved north from Be'er Sheva, the barren landscape slowly transformed into green farmland. Large pasture land for cattle and sheep, and beautiful citrus groves covered the landscape.

Extensive irrigation systems pulling fresh water up from deep aquifers had transformed useless desert land into rich productive farmland. The particular area they were driving through was famous for Jaffa Oranges that were shipped throughout the world.

Farmland slowly gave way to small towns as they approached the capital of Israel. It was Saturday, the Jewish Sabbath, but congestion was still building as they approached the Old City. Orthodox Jews were out on the streets walking to morning services at the many synagogues, but the majority of Israelis, who weren't very religious, were out in their cars getting an early start to a weekend.

Professor Bornstein parked his car just off Via Dolorosa in a large public parking lot, and the three set off on foot. As they walked, Bornstein explained how this catacomb was discovered. "An Arab family owned a small fresh produce store for many generations. Five years ago the owner of the store died, and the man left the store to his nephew who evidently knew nothing of the entrance to the catacomb. It was hidden behind some old crates in the basement. He sold the store, and a Jewish couple bought it and discovered the entrance when they were renovating the place before it opened. They understood the importance of the discovery and showed it to Rabbi Strauss. It's been kept a secret ever since."

As he finished his story, they arrived at the storefront. Neatly arranged stacks of fresh fruit and vegetables created a beautiful invitation to passersby, and a number of shoppers were walking the aisles picking out the best of what the shop had to offer. Professor Bornstein talked to the manager in the back of the store, and the man led the three down a steep staircase leading to the basement. He moved aside a shelf used to hide the entrance and exposed an old iron gate. It was only about one meter in height and two meters wide, certainly not the kind of entrance Lisa was expecting.

Bornstein unlocked the entrance with his key and opened the gate which protested with loud squeaking from its little-used hinges. The manager handed each of them large flashlights and bid them shalom as he returned to his customers.

Ari bent down and directed his flashlight into the dark void. "There're stairs leading down about ten meters; let me go first to take a look. He quickly passed through the small entrance, and his head emerged from the opening a few minutes later with a smile on his face. "There's a long tunnel at the bottom of the steps. You need to be careful on the steps, they're very steep, but once you get to the bottom, everything's fine."

Ari helped Bornstein and then Lisa through the opening, and then all three carefully walked down the steps chiseled in stone with only their flashlights guiding them. At the bottom they regrouped. Lisa's first reaction was the smell. The place was damp and musty. It reminded Lisa of her parent's basement back in Wisconsin after an all-day rain. She zipped up her jacket to keep warm. As she looked around, she noticed the immense size of the tunnel leading away from the steps. It was at least five meters in height and almost ten meters wide.

Ari ran his hand along a wall. "See these tool marks along the wall. This was a quarry. The limestone here is called Royal Limestone because the color is almost pure white. It's a rare color and the stonecutters would have extracted the material for the face of the temple they were building."

Bornstein added, "But these tunnels were used for more than the quarrying of limestone. I'm betting we'll find cisterns used to retain drinking water underground. Water was a precious commodity back then."

Lisa pointed her flashlight down the tunnel, and all she could see was the tunnel wall for another twenty meters. Then everything just turned pitch-black.

Bornstein wanted to map the catacomb. No drawing of these subterranean tunnels had ever been made, and he had promised the rabbi to provide a detailed drawing of the entire catacomb. For the purpose, he had carried a backpack containing a surveyor's walking wheel used for measuring long distances and a compass to plot the changes in direction. He had also brought along a few dozen large Ziploc bags to collect any interesting artifacts they might discover along the way.

After assembling his surveying wheel, he began writing in a small notebook. They began their exploration by heading almost directly north along a straight line. At the 367 meter mark the tunnel turned ninety degrees to the right and headed east. Bornstein made a note in his notebook and reset the surveying wheel to zero. He said, "If we continue on this path, we'll be passing under the Dome of the Rock in less than one kilometer."

Lisa was the first to notice the red six-sided star on the wall about two meters above the floor of the tunnel. Professor Bornstein became very excited and dropped his instrument in order to take a closer look. "It's not a drawing; it's a mark of some kind. It's too crude to be a drawing. You can tell it was painted on the wall quickly, without much attention to detail."

Ari asked, "If it's a mark, then what does it mean?"

Bornstein said, "I don't have a clue."

All three looked around the tunnel trying to identify something that might help explain why the mark had been placed on the wall, but nothing seemed unusual. Lisa took a picture with her i-phone, and the three continued on their journey. At the 1356 meter mark they came to a large opening in the tunnel, and just as Bornstein had predicted, a large circular cistern over five meters in diameter was located in the center of a large room. The height of the ceiling at this point reached almost ten meters. They continued on after the professor had noted the shape of the room in his notebook. He reset his instrument, and after another 113 meters, they came to another large circular room with two tunnels leading off in different directions. One exit turned to the left, and the other exit continued on in a straight line.

This room had a spherically shaped dome ceiling extending up almost ten meters above the floor. Ari pointed to some large cracks in the face of the ceiling. "The roof in this room is very unstable. Look at the size of those cracks. I'm surprised it's held up so long."

Bornstein wanted to continue in a straight line further under the Dome of the Rock. He suggested they could map the other tunnel on their return trip. With the decision having been made, the three entered the tunnel in front of them.

Lisa asked, "How were they able to cut these tunnels?"

Ari answered, "Actually limestone is pretty easy to quarry. Using crude picks and chisels, they would have started at the top of the tunnel and created a horizontal gap across the width of the tunnel. Then they would have chiseled out another gap lower than the first and wedged wooden beams into the lower gap and wet the beams. The wet wood would expand and fracture the rock. You can see the limestone along the walls has been formed into horizontal layers, and as the stones were fractured, they tended to break apart along these lines. Using this method they could easily break free stones of over a half meter in height. Then they would cut the stones to size after they were transported out of the tunnel. If you look at the floor, you can still see small pieces of the limestone left after the stonecutters worked on the stones."

After leaving the room with the domed roof, the three walked another 267 meters and stopped at a second cistern containing water. They sat down against a wall and shared a bottle of water Professor Bornstein had brought in his backpack.

Lisa was the first to notice the change, a strange feeling in the pit of her stomach. Unfortunately, she knew the feeling all too well. Before she could voice the warning, the ground began to shake, slowly at first but building in intensity until the tunnel's walls seemed to sway back and forth. Luckily the three were sitting down as the tunnel shook in defiance at the violent geological attack.

Suddenly a thundering crescendo of noise reverberated along the catacombs. Bornstein screamed, "My God, it's a bomb!"

Lisa screamed back just to be heard. "No, it's an earthquake. I'm from California, and I know an earthquake when I feel it."

Dust, dormant for centuries, suddenly filled the tunnel as the rhythmic vibrations continued. What seemed like minutes was in actuality only forty-three seconds. The calm after the storm was of little comfort.

Ari directed his flashlight back where they had come from. "I think the roof in the last chamber collapsed. I told you it was very weak."

After waiting a few minutes to be sure the event had passed, they slowly stood up and examined each other for injuries. Fine dust particles now suspended in the air made visibility difficult. Without a word being exchanged, they knew they needed to leave the catacombs quickly before the usual aftershocks arrived.

They began walking quickly back toward freedom. Upon reaching the chamber with the spherical dome roof, they were denied entrance. The entire roof had collapsed, and hundreds of tons of rock blocked further progress.

Ari climbed to the top of the rubble and tried to find a pathway to freedom. "There's no way we can get past this area. It's totally blocked off. Once the roof collapsed, the limestone above the ceiling fell down with it."

The three stood at the bottom of the pile of rocks and thought about the implications. With their escape blocked, there seemed to be only one possibility; continue along the tunnel in the direction they were going and hope for another exit to appear. Lisa asked, "Did the rabbi say if there was another way out of the catacombs?"

Professor Bornstein answered, "I never asked him. I was too excited just to get the key."

Ari said, "So let's move quickly to see if there's another way out."

There was no argument. That seemed like the obvious thing to do. They began walking at a brisk pace with Ari carrying the professor's backpack.

With Lisa leading the way with her flashlight, the three walked quickly along the tunnel which continued in a straight-line. Eventually the tunnel split into two directions. They decided to stay together rather than split up. The first tunnel quickly led to a dead-end. The three backtracked and began exploring the second tunnel. It led to a large room with a large circular pit in the center and no other exit.

Ari said, "They must have been digging another cistern but never finished."

They sat down against the wall and contemplated their fate. They were trapped. They had seen nothing to suggest any other opening to the outside world. It seemed their only option was to try and remove the rocks blocking their way back to the fresh produce store.

They walked back to the debris at the entrance to the domed chamber knowing full well that the task of removing the blockage might prove impossible. Bornstein said, "I'm sorry I ever asked you both to come with me. I'm getting old, and I can accept that this will be the end, but both of you have years ahead of you."

Lisa interrupted him. "Stop that talk; we all agreed to come. None of us expected this." To change the subject, she said, "I thought earthquakes were rare in Israel."

Ari answered, "They are. We had a very small one back in 2013. The last major one was back in 1927, and a couple hundred people died. The epicenter was by the Dead Sea."

They arrived back at the pile of rocks blocking their path. Ari climbed to the top of the heap and began handing rocks down to Lisa who passed them along to the professor who dropped them to the ground. They worked silently, and after twenty minutes they took a break. Lisa climbed up to the top of the pile and looked into the mass of rocks with her flashlight. There seemed to be no end to the rubble blocking their escape.

Professor Bornstein said, "I'm sure the store manager will report that we're missing. They'll be looking for us, won't they?"

Lisa told Bornstein the truth. "My experience in California is that it's a triage game. We'll probably be at the bottom of the priority list. They'll be focused on helping the people easier to get to."

The three sat down against a nearby wall and rested. Lisa suddenly became thirsty. She reached into the professor's backpack and removed another bottle of water. There were six left. She opened the bottle, took a sip, and passed it around to the others. Looking at the water brought her mind back to the cistern. She asked a question. "Ari, these cisterns, are they all interconnected or is each a stand-alone water collection system?"

Ari smiled and answered quickly, "Yes, they're almost always interconnected. That way, as one cistern is filled, the water can flow to the next cistern. I know what you're thinking. And maybe that's a way out."

Bornstein asked, "What are you talking about?"

Lisa answered, "If that cistern back in the tunnel is connected to the one closer to the way we came in, then maybe we can bypass the rubble."

All three retraced their steps and then gathered around the cistern with renewed hope. The water level was about three meters below the floor of the tunnel, and two horizontal shafts were cut into the cistern's wall; one leading back in the direction of the first cistern they had encountered, and another leading off in a different direction. The horizontal shaft leading back in the direction of the first cistern appeared to have less than a meter of air space above the waterline.

Ari said, "I'll go down and check out the shaft."

"Wait," Lisa said, "we need to make sure you can get back up."

She opened the backpack and removed everything. The only thing of value was the surveyor's wheel, and it was only one meter long. She attached one of the straps on the backpack to the surveying wheel. If she held onto the backpack and lowered it into the cistern, it just might be long enough to allow Ari to climb back up.

With no time for modesty, Ari removed his shirt and pants, and with Lisa's and the professor's help, he lowered himself into the cistern. He finally let go of the wheel and dropped into the water. Lisa dropped a flashlight into his hand and he swam over to the entrance to the horizontal shaft.

He disappeared into the small tunnel and inspected the possible escape route. The shaft was just tall enough to be able to stand up, and there was about half a meter of air space. As Ari looked down the shaft, he realized the key to escape might be the engineer's ability to build a perfectly horizontal tunnel. He walked slowly along the shaft for about one-hundred meters. The air space seemed to be holding steady. Ari thought about the risk. If they didn't take a chance what was the alternative? He agreed with Lisa; waiting for rescue from the outside wasn't realistic. He reluctantly knew this would be their best chance of escape. He turned around in the narrow shaft and headed back toward the others.

Ari provided a quick summary of his findings, and all three agreed to risk the attempt. Together, they planned the logistics. They would strip down to their underwear and place their clothes and phones in the large Ziploc bags the professor had brought to hold the artifacts. When they arrived at the next cistern, Ari would lift Lisa up onto the floor of the catacomb. Then Lisa could once again use the backpack and surveyor's wheel to lift Ari and the professor to freedom.

Lisa and the professor took off their clothes and sealed everything of importance in the Ziploc bags. Bornstein in a moment of humor said, "You both have fancy underwear, but I'm wearing what you Americans call tidy whities."

Lisa laughed, "At least you're not going commando."

Bornstein asked, "What does that mean?"

"Going commando means not wearing any underwear."

Bornstein laughed, "Oh, you wouldn't want to see that."

They were finally ready to try their luck. Ari eased himself once again into the cistern, and with Lisa using the backpack to lower Bornstein, the professor finally jumped into the water. He came up screaming. "Ari, why didn't you tell me it was so cold?"

Ari laughed, "If I told you, you might not have jumped."

Lisa took aim and carefully tossed the backpack down to Ari, and he easily caught it.

Now it was Lisa's turn. Dressed in Victoria's Secret's finest, she sat on the edge of the cistern and dropped into the pool of water. The water was cold, but not much worse than what she was accustomed to while surfing in the Pacific Ocean.

Lisa led the way with the flashlight followed by Bornstein and then Ari with the backpack. From Bornstein's notes, they knew they had about 400 meters to travel. Lisa figured the water temperature was close to fifty degrees. She knew they had about thirty minutes before they would start feeling the effects of hypothermia. On the positive side, they only needed to travel about the length of four football fields. She advanced steadily along the shaft, making good progress, a little less than one meter with each step. Five hundred steps seemed like a relatively short distance. There was one negative, and it was a big negative. The air space above the water was becoming less as they proceeded along the shaft. They each saw the narrowing gap, but no one said anything.

Lisa had been counting the steps and when she reached five hundred she said, "We should just about be there by now."

Ari answered, "I've been counting the steps myself, and I agree."

The professor was starting to shiver. Lisa knew they needed to reach the cistern soon or they'd never make it. As she shined the flashlight along the shaft, she saw a disturbing sign. The shaft appeared to end, or at least the air space stopped abruptly.

Upon reaching the obstacle, Lisa reached down underwater and could feel the shaft continuing on a half-meter below the surface of the water. The three discussed the problem. Ari and Lisa agreed; they must be very close to the cistern they were trying to reach. Lisa looked at the professor and knew they needed to reach their destination in the next few minutes.

Lisa said, "I'm a good swimmer. I'm going to swim ahead and see if the shaft opens up again."

"Be careful," Ari said. "Make sure you allow enough time to get back here if you have to. Take a flashlight with you. They look like they're waterproof. "

He pulled out a second flashlight from the backpack and handed it to her. Lisa turned on the flashlight, took a few deep breaths, and then disappeared underwater. Lisa kicked forward holding the flashlight in front of her. Lisa was an excellent swimmer and knew she could easily swim the length of a fifty meter swimming pool underwater without any problems. Of course this wasn't as easy as swimming in a pool. She kicked using a steady stroke with her arms extended forward and the light from the flashlight showing the way. Lisa thought about the halfway point, the point of no return. By holding the flashlight in front of her body, she wasn't able to use her arms to pull her through the water.

By the time she thought about turning back, she had already passed the point of no return. Now it was a question of survival. Her lungs were starting to burn. Lisa dropped the flashlight so she could increase her speed. A feeling of desperation turned to pure panic, and then she suddenly emerged into a large circular pool. She kicked to the surface and gulped down the musty air.

She had reached the cistern. After resting a few minutes, she again submerged and headed back to the others. Without a flashlight, she had a more efficient stroke, and she burst to the surface with a smile on her face in front of a startled Professor Bornstein. "The cistern's ahead."

Bornstein asked, "How far do we have to swim underwater?"

"About sixty meters," Lisa answered.

Bornstein looked sad. "I can't make it. I'm not a very good swimmer, and sixty meters underwater isn't in the cards. You'll have to go on without me."

Lisa looked at her friend. "Professor, we're not going to leave you here. We're all going to get out of here together. We won't leave you behind."

Ari said, "I have an idea. He reached into the backpack and took out two large Ziploc bags and opened one. "Professor, if you hold this bag over your head, it will hold enough extra air for you to breath, certainly enough for you to go sixty meters. I'll do the same. We can do this together."

Bornstein thought about the possibility. Finally he said, "Well I guess I can die here from hypothermia in an hour or die a quicker death from drowning. Either way I'm dead, so I'll give it a try.

Lisa swam ahead of the others. Professor Bornstein followed holding the inflated bag open over his head like a deep-sea diver's helmet, while Ari did the same. The water pressure tried to collapse the plastic bags, but the water wasn't very deep, and both Ari and the professor were easily able to keep their plastic helmets open.

Ari's job was to make sure the professor made it to the cistern. Lisa, not encumbered by the flashlight, moved quickly through the water. With plenty of air still in her lungs, she grabbed the flashlight as she passed over it and finally reached the cistern. Lisa dove down again to help pull the professor through the last five meters of the shaft. Ari, who was down the longest without air, gasped for air as he finally lifted off his helmet and surfaced.

The three hugged each other as they rested before the final climb to the top of the cistern. As the professor treaded water, Ari stood on the edge of the horizontal shaft they had just swam through and lifted Lisa onto his shoulders. She tossed the backpack up onto the floor of the tunnel but wasn't quite tall enough to reach the top with her hands. Ari carefully balanced Lisa as he repositioned her feet into his hands. He then lifted Lisa up, all 126 pounds of her. Her fingernails scraped along the stone floor until she was finally able to grab onto an elevated section of the tunnel's floor. She pulled herself up and placed her arms over the edge of the tunnel; and as Ari pushed her vertically with all his strength, she scrambled up over the edge of the cistern and took out a flashlight from the backpack. She quickly scanned the tunnel in both directions. "It looks clear from up here. I think we can make it."

The professor replied, "I'm not as nimble as I once was. I hope I can make the climb."

Lisa hung the backpack with the attached surveyor's wheel over the edge of the cistern. Ari nested both of his hands together, making a place for the professor's foot. The aging Bornstein balanced himself in Ari's hand, and as Ari lifted him out of the water, he reached for the extended backpack. He grabbed it and with Lisa pulling and Ari pushing his legs upward, the professor finally pulled himself to safety.

Now it was Ari's turn, but even with Bornstein and Lisa extending the backpack as low as they could reach, it was still a good two meters away from Ari's extended hand. They needed to find a way to lower the backpack. Lisa took her jacket from a Ziploc bag and tied it to the backpack. Ari tried to reach the extended lifeline, but he was still a good half-meter short of being able to reach the surveyor's wheel.

Lisa had an idea. She told the professor to remove the shoelaces from his gym shoes. She did the same, and Ari threw up his two gym shoes to help out. By the time she was finished, she had used her best hair braiding technique to fashion a rope a half-meter long with a loop in one end. She tied the other end to her jacket. She and Bornstein then lowered the backpack once again. This time Ari was able to jump up and grab onto the makeshift noose. With Ari holding on, it was now only a matter of Lisa and the professor pulling him up to safety. Easier said than done. Ari weighed almost 195 pounds and was just too heavy for the two to lift. It was all they could do to hold the straps of the backpack steady while Ari tried to climb up the makeshift ladder. Luckily, Lisa was able to brace herself against a raised section of the tunnel's floor, and Ari slowly pulled himself upward and finally slipped over the top of the cistern.

They had made it, all three of them, but they were absolutely exhausted and they rested for the next few minutes. Finally Lisa said, "I don't know about the two of you, but I'm getting dressed. You've both seen too much of me already."

Although the backpack was soaking wet, the Ziploc bags had kept all of their clothes dry. They slowly dressed and began walking toward the gate leading to the produce market.

Lisa was the first to notice the stones littering the floor of the tunnel. She didn't think it was strange until she looked up and noticed the blood-red mark of the star. She suddenly stopped and pointed to an opening in the wall just below the mark. Bornstein became very excited. "Look," he said, "the stones must have been covering up this alcove in the wall."

Lisa shined her flashlight into the space in the wall, and there was certainly something hidden in the alcove. Ari began removing more stones from the opening in the wall. After clearing more space, Bornstein looked into the alcove and said, "Oh my God, it's an urn, the kind the ancient Israelites used to store scrolls."

He reached into the alcove and carefully, almost reverently, removed the small clay vessel. "Look," he said, "It's been sealed with wax. Do you realize how important this discovery could be? I'm not an expert on pottery, but this looks very old. It certainly predates the Roman period. We have to bring this back to my lab to study it."

Neither Ari nor Lisa was going to argue with Bornstein. They just wanted to get out of the tunnel before any of the expected aftershocks hit. The professor cradled the precious urn in his arms as they quickly walked back to the iron gate leading to safety. They found the manager cleaning up vegetables and debris from the floor of the store. The place was a mess. He greeted the group. He had contacted the emergency telephone number to explain there were three people trapped below ground in the catacombs, but as Lisa expected, there were too many other injured people to be cared for.

As they left the produce market, a symphony of wailing sirens from dozens of ambulances and fire trucks filled the air. Amidst the debris littering the streets of the commercial district, the three walked down the street with the professor clutching his newly discovered urn.

Chapter 4

Jamal Hashem had been paid a small stipend indirectly by the Grand Mufti of Jerusalem to watch the produce market. The existence of the gate to the catacomb had been known for generations. It had come as a shock that the store previously owned by an Arab had been sold to an Israeli family. If the Grand Mufti had known of the man's death, he would have taken steps to purchase the property. That, however, was water over the dam.

Jamal had been paid to watch for people entering the catacomb or other suspicious activities. For years nothing out of the ordinary had ever happened, just a few visitors from time to time who never purchased any food but disappeared into the store's basement. Now, however, Jamal had just seen an older man clutching an ancient artifact, some type of vessel.

He immediately called his contact who insisted that he follow the suspicious person to see where the artifact was being taken. Jamal quickly jumped on his moped and followed the three strangers to the professor's car. He called his contact who instructed him to follow the group until help arrived. Jamal smiled; he had actually accomplished something to earn his money. He followed the professor's car and waited for support to arrive.

Chapter 5

The city was in a state of mass confusion: collapsed houses, children crying, car alarms blaring, people wandering aimlessly in the streets. Lisa's waterlogged gym shoes squished with every step. Bornstein said, "We've got to get this back to my lab."

Lisa said, "You know for a person who almost died, you're in rare form."

Bornstein answered, "You don't understand. This is the find of a lifetime. Most archeologists work their entire careers without ever finding something like this. I've got to find out what's inside."

Ari drove the professor's car while Bornstein sat in the backseat clutching his prized possession. As Ari headed for the Hebrew University north of the Temple Mount, they passed thousands of people standing in the streets. Even though earthquakes were a rare event in Israel, the residents of the city knew enough about aftershocks to leave their houses and stay in the streets.

They parked in the university's faculty parking lot just off Zalman Schocken Street and walked over to the six-story ultra-modern Science Building. The professor talked to the guard in the lobby. They both obviously knew each other. It seemed the building had held up pretty well to the earthquake, although some of the labs, particularly the chemistry labs, were in a bad state and much of the glassware lay shattered on the floor.

The group took the elevator up to the fourth floor. The professor's lab seemed to be in pretty good shape. His biggest concern was the artifacts in his storage room, and a quick check confirmed his precious possessions in storage had not been damaged. Some artifacts on workbenches, however, were scattered over the lab's floor.

Bornstein ignored the damage. He swept away some broken pieces of pottery with his hand and carefully placed the urn on a workbench. He asked Lisa to take a series of pictures with her iPhone to document the find. He hurried over to a cabinet and returned with a number of tools. As Lisa began taking pictures of the urn, Bornstein, with disposable gloves on his hands, removed a portion of the material sealing the lid to the top of the urn. "It looks like bee's wax," he said.

He placed a sample of the material inside a covered petri dish for later analysis and then, using a scalpel, cut through the wax seal. After placing a large sterile disposable plastic drape next to the urn, he repositioned the vessel onto the drape and then carefully and slowly pried open the urn's lid with the tip of a knife. He looked at his two friends. "Here we go. Let's see what gift our ancestors left for us."

He lifted the lid off of the urn and placed it in a Ziploc bag. He asked Lisa to take some pictures of whatever was inside. Lisa, without looking inside, took a few pictures. The three viewed the photos on her cellphone. Ari said, "It looks like a scroll."

Bornstein, now in an excited state, said, "Yes it does look like a scroll. Let's get it out of there."

Bornstein thought about how to remove the artifact from the urn with the least amount of damage. A tweezers might damage the fragile document. In the end, after looking again at the picture, he decided to tip the urn over and let gravity help remove the scroll. He carefully lifted the urn and began tipping it over above the protective drape. Luckily, the scroll was rolled up and easily dropped out onto the white plastic cloth. He set the urn back down. The rolled up scroll was tied with a fragile hemp string, and the string was secured with a brown wax seal.

Lisa took a few more pictures and the professor thought about the next step. He walked over to a large cabinet in the corner of the room and set some dials. "We need to store the scroll in a temperature and humidity controlled environment. I'm going to open the scroll, and then after taking some pictures and examining it, we'll place it in the cabinet. It looks like ancient parchment material."

Ari said, "Isn't parchment like paper?"

Bornstein answered, "No Ari, parchment is actually made from the skin of an animal. It's treated in a very special way to make it a very durable writing surface. It was a time consuming process, so it was only used for the most important documents."

Lisa asked, "If you unroll it, will it break apart?"

Bornstein answered, "If it was papyrus, definitely yes, but parchment is very flexible and durable. I think we'll be okay. I'll cut the string with a scissors, unroll it slowly, and then I'll get some pinchers to hold down the corners of the document. If it begins to crack, I'll stop."

The professor went to a cabinet and removed a package of large sterile clips and secured them to the two exposed corners of the scroll after cutting the string. Then he slowly began unrolling the old parchment scroll.

Two minutes later, Lisa was taking a number of pictures of the document while Bornstein was in apparent ecstasy. "It's written in a very old early form of Hebrew. I can't translate it without a special dictionary. My God I think this must have been written before the Roman period, maybe even during the time of the First Temple, and if it's from that earlier period, it may provide the proof of the existence of the First Temple. This could be the most important find of the millennium."

Lisa asked, "Why is that so important?"

Ari answered, "It gets back to the political problem we were talking about. Professor, correct me if I'm wrong, but archeologists have never found definitive proof of the existence of the First Temple or even that King David and King Solomon set up Jerusalem as the capital of Israel."

Bornstein answered, "You're absolutely right Ari. Let's put this into the chamber to keep it in good condition. I'm going to go to the library to get the special dictionary to translate this."

Ari suggested, "Why don't Lisa and I go back to my apartment to get cleaned up. We can upload Lisa's pictures to my computer, and I'll send you an e-mail. We'll come back here after we dry off."

The professor said, "I've got a change of clothes in my office. I'll go there first, and then I'll go to the library. You guys can take my car."

Bornstein placed the lid once again on the top of the urn, and Ari helped the professor place the scroll inside the controlled environmental chamber. As they parted ways in the hallway, the professor hugged them both and said, "In my excitement I forgot to thank both of you. The scroll's important, but not as important as our lives. I owe my life to both of you, and I'll never forget it."

Chapter 6

Ari and Lisa never noticed the small moped following their car. They were too busy reliving their recent ordeal in the tunnel beneath the Temple Mount. They both realized how lucky they were to be alive, and then the discovery of the urn had transformed a horrid day into something significantly more interesting.

Ari lived in a small apartment about ten minutes from the university on Revadin Street. Ari parked on the street outside his five story apartment building, and they walked to the front entrance. This area of the city looked to have sustained only minor damage. Ari opened the door to his one bedroom bachelor pad, and the two walked inside. Lisa was impressed. The place actually looked neat. Ari sensing her stare said, "I have a maid who comes in once a week to keep the place clean."

"So this is what an architect's apartment looks like?" Lisa said. "I see drawing boards have become obsolete. Your computer screen is about the biggest I've ever seen."

"I do everything on my computer now. I was thinking of buying a drawing board, but only for decoration. Why don't you take a shower first while I put our dirty clothes in the washer and dryer? I've got a robe you can use until everything dries."

Ari handed Lisa a long white terrycloth robe and towel and led her to the bathroom. She took off her clothes. Her underwear was still damp and clung to her body. After putting on Ari's robe, she handed him her clothes and prepared to shower. The hot water felt therapeutic as she removed the dirt and dust from her body. Her mind returned to the excitement of finding the urn, and it seemed to temper the shock of being trapped underground.

After finishing her shower, she blow-dried her hair, put on her robe, and found Ari at his computer. He had managed to upload her pictures and e-mail them to the professor. He looked approvingly at her. "You look much better now. Of course I really liked you in your underwear."

Lisa smiled, "I'm glad you enjoyed the experience, and I loved your Calvin Kleins."

"I was lucky I didn't wear my old torn ones. I guess it's time for me to take my shower."

Ari disappeared into the bathroom with a change of clothes. Actually, she had really enjoyed seeing Ari in his underwear, much more than she was ready to admit to him. Lisa heard the washing machine signal the end of the wash cycle. She located the machine in a closet and transferred all of the clothes into the dryer. She set the timer and then wandered around Ai's apartment. It wasn't very big, but it had a beautiful view east toward the Temple Mount and the Jordan valley far in the distance. She didn't notice any damage from the earthquake, and she realized the damage must have been very localized.

She suddenly realized she hadn't eaten anything since before they left Be'er Sheva early in the morning. Ari's refrigerator was basically empty. He must have thrown out anything that could spoil before he left. She did, however, find two frozen chicken dinners. She microwaved both and set two place settings at his kitchen table.

Ari suddenly appeared in clean clothes. "Well I see you've made yourself at home, and I guess we'll both have a late lunch."

"I thought you'd be hungry; I know I am."

The two ate quickly, neither one realizing how hungry they were.

Chapter 7

Two college-age girls, carrying school books and laughing, entered the Science Building. The guard at the desk asked to see their IDs. The tallest girl opened her purse, withdrew a gun with a silencer, and shot the security guard in the head. As the man fell to the floor, two men carrying assault rifles and dressed in black masks entered the building and moved the guard's body into a nearby closet. The second girl took possession of the guard's gun.

The four proceeded to the fourth floor and quickly found the professor's lab. Bornstein was startled when they barged into his laboratory. He asked, "What are you doing here, and what's with the guns and the masks?"

The leader of the assault team demanded, "Where's the urn you took from the catacombs?"

Bornstein pointed to the workbench. The leader looked inside and seeing nothing asked, "Where did you put what was inside?"

Bornstein tried to cover up the pictures sent from Ari. "The urn was empty!"

The leader looked again at the urn and the opened lid. He doubted the urn was empty. Then he noticed the professor trying to hide the papers on his desk. The leader looked at the pictures and demanded, "Where's the scroll you found in the urn?"

Bornstein said, "The urn was empty."

"Bullshit," the man said. He pushed Bornstein back against the workbench and placed the barrel of the gun into Bornstein's mouth. "I'm going to ask you just once more. If you don't tell me where you put it, I'm going to kill you. Where's the scroll?"

Bornstein had no intention of dying. He'd already translated the scroll. He knew what it said, and although the scroll was important, he already knew the message on the scroll by heart. He led the leader of the group over to the environmental chamber and opened the door.

The leader carefully removed the scroll, and then asked the professor what the scroll said. Bornstein replied, "I don't know; it's written in ancient Hebrew, and I couldn't translate it without a special book."

The leader looked at the professor's pictures and decided the professor had outlived his usefulness. He thought about killing the man with a single bullet to the head but wanted to make him suffer. Instead, he shot him in the stomach and said, "That's for violating the law. You know you're not supposed to go under the Temple Mount."

The leader placed the scroll back in the urn and reattached the lid. He gathered all of the professor's pictures, and then the four left Professor Bornstein bleeding out on the floor.

Chapter 8

Ari parked their car in the professor's reserved spot. The guard at the front desk was nowhere to be seen, but Ari did notice a trail of blood leading to a closet behind the desk. He opened the door, and the guard's body fell down at his feet. Ari immediately pulled out his cellphone and dialed 100, the Israeli emergency telephone number. He explained the situation and asked for an armed response by the police and an ambulance. His bigger concern was the professor. Somehow he knew the guard's death had something to do with the ancient urn, and he was worried about Bornstein.

Lisa, who couldn't figure out what was happening, followed Ari as he moved cautiously up the stairs. If the guard's killer was still in the building, he didn't want to risk taking the elevator. The fourth floor hallway looked vacant, but the light in the professor's lab was still on. Without a weapon, Ari advanced cautiously down the hallway and into the lab with Lisa following close behind. Bornstein was lying in a pool of blood on the floor by his desk, and the urn was missing from the workbench.

Ari felt for a pulse. It was there but very weak. Ari called out to the professor, and he slowly opened his eyes. He smiled in recognition and asked for some water. Lisa ran to a nearby sink and found an empty coffee cup. She filled the cup and lifted the professor's head so he could drink. The water seemed to restore his strength. He looked at both of them, and with his last bit of strength whispered, "It's the proof."

That was all he said, and then he shut his eyes for the last time. Ari felt for a pulse and found none. He turned to Lisa and shook his head no. Lisa was horrified. The tunnel, the shooting of the guard, and now the death of the professor were almost too much to accept in the space of a few hours. She reached out to hold Bornstein's limp hand and began to cry.

Ari knelt down next to Lisa and held her in his arms. "It's all about that lousy urn. Is that piece of ancient history really worth two lives? Who did this?

A pudgy middle-aged balding man standing at the door answered, "That's my job to find out. I'm Detective Moshe Stern. An ambulance is on the way."

Ari replied, "The professor's dead. He was shot in the stomach. He died a few minutes ago."

Detective Stern spoke into his police phone. A few minutes later he was interrupted by two paramedics. "It's too late Stern said, leave the body there until Forensics is done."

The lead paramedic said, "There are many people injured from the earthquake. Call us when you're ready."

Meanwhile Ari had gone over to the environmental chamber. "The scroll's been taken," he told Lisa

Stern overheard him. "What scroll?" he asked.

Ari said, "It's a long story Detective Stern."

"I've got plenty of time, so let's sit down in the far corner of the lab, and you can tell me what happened."

Ari held Lisa's hand as the three found a place to sit down as far away as possible from the crime scene. Lisa chose a chair with her back to Professor Bornstein's body. It took the two of them almost half an hour to brief Detective Stern on their day. Their story was interrupted for a few minutes when Forensics arrived. Stern took many notes, and when they were finished updating him, he scratched his nose and finally said. "Religious artifacts, and this time underneath the Temple Mount; that always leads to trouble. Me, I don't know urns from vases, but my niece, Dalia Herbst, works for the Antiquities Authority. I'm going to ask her to come here and talk to you."

He walked to the far side of the lab and called her on his cellphone. They spoke for a few minutes, and then he returned. "She's at the main museum. There's been some damage there from the earthquake. She'll be here as soon as she can. You said you have pictures of the urn and scroll?"

Lisa showed him the pictures on her iPhone, and at his request, she forwarded them to the detective's phone. Another detective, a woman by the name of Elsi Fischer, walked into the lab and introduced herself. "Moshe, we've got the surveillance tapes on the monitor. Do you want to see them?"

"Yes," he said, "and I'd like you both to join me. Maybe you can recognize someone."

Lisa had never been at a crime scene before, and she avoided the Forensics people taking their pictures and dusting for fingerprints. She couldn't bring herself to look at the professor's body as she left the lab and followed Detective Stern down to the basement of the Science Building and into a room labelled Security.

Detective Fischer sat down at a monitor next to one of the university guards. A few seconds later they were looking at two innocent looking girls entering the building and walking up to the guard's desk. A few seconds later the man was shot in the head. Lisa cringed in disbelief as he fell to the floor. Two men wearing black ski masks rushed into the lobby. The security guard kept changing cameras as the four killers took the elevator up to the fourth floor. Five minutes later the group left the professor's lab. One of the men was carrying the urn, and one of the girls was carrying a handful of papers. The videos ended with the four leaving the university grounds.

Ari and Lisa had never seen the girls before, and the two men's faces were covered. "So," Detective Stern said, "We know there were four of them. The girls were there to gain entrance to the building. She was using a Glock with a silencer, and the man carrying the urn is probably left-handed because he's wearing a watch on his right arm. Elsi, let's get these tapes back to the lab. I want them looked at again to see if we can learn anything else."

Just then a striking young woman walked into the room and gave Moshe Stern a kiss on the cheek. He turned to Ari and Lisa. Let me introduce my niece Doctor Dalia Herbst. She's the lead investigator with the Antiquities Authority. Dalia Herbst shook hands with Lisa and Ari. "I understand you discovered an ancient urn and a scroll today. My uncle sent me the pictures, but I need to get a full briefing from both of you. I know this will be difficult, and my sympathies for your friend Professor Bornstein. I knew him well. We worked together on a number of projects. I have some ideas about what happened, but I want to listen to your story first."

Dalia Herbst was clearly a take-charge woman. Her six-foot height and commanding presence demanded attention. She had beautiful long red hair and mysterious green penetrating eyes. Ari eyed her with more than just politeness, and Lisa was too distraught to notice. Herbst looked at both of them and said, "Listen, why don't the three of us go someplace for some coffee. Uncle, I'm assuming you're done with them?"

"Yes Dalia, they're yours as soon as they give me some contact information."

Ari and Lisa exchanged information with Detective Stern and then left the building. "There's an outdoor coffee shop over on Sderot Churchill," Dalia said. "Do you know the spot?"

Ari answered yes, and they agreed to meet there. Ari drove the professor's car and the ride took less than five minutes.

Chapter 9

The outdoor café was located on a tree-lined peaceful corner across the street from a small park. Dalia was waiting for them when they arrived, and she had managed to find a vacant table under an awning in the corner of the patio.

They ordered coffees, and Dalia took out her notebook. "I know you must have told your story to my uncle, but I need to hear everything again and in great detail."

Ari asked, "What's your role in all of this?"

Dalia smiled, "Ari, I'm the person who's going to help get back the professor's urn and scroll."

Between Lisa and Ari they spent the better part of an hour explaining their day in excruciating detail. Dalia was busy taking notes, and never interrupted. At the end of the tale, she began asking questions. "Tell me more about the hidden alcove."

Lisa said, "The six-pointed star was blood-red. Bornstein said it was drawn in a hurry. He said it was a mark. We couldn't see the alcove in the beginning before the earthquake. It was hidden from view by perfectly cut stones. We were looking right at it, and we never saw it. After the earthquake, some of the stones sealing the alcove broke apart and fell to the ground. That's how we saw it."

"Tell me more about the urn. Were there any markings on the bottom?"

"We never looked," Ari said. "and I never saw any makings or decorations of any kind. It was just a reddish-grey color."

Lisa agreed and then Dalia asked another question. "Was the urn under the Temple Mount?"

Lisa asked, "Why is that important?"

Dalia answered, "After the 1967 war, the agreement was that the Waqf would control the Temple Mount and everything beneath it. So if the urn was found under the Temple Mount, it needs to be turned over to them. And by the way, the agreement also stated that nobody was allowed in the catacombs below the Temple Mount without their approval. The good news is the three of us aren't going to tell the Waqf about your adventure."

Ari said, "The professor was mapping the tunnel. He had a notebook with all of the distances and directions."

"Where is it?" Dalia asked.

Lisa answered, "The last time I saw it; it was in a Ziploc bag in his backpack."

"Where's the backpack?" Dalia asked.

Ari said, "When we came into the professor's lab I put it on the floor next to his desk."

Dalia immediately called her uncle. "Uncle Moshe, are you still at the crime scene?

"Yes."

"Is there a backpack on the floor next to the professor's desk?"

There was silence for a minute and then Dalia said, "Good, is there a notebook in the backpack with distances and compass headings written down?"

Silence and then, "Please text me pictures of the information."

Dalia thanked him and then turned her attention back to Ari and Lisa. Where exactly is this entrance to the catacomb?"

Ari took out his cellphone and used his map app to show Dalia the location of the produce store.

Dalia thought for a minute. "I'm going to need to go back down there again. I want to get scrapings of the red star. If it's blood, which I think it is, I should be able to get a Carbon 14 dating. That will be very important in establishing the date the urn was placed in the alcove.

Lisa said, "You need to wait at least twenty-four hours until the aftershocks subside."

Lisa had been thinking about how to broach the subject with Dalia. She finally just spoke frankly. "You say you're going to find the urn. Ari and I have a lot invested in that urn. It's not just important because of its potential historical significance. It's really about completing what Professor Bornstein wanted done. I don't know how Ari and I can help, but I certainly want to be a part of the search."

Dalia considered Lisa's request. "You're welcome to help me, but if it becomes dangerous then all bets are off. At some point we're probably going to have to get my uncle involved. We don't have a police force in my department."

Ari asked, "What kind of resources will you have to help?"

"Not many I'm afraid. The earthquake caused damage in many of the museums we control, and most of our people are tied up sorting out the mess."

Ari said, "We should go back down with you to show you exactly where the alcove is located, but we're going to need a key to open the gate. The professor put it in the backpack. Call your uncle and see if it's still there."

A quick call to Uncle Moshe confirmed the key was still in the backpack, and he said he would drop it off at his niece's office.

Lisa asked, "So what's next?"

Dalia looked at the picture of the scroll on Lisa's cellphone. "The scroll is written in a very old form of Hebrew. That's why the professor needed a dictionary to translate the words. There's an expert on this old language in my department. I'll set up a meeting with him for tomorrow morning. We need to get an exact translation."

Ari asked, "What about recovering the urn?"

"I have an idea about that," Dalia said, "In the past we have found that the Waqf has all the entrances to the catacombs constantly under surveillance, just in case people like you remove ancient artifacts. That's what I'm guessing happened. One of their people followed you to the Science Building, and then they sent in a team to recover the urn. Tomorrow morning I'm going to check things out at the produce store and see if anyone is watching the place."

"But why did they have to kill two people?" Lisa asked.

Dalia answered, "Because they wanted to send a message; don't ever do anything like this again."

Dalia looked at her watch. "Listen, it's getting late. You guys have been through a lot in one day. Let's meet tomorrow morning at my office; let's say ten o'clock. That will give me time to check out the store and set up a meeting with Professor Braverman; he's our expert on this old language."

Lisa suddenly realized how tired she really was. Dalia paid for the coffees and the three left the restaurant just as a minor aftershock rumbled underground. Luckily, it was very minor, but the residents of the city, already on edge, streamed out into the streets to avoid being trapped in their homes.

Chapter 10

Ari insisted that Lisa spend the night in his apartment, and she wasn't about to argue. She had no desire to be alone. After parking the professor's car out on the street, they began walking toward Ari's building. He stopped suddenly and looked up at his dark apartment. "I know I left the living room light on when we left. All the lights are off in my unit, and there's power to the rest of the building. Someone's inside."

Lisa stared at the dark apartment. "Who could be up there?"

"Let's try the people who killed the professor for starters."

Ari handed Lisa his cellphone. "Call Stern and get the police out here. I'm going to find out what's going on."

"Ari, I'm afraid; just wait here until the police get here."

"No, with all of this earthquake confusion, they'll have no time for our little problem."

Lisa pulled him back as he tried to leave, but he broke free and sprinted across the street. Ari had a plan, and his first stop was his storage locker in the basement of the building. He opened the combination lock to the small locker and pulled out his army reserve bag. He wasn't authorized to carry a gun, but he had two commando knives, and he knew how to use them. He placed one knife in its specially designed leather belt and secured it around his waist. With the other knife in his right hand, he left the building by a backdoor and headed for the stairway leading up to his back porch.

Meanwhile, Lisa called Detective Stern and explained what was happening. Stern said, "We won't be able to make it for another fifteen minutes. I'll call the office and have them send out a police car, but with all this confusion, I'm not sure when it will get there. I'll have my partner leave for your apartment right now. What's the address?"

Lisa realized she didn't know the address. She told Stern to wait as she ran to the corner of the street to look for a street sign. She finally found it and gave Stern the names of the two intersecting streets. She then ran back to the front of the building and looked at Ari's apartment, not knowing what to do.

Ari had quietly climbed the steel staircase leading to his back porch, and was now looking through a corner of the sliding glass door leading to the kitchen. He lay down on the cement floor, keeping his body out of sight, and let his eyes adjust to the darkness inside his apartment. The kitchen and living room appeared empty, but eventually he spotted some slight movement behind a chair in the corner of the living room. He continued to stare at the wall behind the chair, and finally a man dressed in a black mask stuck his head above the chair, scanned the room, and ducked down once again out of sight.

Ari crept slowly along the back porch until he reached the French door leading to his bedroom. Once again he waited silently outside searching for any movement. After concluding there was only one person waiting in the living room, he quietly unlocked the French door and entered his bedroom.

He waited for several minutes, wanting to be certain the intruder had not heard him enter the apartment. Ari moved silently over the bedroom carpet until he was able to see the outline of a man still crouching behind the living room chair. He could throw the knife in his right hand, but it would be a difficult throw. He really wanted the man to stand up; that would be the best option. He thought about the tactical problem and finally reached for a tennis ball sitting on his dresser.

The man was carrying a gun. If he threw the ball against the kitchen wall, the man's natural reaction might be to stay hidden behind the chair, but if he threw the ball right at him, his natural reaction would be to stand up and turn toward the source of the throw. That would present an inviting target for his knife. Of course if he missed, the man with the pistol would have the advantage. Why not just wait for the police to arrive? If the guy heard a siren, then he might try to leave by the back kitchen door, and that would also present an inviting target. But what if the police arrived with their sirens turned off; what then? There were too many unanswerable questions. It was time to act.

Ari shifted his throwing knife to his left hand and held the tennis ball in his right hand. He threw the ball toward the man and quickly shifted the knife back into his right hand. The ball missed the man's head, but hit the back of the chair and bounced back into his chest. The man flinched and was confused, but the intruder knew the object had been thrown from behind his back. He jumped up and turned to face the source of the threat with his gun pointed in the general direction of the bedroom.

Before he had a chance to focus on the source of the danger, Ari threw the knife and the blade struck him in the chest. The man reflexively pulled the trigger as he fell backwards onto the tile floor. The gun's bullet passed harmlessly to Ari's right, and before the man hit the ground, Ari had pulled the second knife from its sheath and was ready to throw it if necessary.

The knife struck the man in the center of his chest, just below his ribs, and he was doubled over in pain as he bled out onto the floor. Ari bolted to his side and kicked the intruder's gun into the far corner of the living room. He lifted the dying man's head and demanded, "Who sent you?"

The man looked up at him and smiled. Then he coughed up a mouthful of blood and closed his eyes. Ari felt for a pulse, but the man was dead.

Lisa, heard the single shot, and against her better judgment, raced into the apartment building and took the elevator up to Ari's floor. She had no idea what she would do when she got there, but she had to find Ari and protect him against whoever had shot him. She screamed Ari's name at his front door and waited for an answer.

Instead of an answer, the front door opened, and Ari was smiling at her. He pulled her into his body and comforted her. Then Lisa suddenly pushed herself away and slapped him across the face. "Why did you do that? You could have gotten yourself killed. What is this, some kind of macho male game? Why couldn't you wait for the police to get here?"

Lisa was crying and Ari was in shock from Lisa's rebuke. He stared at her crying in front of him, and then she looked back into his eyes and leaned forward into his arms. They held onto each other until Lisa's crying slowly subsided. She looked up into his large brown eyes and said, "Oh Ari, I'm so sorry, but when I heard the gunshot, I was sure you were hit."

"So if you knew there was danger, why did you risk your life to save me?"

It was a good question, a very good question. Without thinking of the consequences Lisa blurted out, "Because I love you stupid. I fell in love with you when I saw you in your Calvin Kleins."

Lisa was laughing with tears still in her eyes, and Ari laughed at her funny explanation. He then bent over and kissed her deeply on her lips. Ari couldn't believe she had risked her life to save him. She was quite a girl.

Lisa could see a man's body partially hidden behind the living room chair, and she could see a large pool of blood flowing slowly along a grout line between two rows of tile.

Suddenly, Detective Elsi Fischer appeared at the front door with her gun drawn. As soon as she saw the man's body lying on the floor, she put her pistol back in its holster. "I'd say you two have had one hell of an exciting day. What happened?"

The three sat down at the kitchen table. Elsi immediately called Forensics and an ambulance, and then she waited to hear Ari's explanation of the details of his encounter with the would-be assassin. It took Ari several minutes to explain what had happened. Detective Fischer never asked why Ari had killed the man. Lisa thought it was as if it was the natural and only thing to do under the circumstances. These Israelis were just too accustomed to violence. In the United States, Ari would have already been hauled down to the police station for questioning.

The same forensics team Lisa had seen at the university arrived, and after they had taken pictures of the crime scene, Elsi searched the dead man's body for any identification. Not surprisingly, she found nothing. The man's fingerprints would be the only way he might ever be identified. Two beat cops arrived and Detective Fischer asked them to search the street looking for a car the man might have used, but without finding any car keys on the body, she doubted whether he had driven to the apartment.

He had probably been dropped off by someone with instructions to meet a pick up car near the apartment after he had finished his job. That's the way it usually worked. An accomplice might be waiting in a car at a nearby corner, but the visible presence of the police made that very unlikely. He had probably left as soon as the first police car arrived.

By this time a number of Ari's neighbors had gathered in the hallway. He finally left to explain what had happened and to assure them that he was unharmed. Lisa sat at the kitchen table shaking as she looked at the body. Three people now dead because of an ancient artifact. What was this turning into? Whatever it was, she was knee-deep into it; and one thing for sure, this was an entirely new experience for her. The reality of several near-death experiences was hard to digest.

Detective Fischer said, "They must have followed you here when you left the professor. Maybe they were checking to see if you had any other artifacts."

It was after midnight before Elsi Fischer left the apartment. The body had been removed, and the forensics team had tried to clean up the blood, but some had seeped into the grout between tiles and would require some major cleaning. Detective Fischer had insisted on stationing a police car outside the building just to be certain no further attempts were made on their lives.

Lisa said, "I don't want to spend the night here. Can't we find another place to stay?"

"There's a small hotel a few minutes from here. We can spend the night there."

The Hotel Sampson was nothing more than an upscale B&B. Ari asked the clerk for two rooms, and Lisa immediately corrected him. "I'm not sleeping alone tonight."

Once inside their room with the door locked and bolted, Ari said, "I think it's safe to spend the night here. I'll block the door to prevent anyone from sneaking in while we're asleep."

Lisa helped Ari move a couch to block the entrance to their hotel room. They both laughed as they finished the barricade and sat on the double bed.

Lisa held Ari's hand as she thought about the assassin. "Where did you learn to do things like that?" Lisa asked.

"We all have to serve in the Israeli Defense Force, even women. I was assigned to a commando unit. Our job was to insert ourselves behind enemy lines to create havoc and laser-target enemy installations for our fighter planes. I'm pretty good with a knife."

Lisa shuddered at the thought, but it was late and she was tired. Ari said, "I'll sleep on the couch."

Lisa smiled, "I don't want to sleep alone, not after what happened today, and I've already seen you in your underwear. Let's share the bed."

Who was Ari to fault Lisa's logic? It even made sense to him. After Lisa finished in the bathroom, she found Ari already in bed. "I set the alarm for seven o'clock. Is that okay?" he asked.

Lisa nodded in agreement. Ari pulled the covers back and Lisa lay down with her back to him. She then inched back against his warmth. Ari wondered whether her move was an invitation to get a little more serious. She looked so beautiful just lying next to him, her long blond hair scattered over her face. What an opportunity he thought. Was she just flirting with him or did she really want him to take things to the next level?

His mind returned to the worst day in his life. His fighting in two wars was nothing compared to their ordeal in the catacombs, and Lisa had handled herself perfectly in the heat of the moment.

He finally thought he would test the waters. He carefully pulled back her hair from the side of her face and waited for a reaction, but there wasn't one. He whispered her name and there was no answer. Shit, he thought; she's asleep already.

Lisa, who would have welcomed Ari's advances, had instantly fallen asleep. The day had sucked every bit of strength from her body. Ari, feeling disappointment, put his head back down on his pillow and was soon asleep.

Lisa awoke from a bad dream about six o'clock. The nightmare had something to do with drowning in a pool of water. It instantly faded into one more forgotten memory. She rolled over and looked at Ari. He was lying on his back, still in a deep sleep. Once again she thought about him as a full-time lover, and once again she thought about what she knew would be a sad departure when she returned home to California.

She ran her fingers gently across his face. He needed a shave, but his day-old beard felt kind of sexy. She leaned over and kissed him gently on the cheek. He wrinkled his nose and began to wake up. He slowly opened his eyes, and Lisa leaned over and gave him a sensual kiss on his lips. "What a nice way to wake up," he said.

"I wanted to do that last night to thank you," she said.

"I'm the one who should be thanking you. You were the one who thought of escaping through the cisterns."

Lisa put her arms around his neck and kissed him again. This time there was little room for doubt, and Ari turned onto his side and pulled her body into his. Lisa giggled as they both shed their clothes, but her sexual desire soon overcame her nervousness. She longed for Ari's body being a part of hers, and as she felt between his legs, she knew he was ready as well. Their pleasure slowly built as both their hands and kisses attempted to visit every part of each other's bodies, and then it was over.

Ari kissed her on the cheek. "That was the best thank you anyone ever gave me."

"Mine was pretty good too," she said.

"Just pretty good, or the best?"

"Well there's always room for improvement, but okay, I admit it; it was the best."

Ari held her in his arms and said, "I've wanted to do that for a long time, but I thought you just wanted to be good friends."

"I wanted to do it too, but I kept thinking about what would happen when I go back to California; and then what happened yesterday; we almost died, and I thought we really have to take each day for what it is and enjoy life."

The alarm clock sounded and it was time to get ready for a new day. Somehow taking a shower together seemed like the right thing to do. They helped each other get clean, and then they toweled each other dry. Lisa said, "I need to buy some clothes today. I thought we'd be back in Be'er Sheva last night."

"I know a place near here. We can stop there on the way to see Dalia if we have some time. I also need to buy some food. I think we'll be here for a couple of days."

After getting dressed, they both had breakfast in the hotel's small dining area. Lisa said, "I'm still trying to process what happened last night. They're going to try to kill us again, aren't they?"

Ari thought about how to answer the question. "I've been thinking about that too. I think they want to kill us to prevent others from finding out what we know. But now they understand that a lot of people know everything we know. So what's their point? Punishment is all I can think of right now. Maybe that or they want to make an example of us so others don't venture into the catacombs to find artifacts. These aren't sensible people we're dealing with. They're fanatics. They're obsessed with protecting their rights to Jerusalem."

"So we'll never be safe again," Lisa said.

"Time heals all wounds, or the other option is to find the people who did this and prevent them from hurting us in the future."

"I don't think time will take care of this one, and from what Dalia was saying, there're probably hundreds of people who want to kill us."

"Welcome to the Middle East my love. Arabs fighting Jews is an everyday occurrence here in Israel."

Chapter 11

Dalia Herbst parked near the produce market and scanned the street outside the store looking for anyone who might be monitoring people going down into the catacombs. There was a young man sitting in the front of a tobacco shop across the street smoking a cigarette, and he looked like the ideal candidate.

Dalia walked into the fresh produce store and found the manager in the back helping a customer select some Japanese eggplants. After the customer left, she showed the manager, Mr. Simon, her credentials and introduced herself. "Mr. Simon, yesterday Professor Bornstein and two of his colleagues were here to visit the catacombs. The professor was killed last night, and the urn he found was stolen from his lab. The police are looking for the killers, and in my experience, the Waqf almost always have people monitoring the entrances to the catacombs to make sure artifacts are not removed. So the question for you is whether anyone seems to be constantly watching your store."

Mr. Simon thought for a split-second and said, "That would be the young man who works at the tobacco shop across the street. He's always looking over here, and he's been doing that since the day we opened for business. You can see him now. He's just sitting there smoking a cigarette. I rarely see him doing much of anything. He just sits there looking at my store all day long."

Dalia said, "Tomorrow, I'm going to need to go back into the catacombs. I have the key for the gate. Please don't allow anyone else to enter the catacombs without notifying me."

She handed the manager her business card and then walked to the front of the store where she secretly took several pictures of the young man. Back in her car, she called her uncle. "Uncle Moshe, I'm going to need some help, and I also have a good lead for you on the professor's killers. There's a young man who works across from the fresh produce store in a tobacco shop. He's probably been watching the catacombs to see who might be entering; at least the manager thinks so. He probably followed the professor back to the Science Building and then called the Waqf. I'd like you to pick him up for questioning tomorrow morning a little before nine o'clock. While you question him back at the police station, I'm going to go back into the catacomb to check out where the urn was found. I'm texting you his picture now."

Stern listened to his niece and agreed to pick the young man up the next morning. "By the way Dalia, someone tried to kill Lisa and Ari last night in Waldstein's apartment. Ari was able to kill the person first, but you all need to be very careful. Whoever killed the professor is also trying to kill everyone else involved with the urn."

Dalia was not surprised. "I'll bet the same guy who followed them back to the Science Building also followed them back to Ari's apartment."

"Makes sense. Listen, I've got to go now, but I left the key to the catacombs on your desk."

"Take care uncle."

"You too honey."

Dalia stopped at a café for some coffee and then called her colleague Professor Braverman. "Andre, good morning; it's Dalia. I have an interesting opportunity for you. I'm going to e-mail you a picture of a scroll taken from an ancient urn. The writing is definitely very early Hebrew. I need a quick translation, and you're the best person I know to do the job."

"Sure Dalia. How long is the document?"

"Only a couple hundred words at most."

"Okay, stop by my office at eleven o'clock. I should have it done by then."

"Thanks Andre, see you then."

Chapter 12

By the time Lisa and Ari left the hotel, it was already close to nine o'clock. They had an hour before their meeting with Dalia, barely enough time for Lisa to buy much of anything, but Ari stopped at a nearby shopping mall. Lisa started with a pair of jeans and two loose fitting blouses. After a quick stop at the lingerie department, she had at least one full change of clothes, clearly not enough, but it would have to do.

Much to Ari's delight, she changed out of her day old clothes in the front seat of their car. "Do you need any help?"

"No," she said laughing, "I think I can manage it all by myself, but thanks for asking."

They parked in the visitor's parking lot outside the Antiquities Authority building and arrived at Dalia's office a few minutes after ten o'clock.

Her office was piled to the ceiling with a variety of textbooks, and dozens of ancient artifacts filled every empty space. The most interesting piece was a very old clay tablet with cuneiform writing leaning against the wall on the top of her bookcase. As Ari and Lisa marveled at its remarkable condition Lisa laughed, "It's a fake," she said. "The guy who was going to sell it to me claimed it was from the Negev Desert around

1200 BC, but the clay used to make the tablet came from the Nile river; you can tell from the reddish colored grains of sand mixed in with the clay, a dead giveaway. That guy's in jail now for selling forgeries, and I bought the tablet at the police auction as a reminder."

"It certainly looks real," Lisa said.

"Yes, the forgers are pretty good here. As they say in Latin, *caveat emptor*, let the buyer beware. Listen, Professor Braverman says he'll have the scroll translated by eleven o'clock. Let's get some coffee in the commissary, and I'll tell you what I've been up to."

Dalia led the way to the small self-service eating area in the basement of the building. They sat at a table in an out of the way spot with their coffees. "This morning I visited the produce market and talked to the manager. A young man who works in the tobacco shop across the street seems to be constantly monitoring his store. These people are paid by the Waqf to keep an eye on the entrances to the catacombs. This guy probably followed you back to the Science Building. The professor carrying the old urn would have aroused suspicions."

Ari said, "So that's how they found out about the urn."

"It seems like it, and then the same guy probably followed you to your apartment; and when you left to go back to the lab, they broke into your place. It seems they want to kill everyone who knows anything about the urn."

Lisa didn't want to think about another attempt on their lives, so she changed the subject. "What do you think the scroll says? Just before the professor died, he said *it's the proof.*"

Dalia answered, "I have no idea, but it must be important. Otherwise why would they have gone to all the trouble to conceal it in the alcove?"

Dalia's cellphone interrupted her. After a minute she ended the call. "That was Braverman. He's finished and he says it's the most exciting find of the century. He could hardly contain himself. I told him we'd be right there."

They took the elevator up to the seventh floor. Lisa had no idea about what the scroll said, but she was excited. Ari and Dalia also seemed ready for a surprise. Andre Braverman met them at the door and Dalia made the introductions. Braverman seemed unconcerned with his other guests. He spoke only to Dalia. "You have to see this. It's absolutely unbelievable, and I pray it's authentic."

They sat down around Braverman's desk. "It's a preliminary translation you understand. It's so important that I'll have to get some other experts to verify it."

Dalia said, "We understand Andre, but what does it say?"

Braverman put on his reading glasses, picked up his notes, and cleared his throat. "Okay, here it is. The date at the top of the scroll says *the 7th of Av in the year of our lord 3337*. That's 425 BC in our calendar. The body of the text reads, *the prophet Jeremiah warned the people of Israel and Judah of the terrible devastation they would incur if they continued to worship false idols and mistreat each other, but they did not listen. Jeremiah spoke unto the people, telling them of all the evil that the Lord planned to do unto them in order that they might repent for their evil ways.*

"The people did not listen, and because they did not listen to the word of the Lord, he sent the Babylonian king to punish our people.

"Therefore, before the final Babylonian onslaught, the Lord said unto King Zedekiah, save the history of the Jewish people; the descendants of Abraham, Isaac, and Jacob.

"King Zedekiah then decreed that all of the records of our people, even from the times before King David and King Solomon, be removed from our Temple and moved to a secret cave.

"With the help of our Lord, the entrance to that cave may be found. The High Priest must stand at the birthplace of the Columns of Solomon on the morning of the summer solstice. At sunrise, the shadow of the finger of God will point the way to the secret entrance.

"The King has also decreed that the Senior Priests move the Holy of Holies to a place known only to them. The records and the Holy of Holies will be returned to the Temple only after peace is restored to our land."

As Braverman finished reading the translation, Dalia blurted out, "It is the proof! My god it really is the proof!"

Ari said, "This is the first and only written record, other than in the Torah, of the name of King David or the First Temple. Up until now the Palestinians have always claimed the First Temple never existed. This document proves it did, and because it was found near the site of the Temple Mount proves the First Temple was indeed built here in Jerusalem."

"We have a problem." Dalia said. "If this document has been stolen by the Waqf, they'll certainly be able to get it translated, and when they realize what it says, they'll destroy it for sure."

Lisa said, "But even if they do destroy the scroll, the translation tells us where to find all of the ancient records of the Jewish people. Surely that is even more valuable than the scroll."

Braverman lamented, "But a bird in the hand is worth two in the bush as you Americans are fond of saying, and we don't have the scrolls in our possession; and I have no idea where the birthplace of the Columns of Solomon is located; and I don't know what the finger of God is. Do any of you?"

Ari said, "Can't we check with some experts on ancient Israel? Whether they're rabbis or secular scholars, you'd think someone would know what these words mean."

Dalia said, "I don't just want to hand the information on this scroll over to some religious fanatics. They'll just use the scroll to forward their political agendas."

Lisa said, "So just ask them where the birthplace of the Columns of Solomon is located or what the Finger of God means."

Dalia asked, "Andre, if we ask some people, who should we talk to?"

Braverman thought for a few moments. "Professor Engle is good and so is Professor Gold."

Dalia said, "I know Ellie Gold. I can trust her to keep a secret. What about on the religious side of this. Who's the best religious scholar?"

Braverman answered, "I don't know, but Rabbi Horvitz would know who to talk to."

Dalia said, "So let's make some calls."

Braverman led them to a conference room with a speakerphone. Dalia called her friend Ellie Gold first because she had the number handy. "Professor Gold, hello, it's Dalia Herbst."

"Hello Dalia."

"I'm sitting here with Andre Braverman, Ari Waldstein, and Lisa Green, both of whom work at Professor Bornstein's dig. I hate to be the bearer of bad news, but Professor Bornstein was killed last night."

"My God! What happened?"

"He was murdered over an artifact he found in the catacombs. Ellie, the reason we're calling is that we have found some ancient writing that refers to the birthplace of the Columns of Solomon. Do you have any idea where in ancient Israel that might be located?"

Professor Gold thought for a few moments and then answered. "Not the Columns of Solomon, but I have heard of the Pillars of Solomon. They're located near Mount Timna, about twenty-five kilometers northwest of Eilat."

Braverman admitted, "My translation could also be pillars instead of columns. Ellie, what's the ancient history of that area?"

Professor Gold answered, "You've heard of King Solomon's Mines; well there was a lot of copper mining done in the area. It was the source of copper for ancient Egypt and was active as a mining community for about a thousand years."

Dalia asked, "Ellie do you know the location well enough to show it on a map?"

"Sure, I'll send you an old map that shows the exact location."

"One more thing Ellie; do you have any idea what the Finger of God is?"

Again Professor Gold thought about the question. "It sounds like a thing or a place, but I've never heard of the name before."

"Any idea who might know?"

"You can try Rabbi Friedman at the Beit El Synagogue in Jerusalem. He's the most knowledgeable religious scholar I know."

"Do you have his telephone number handy?"

"I think I do. Hold on for a second while I check my phonebook."

A minute later she was back on the phone and gave Dalia Rabbi Friedman's telephone number. Dalia called the rabbi's number. His administrative assistant answered the call. The rabbi was not available but Dalia left her cellphone number and an explanation of who she was. The assistant insisted the rabbi would return her call just as soon as he returned to the office.

After thanking Andre for his help, the three left his office with a copy of Braverman's translation. Ari said, "Let me buy you ladies lunch while we wait for the rabbi's call.

The three walked to a nearby outdoor restaurant close to the Antiquities Authority building. After ordering, Dalia said, "It's hard for me to process the enormity of this discovery, but one thing's for sure; we need to try to find these hidden documents before the people from the Waqf, and you can be sure they'll be searching for them. They can't allow these documents to ever be brought to the public's attention."

Ari said, "I think this Finger of God is a place. Think about it, the scroll talks about a shadow at dawn from the Finger of God pointing the way. We need to get out to this Pillars of Solomon place and look for something that looks like a finger."

Dalia said, "But then we need to wait for the Summer Solstice. That's months away."

Lisa interrupted, "We may not have to wait. I have a friend back in California who's an astronomer. I'm going to ask her for some help. Lisa looked at her watch. Her friend, Carol Winslow, would probably just be getting up, but it was worth a try. She answered on the second ring.

"Carol, it's Lisa; I hope I didn't wake you up."

"No, when did you get back in town?"

"I'm not; I'm calling from Jerusalem. I've got an astronomy problem that you can probably help us solve. We have a very old document that says we can find something by waiting for sunrise on the Summer Solstice, and a shadow from the top of a certain rock will point the way. We don't want to wait for the Summer Solstice. If we know where the shadow points today, can we predict where it will point at sunrise on the Summer Solstice?"

"Well my dear. It sounds like you're after buried treasure. It sounds like fun."

"You have no idea. I'll tell you the full story in a couple of months."

"Well to answer your question. I can definitely help. It's going to essentially be a geometry problem.

You're going to need surveying equipment. I'll need to know the elevation of the point on the horizon where the sunrise occurs, and the range to whatever the shadow is pointing to. I'll also need the elevation of the thing casting the shadow, and since you've said this is a very old document, I need its date so I can correct for time. But most importantly, if I do this for you, it'll cost you a dinner at Charlie's."

Lisa laughed at her old college roommate. "Only if you buy the Margaritas."

The rabbi's callback to Dalia ended Lisa's conversation early. She thanked Carol for her help and began listening into Dalia's conversation which she had put on speaker. The rabbi was talking. "The Finger of God is a biblical phrase. It describes the means by which words spoken by the Lord were said to be written onto the stone tablets brought down from Mt. Sinai by Moses."

"Rabbi, have you ever heard of the words being used to describe a place?"

"Well now that you mention it, many years ago, someone told me of a tall spire located in the Negev desert that the local Bedouins called the Finger of God, but it's been so long ago, I can't even remember who told me. I guess that's what happens when you get old."

Dalia said, "Rabbi, if you remember, please give me a call; it's very important."

"I'll certainly do that Doctor Herbst."

Ari summarized, "So here's what we know. These documents are in a hidden cave, maybe near a place called the Pillars of Solomon, and if we stand there at sunrise and observe the shadow from a rock formation called the Finger of God on the longest day of the year, the shadow will point to the hidden cave."

Dalia said, "That about sums it up."

Ari asked, "So what are we going to do to find this place?"

Dalia said, "After lunch, I'm going to talk to the head of the Antiquities Authority. I'll show him the translation and your pictures and explain the situation. I'm sure he'll fund an expedition to find the documents."

Ari asked, "And if he doesn't, what then?"

Dalia answered, "We'll worry about that if he says no."

Ari said, "I have a friend who takes people out on camping tours in the desert. He's got all the equipment we'd need to find this place. I'll ask him to help us, and I know where I can get some pretty sophisticated survey equipment. So when we find this place, we'll take the measurements we need to locate the cave."

Lisa said, "We need to contact the workers at the dig and let them know Professor Bornstein is dead. I'm assuming your uncle will notify his family."

Dalia answered, "I'm sure he will."

Ari called Bornstein's Administrative Assistant who worked at the site. The university had already called to inform her of the professor's death. She indicated the funeral would be held tomorrow. The entire group working at the dig would be coming in for the memorial service. Ari asked about the professor's car, and his assistant told him it was the university's car, and he could keep it until they returned.

Lisa said, "You know it's easy to get wrapped up in this scroll thing and forget that our good friend was killed, but I know he would want us to be following up on these documents."

Dalia excused herself, but promised she would contact them after her meeting with the head of the Authority. She thanked Ari for the lunch and left the restaurant.

Lisa asked, "So what are we going to do for the rest of the day?"

"Well I'm going to stop by the place I work and borrow some survey equipment, and we need to get you some more clothes and buy some food."

Chapter 13

Sheikh Muhammad Hussein, the Grand Mufti of Jerusalem, looked up to see his assistant enter his office. The man held an envelope in his hand, the one the head of the Waqf had been waiting for. The assistant said, "Imam Wadi told me you will not like what the scroll says."

The Grand Mufti opened the envelope and read the imam's translation. His face suddenly turned blood-red, and with veins bulging from his forehead, he repeatedly pounded the desk with his fist. He re-read the translation and buried his head in his hands. He finally looked at his assistant, and in a calm voice asked to speak with Imam Wadi.

The call came through a few minutes later. Sheikh Hussein asked, "What does the letter mean?"

The imam answered, "It means that if the Israelis find the documents, we've lost all hope of ever proving our legitimate claim to Jerusalem."

"I know that Farouk; I'm asking what the birthplace of the columns of Solomon and the Finger of God means. I'm hoping you have an answer; otherwise we have no way of knowing where to look for these documents."

There was prolonged silence from the imam. Finally he said, "Muhammad, I know you don't want to hear my answer, because the truth is I have no idea of what those words mean. More importantly, I believe the only people who might understand the meaning are Israeli scholars, and they certainly won't help us."

The Grand Mufti slammed the telephone back into its receiver and screamed at his assistant. "I want to see the head of security now."

A few minutes later Hakeem Kassab entered the Grand Mufti's office. The Grand Mufti handed him the translation, and after Kassab finished reading it, Sheikh Hussein said, "This could be an incredible disaster. If the Israelis find these documents, they will have the facts to support their claim to Jerusalem. We can't allow that to happen."

Kassab said, "We have the urn and the scroll. And we killed the professor."

Hussein interrupted him, "But the two others still live, and we don't know how much they know and what they've told the authorities; and now we know they're both dealing with the Antiquities Authority."

"If you want, I will have them all killed."

"Here's what I want Kassab; I want you to assume these people also have a translation to the scroll, and they will be able to find out where the documents are hidden. Follow them; let them lead us to the hidden treasure, and then after you takeover these documents, kill them all, every last one of them. Call me when you have the documents. You must not fail. The future of Palestine rests with you my friend."

Chapter 14

Dalia Herbst sat in Director Berger's office. She had shown him the translation of the scroll. He had seen the pictures of the urn and scroll, and he had heard Dalia tell the detailed story of what had happened. Now he was considering alternatives. His heart wanted to mount an immediate expedition to find the hidden documents, but the earthquake had created severe damage to treasures already under his control.

Yes, time was of the essence, but so too was the repair of the devastation caused by nature. He looked at one of his favorite senior employees with a saddened face. "Dalia, I understand this is probably the find of a lifetime, and I want to give you the resources to find these documents, but I can't right now. After we clean up the mess from the earthquake, you'll have whatever resources you'll need, but I can't give them to you now."

"But Jacob, the Waqf will be looking for these documents right now. We can't wait a couple of weeks; we have to act now."

"I'm sorry, in two weeks you can have the resources, but not now. That's my final decision."

Dalia played her final card. "I have access to outside resources that can help. Will you at least approve their assistance, and fund the expedition."

Director Berger thought for a moment and smiled at his friend. "Dalia, you're one persistent lady. Yes, you can use outside resources, and yes I'll fund the project. Now get out of my office before I change my mind, and by the way, good luck."

Chapter 15

They had split up at the shopping mall. Ari was stocking up on some fresh food, and Lisa was exploring some of the clothing shops. When they met back at the car, Lisa had a smile on her face. Ari said, "I guess you were successful, from the size of the shopping bags."

"I thought you deserved to see clean clothes."

Ari smiled that special smile of his. "Does that mean I'm going to get lucky tonight?"

"That depends on whether you're nice."

"I'll be sure to be on my best behavior."

Ari's phone rang; it was Dalia. Ari turned the cellphone's speaker on, and she briefed them on her meeting with Director Berger. Ari said, "I'll contact my friend and see if he's available."

"Okay, and let's meet in the parking lot near the produce store tomorrow morning at exactly nine o'clock, and make sure nobody at the tobacco shop sees you."

After disconnecting, Ari said, "So it looks like we're in on the treasure hunt."

Lisa replied, "I'm a little worried about the Waqf, but I'm glad we're doing it."

Ari drove the professor's jeep over to a tall glass and steel building in the newer business section of the city. Lisa waited in the car as Ari walked into his company's office building. He showed his ID to the guard in the lobby and signed in. He took the elevator up to the tenth floor and opened the door to the equipment storage locker. He signed out the best survey equipment in the company, a CST 2" Reflectorless Total Survey Station manufactured by Allen Precision. He placed the equipment in the back of the jeep.

Ari took out his cellphone, and using his speaker, called his friend Uri Shafer. "Uri, it's Ari; did I catch you at a good time?"

"Sure, what's up?"

"Listen, I need your help on something very important. It involves a few days out in the Negev, and it could be very dangerous, but I can tell you without a doubt, it's very important."

Uri interrupted, "Enough already, I owe you my life; anything you want me to do, I'm in; just tell me more about how I can help."

"Well first, a friend of mine and I need a place to stay for a few nights."

"No problem, what else?"

"It's a long story Uri; why don't we come over, and Lisa and I will brief you on the problem."

"Well, I've made arrangements with six girls for tonight, but I guess I can manage to change my plans. I'll put some steaks on the grill. You bring the wine. Can you make it at six o'clock?"

"I'll be there my friend, and I'll bring the wine; shalom."

Lisa asked, "He said he owed you his life. What was that all about?"

"Uri's in my Army Reserve Unit. We were called up in 2008 to stop the Gaza rockets. Our commando unit was doing secret advanced reconnaissance in the town of Beit Hanoun. We both got separated from our unit and hid out in an apartment building. Hamas tried to break into the place to capture us. We stopped them, but Uri was hit in the leg by some shrapnel from a grenade that was thrown, and he couldn't walk.

"After dark, I carried him out the back of the building and back to our own lines. Our soldiers almost shot us, but we signaled them with the right password, and we made it back safely."

"So I guess he really does owe you his life."

Ari said, "We need to risk going back to my apartment. I need to get some clothes if we're going to be staying at Uri's"

They drove back to Ari's apartment. Ari parked on the street behind his apartment and walked up the back stairway. After checking for any intruders, Ari unlocked the kitchen door and then checked for anyone hiding inside before he allowed Lisa to enter. Lisa unpacked the groceries while Ari began packing his clothes in a backpack.

"Ari you promised to show me some of your work. I want to see all of your sketches. I'm interested, I really am."

Ari went to his office and brought out several sketch books. Lisa slowly looked at page after page of sketches. Ari's early work was uncertain and without a common theme, but she could see a style evolve with each new drawing. Ari had talked about combining ancient architectural themes into modern construction, and she could see those elements in his work. The office buildings made use of Grecian columns and stone, and some of his single family homes gave the impression of Egyptian pyramids, but with a modern flare. She was truly impressed.

She placed the sketches back in his office and snuck up behind him. She kissed him on the back of his neck. "They're beautiful," She said. "How many have been built?"

"Three," he said, "one office building and two homes. I think I'm getting a reputation."

Ari grabbed two bottles of wine from his pantry, and the two left for Uri's apartment.

Uri opened the door and eyed Lisa, trying to determine the relationship between his friend and this new addition to the scene. Was it business that brought them together or something more? Lisa, sensing his unspoken question, moved unconsciously closer to Ari, who made the introductions.

Ari said, "Let's go out on your balcony and have a drink. We'll bring you up to speed, and then we'll have dinner."

Ari walked to the fridge and pulled out three beers. He obviously had been here many times. It took them about an hour to brief Uri. Lisa showed him pictures of the urn and scroll. He read the translation several times. "I've got two comments," he said, "and they're both related. First, if we find the documents it's a game-changer. The Palestinians will have no rightful claim to Jerusalem. The second is that the Waqf is going to try to kill the three of us, and probably this Dalia Herbst as well."

Lisa said, "They tried to kill us already."

Uri answered, "Sure, and then again they may rethink their desire to kill you right away. Maybe they don't understand how much you really know. Sure they have the scroll, and sure they've had it translated, but what does it really mean: the birthplace of the Pillars of Solomon, the Finger of God. Maybe they don't have a clue what it all means, and if they think you two know the answers, you're better off alive than dead. But the time will come when you're of no more use to them, and then they'll try to kill you both."

Ari smiled, "We've been through a great deal already: an earthquake, swimming underwater in cisterns, seeing our friend the professor get killed, and their attempt to kill us. I guess Lisa and I owe it to ourselves to finish this. What do you think Lisa?"

Lisa answered without hesitation, "We owe it to Professor Bornstein."

"So now you want to bring me into it," Uri said. "Okay, I'm in, and besides business has been very slow lately. I don't have a tour party for the next two weeks."

Ari asked, "What do you know about the Pillars of Solomon?"

"Nothing really, but I've been to the Timna Valley before. It's a strange place geologically: strange shaped rocks, barren, and rich in minerals. I took a geologist there once; he said it was underwater a million years ago. He showed me fossils of fish to prove it."

Ari left to go to the bathroom, and Uri took the opportunity to ask Lisa, "Are you two....?"

He moved his hand back and forth in a gesture meaning in some special type of relationship. Lisa laughed and gave the same gesture back. "We're working at it," she said.

Over dinner, the three made plans. Uri had everything they needed to mount the expedition. He would stock up on supplies, enough for four people for a week, and he would go with them to the produce market.

It was almost midnight when they went to bed. Uri gave Ari and Lisa his bed and he slept on the couch. Lisa put her arms around Ari. "I like Uri, but I like you better."

"Did he make a pass at you? He's done it with every woman I've ever known."

"Well, he sort of asked if you and I were an item."

"And what did you say?"

"I told him we're working on it."

Ari laughed, "So let's work on it."

Chapter 16

Dalia arrived early at the parking lot near the produce store. She sat in her car with a clear view of the tobacco shop. A few minutes before nine o'clock, a police car pulled up in front of the tobacco shop. Uncle Moshe and his assistant walked in and with the picture Dalia had sent them, they knew exactly who they were looking for. They found the young man sitting near the front of the store watching the street.

Moshe showed him his ID. Moshe's approach was to be direct, to put the person immediately on the defensive. "What were you doing at the University Science Building two nights ago?"

Jamal Hashem was shocked to say the least. Caught off guard, he wasn't really sure how to answer the question, so he just stood there in silence. Stern continued, "We have pictures of you taken with our security cameras. What were you doing there?"

Hashem knew they probably did have pictures of him, but then again he had a right to be there. "I was going there to meet a friend, but she never showed."

Stern laughed at the reason. "Actually, we have reason to believe you were involved in two murders at the university, and we're taking you in for questioning."

They handcuffed the young man and helped him into the backseat of their police car. A small crowd gathered in front of the store, a mixture of Arabs and Jews. Whatever the ethnic origin, people were people, and were always interested in a police arrest.

Dalia smiled as the police car pulled away. She knew she could count on Uncle Moshe to keep the young man occupied at the police station for several hours. Ari and Lisa, followed by Uri, pulled into the parking lot a few minutes later, and Ari introduced his good friend Uri.

Dalia said, "So this is the team that's going to fight the forces of evil and save the Israeli nation from its enemies?"

Uri answered, "Yes, and we're the best in all of Israel. You can bet your life on it."

Dalia answered in a serious tone. "I am betting my life on it!"

After a moment of silence Dalia continued. "Uncle Moshe has already taken the young man into custody, so we've got a couple of hours without being observed. Just to play it safe, let's each go separately into the shop. I'll go first with the key. I'll talk to the manager and meet you at the entrance to the catacomb."

Dalia left and Uri said, "I'm in love already. I noticed she wasn't wearing a ring. Does she have a boyfriend?"

Lisa answered, "You're certainly quick Uri. I think you'll have to find out for yourself about any boyfriends."

By the time Lisa walked into the back of the store, the others were already waiting by the open wrought iron gate. She had no desire to relive that terrible experience in the catacombs. It wasn't that she was claustrophobic; it was just that she feared another aftershock, and her experience in California made the possibility all too real.

As they descended the stairs into the catacombs, their flashlights could barely see ten meters in front of them. The earthquake had shaken the dust from over two-thousand years into the air, and the fine particles of limestone still suspended in the air made breathing difficult.

Ari led the way along the tunnel. At least this time Lisa and Ari knew what to expect, and it only took about ten minutes to locate the alcove and the blood mark on the tunnel wall. Dalia removed a chisel from her backpack and chipped off several samples of the red mark. She took samples of the stones that had hidden the secret hiding place. Then a bit of real luck. She found a sliver of what looked like wood inside the alcove; perhaps part of the handle from a stone cutting tool. Regardless of the origin, it would give Dalia the opportunity to get a Carbon 14 dating.

Chapter 17

Jamal Hashem sat alone at a table in a locked interrogation room. He had been fingerprinted as soon as he arrived. Then the detective who arrested him entered the room and asked to see Jamal's identification papers. He studied the documents and sat down across from the young man. "So Jamal, why were you at the University Science Building?"

"I already told you; I was meeting a girl."

"And what was the girl's name?"

"I don't know her name. I met her the other night in the park."

"Tell me Jamal, how long have you worked at the tobacco shop."

"Twelve years."

"And what do you do there?"

"Whatever they ask me to do."

"How do they keep track of your time?"

"I use a timecard."

"And how late did you work two days ago?"

"I don't remember."

It went on and on. Moshe's only purpose was to keep Jamal occupied for two hours. Detective Stern finally said, "Jamal, I'm sending my assistant to the tobacco store to get your timecard. I'm afraid you're going to be here for several more hours."

Jamal said, "I'm getting hungry. Can I have some food?"

Stern answered, "I'll get you something."

He left the interrogation room, and Elsi spoke to him. "Do you want me to check out his timecard?"

"Yes, and I noticed he has a cellphone in his pocket. He probably used it to contact the Waqf. I want to look at the call history without his knowing it. I'm going to slip some Rohypnol into some orange juice. He asked for lunch. When he falls asleep, I'll take his cellphone and upload all the history data."

Elsi gave him a surprised look. "Don't look at me that way!" Stern said. "This kid didn't do it, but he reports to someone who knows who did, and I want to find out who that person is. Now go get the information while I check out his cellphone."

Stern called the cafeteria and ordered a sandwich and a glass of orange juice. The food arrived ten minutes later on a plastic tray. He thanked the delivery person and then went to his desk and pulled out two small capsules of Rohypnol from a vial he kept hidden in his bottom drawer. After confirming nobody was watching, he opened the capsules and added the white powder to the glass of juice. He stirred it with his finger, brought the food into the interrogation room, and left Jamal alone.

Stern watched Jamal devour his lunch through the one-way mirror. He knew he was doing something illegal, but two people were dead, and sometimes the end does justify the means; and besides, he was close to retirement anyway, so if he lost his job, so be it.

With his lunch over, Jamal sat back in his chair with nothing to do but wait. He kept looking at his watch, then he began nodding his head, and finally he put his head down on the table and closed his eyes.

Stern waited for the drug to take full effect and then entered the room. He called Jamal's name, but he didn't respond. Stern reached into the young man's pocket and carefully removed his cellphone. Back at his desk, Stern quickly removed the phone's microchip, and using a special system, he uploaded the history data onto his desktop computer.

He returned the cellphone to Jamal's pocket and left the room while Jamal slept off his drug-induced state. Stern opened the file containing the cellphone's history and printed out a long list of telephone numbers. He gave the list to one of the junior officers and asked him to get the names and addresses of each of the phone numbers.

Just as Jamal was waking up, Elsi returned with the timecard Jamal had filled out. She had taken the timesheet as evidence without too much objection from the owner of the tobacco shop. She had asked him about when Jamal left the shop two days ago, but the owner said he didn't remember. The timecard said he had worked until six o'clock when the shop closed for the day. It was the same every day. He started at exactly the same time and checked out at exactly six o'clock each day.

Elsi said, "It's all bullshit. Nobody starts work at the exact same time every day. We need to check on his paychecks. I'll bet he doesn't even get paid by the store. I'm betting the Waqf pays him to watch the catacombs."

Moshe Stern agreed. "Let's check the owner's tax filings. He'd have to include a list of every employee on his payroll."

Jamal was sitting up in his chair looking around the room, probably wondering why he had fallen asleep. Stern decided to let him sit there another hour to make sure the drug had left his system.

When Stern eventually entered the room, Jamal was pacing back and forth. Stern handed Jamal's identity papers back to him and told him not to leave Jerusalem without notifying the police.

Jamal asked, "How do I get back to work?"

Stern smiled and said, "That's your problem Mr. Hashem."

Jamal Hashem left police headquarters and began walking back to the tobacco shop. Halfway there he stopped for a rest at a small park. He sat down on a park bench and called his contact. After describing his interrogation by the police to the voice on the other end, the man asked, "Did they look at you cellphone?"

Jamal answered, "Absolutely not, it was in my pocket the whole time I was there."

After a few more questions, the man praised Jamal for his good work and asked him to resume surveillance of the entrance to the catacombs.

Chapter 18

Dalia dropped her samples off in sealed containers at the Antiquity Authority's laboratory, and the four decided to make plans over lunch in the building's cafeteria. The discussion had switched from the visit to the catacombs to the search for the hidden treasure.

Uri said, "I'll have the last of the supplies loaded into my pickup first thing tomorrow, and we can leave anytime tomorrow."

Lisa said, "I want to go to the professor's funeral this afternoon."

Ari wanted to join her. Everyone turned to Dalia. "We'll leave tomorrow at seven. Uri give me all your receipts. Director Berger said he'll fund the expedition. I've been thinking the Waqf is definitely going to be trying to beat us to the documents. I'm sure they'll be well-armed and will have no problem killing us in order to find the treasure. What are we going to do for weapons?"

Uri smiled, "Taken care of. One thing about being a tourist guide is that I'm allowed to buy and carry weapons. I've got enough in my truck to take care of business if it becomes necessary."

Lisa was starting to get worried. It was one thing to go on an exciting treasure hunt but quite another to be risking a fight to the death with fanatics. Personal safety, however, lost out to the excitement of the hunt. She would just have to be extra cautious. Lisa asked, "How many days do you think we'll be gone?"

Dalia said, "It's hard to tell; it could be just a couple of days, but might drag into weeks. We'll know more in a couple of days."

Uri said, "If we run low on supplies, I can always drive into Eilat. It's only an hour away from the Timna Valley."

Ari asked, "What's the cellphone reception like where we're going?"

Uri answered, "The last time I was there it was very spotty. The further we get away from the main roads, the worse it becomes."

Dalia thought out loud. "Maybe I'll get a satellite phone from the supply storeroom. I know they have a couple."

Ari, who was used to meticulous planning as part of a military operation, felt uneasy. His instincts told him they were taking things too lightly. This was not some simple archeological expedition. This was going to be more like an Indiana Jones adventure, and he knew the Waqf would be armed to the teeth and trying to find the documents before they did. His commando training kept him going over and over the things they would need. It finally occurred to him. "What will the entrance to the cave be covered with? If it's a ten-ton boulder, we're not going to be able to move it with our hands, and we certainly don't want to use dynamite."

Uri said, "I'll get some strong rope. If it's a boulder, we may be able to pull it away by using the hitch on the back of my truck."

Lisa said, "We need mountain climbing equipment. This Pillars of Solomon area is in the Timna Mountains. Placing a hidden cave at ground level makes it pretty easy for people to accidentally discover the entrance, and consider how they were able to camouflage the alcove where the scroll was hidden. If we find the cave, we may only need a pickaxe to open up the entrance."

Ari said, "Lisa and I will get all the mountain climbing gear this afternoon."

Dalai added, "I'll bring some excavation tools. We've got plenty in our storeroom. Let's meet outside my building at seven o'clock tomorrow morning."

After lunch, Lisa and Ari drove over to a sports supply store catering to outdoor activities. Neither knew much about mountain climbing, so they relied heavily on the expertise of the salesman helping them. They explained where they were going, and they might have to do some mountain climbing. The sales guy wanted more details but they wouldn't describe exactly what they were doing.

It took them almost two hours and 5000 shekels, or about one-thousand dollars, to fully equip the expedition. Ari charged it and saved the receipt for Dalia. It was almost time to attend the professor's funeral. They made a quick stop at a women's clothing store where Lisa could buy something appropriate to wear to the funeral and then drove back to Ari's apartment to change clothes. Once again they entered his apartment from the back stairs. They then headed over to the synagogue where the service was being held. The police were at the synagogue in force. Moshe Stern was concerned the Waqf might try to attack Ari and Lisa again.

The professor was a widower, but his two sons and three grandchildren were greeting friends and family as they arrived. After extending their condolences to the professor's family, they sat down in the back of the synagogue with their friends from the dig. They both hugged and kissed the professor's administrative assistant who had worked for the professor for over twenty years. Understandably, she looked totally devastated. She whispered to Lisa, "I want to talk to you both after the service."

Lisa nodded yes and took a seat next to Ari. The sanctuary was filled to overflowing. Bornstein had been liked by the faculty and students alike, and they were all there to show their respect for the professor. The rabbi eventually walked to the podium and began the service. Bornstein never struck Lisa as a very religious person, but in death families go back to their roots, and the rabbi seemed to have known the professor for a very long time.

Lisa sat through the service, understanding very little, but feeling good just being there. She did recognize the Mourner's Kaddish, the prayer for the dead, and she stood up with the others, but her mind was far away. She was thinking about her own parents who had both died when she was in her early twenties. She missed them both, and although she didn't think of them every day, like she had for many years after their death, she still wished she could have had more time with them. Now it was just Lisa and her older sister Ruth.

She owed Ruth a phone call or at least an e-mail to explain what she was doing. Two people had already been killed because of that scroll, and she could easily envision the list of casualties growing. She looked at Ari. He too seemed to be lost in personal thoughts. She reached for his hand and squeezed it. Ari looked at her, smiled, and kissed her on the cheek.

Lisa had fallen for him hook line and sinker. What was she going to do when it was time for her to leave? She had no idea, but it was too late to turn back now, and this quest for the documents had brought them together in dramatic fashion. How would this all end?

The service finally ended and everyone filed out of the synagogue. Their friends gathered at the front steps, and they all wanted to know what had happened. Ari explained where they had been the day the professor was killed, and how they had taken an artifact back to the professor's lab. When they returned later in the day, their friend and a security guard had both been killed, and the artifact was stolen.

Dalia had cautioned against saying anything about the scroll, and Ari had followed her instructions. There were more questions from the group with the professor's assistant still almost in total shock. His death was particularly hard on her.

The group finally broke up. Ari and Lisa indicated they needed to stay in Jerusalem as part of the ongoing investigation, and the archeological team seemed to accept the little white lie.

The professor's assistant met with them after the others had drifted off to other activities. "What was in the urn?" she asked.

Ari felt the need to provide some additional information. "Rachel, the police don't want us to talk about it, but it was something very important. We're working with the Antiquities Authority to recover everything. We owe that much to the professor."

Rachel Goodman smiled a knowing smile. "The Professor sent me a text message just before he was killed. It said he had found the proof of the First Temple being built under the Temple Mount. Let me know if I can help in any way, and you can keep the professor's car for as long as you need it."

When they finally returned to Uri's apartment, Ari took out a bottle of scotch and poured two shots. "To Professor Bornstein," he said. "a good friend who we will honor by finding the hidden documents."

Both touched glasses and downed the whiskey. They changed into casual clothes and when Uri returned, they walked to a nearby restaurant for dinner. After dinner they went for a long walk and stopped for a coffee at an Aroma, the Israeli equivalent of Starbucks. Lisa wasn't sure why the three were so silent; perhaps it was the professor's death, but more likely the recognition that they were all about to embark on a very dangerous adventure.

Back in Uri's apartment, they all packed backpacks with everything they would need for a week away from civilization. Lisa had never been on a camping trip, but Uri seemed to know what needed to be taken, including a variety of medical supplies.

They settled into bed around eleven o'clock. They faced each other and Lisa began to cry. "Ari, I don't know where this will all end, but I want you to know I love you so much. I don't know what's going to happen when it's time for me to go back to California, but I've decided I can't think about it anymore."

Ari also had tears in his eyes. He kissed her gently on the lips, not a passionate kiss, but a gentle loving kiss. "I love you too my little California beach bum. I don't really know why; I haven't figured it out yet, but at the end of the day all I know is that I'm in love with you, and I guess that's all that really matters."

Lisa leaned against the man she loved and drove her tongue into his mouth. They were experienced now, and the sex was both experimental and enjoyable. They fell asleep in each other's arms, content that at least for the moment they were at peace with their devotion to each other.

Chapter 19

Uri had left early to pick up ice to refrigerate some of their supplies. Lisa sat at the kitchen table playing with her yogurt, she wasn't very hungry, and she was thinking once again about the risks of their upcoming adventure. Ari knew something was definitely troubling her. "What's wrong?" he asked.

At first Lisa said nothing, but then she realized Ari deserved the truth. "I'm scared Ari, really scared, Last night I dreamed I was dead with a bullet in my head. I want to go ahead, but I'm scared."

Ari thought for a moment and beckoned her to come sit on his lap. She did and then he put his arms around her. "You know there're all kinds of being scared: a child thinking there's a Boogie man hiding in the closet, the uncertainty of starting a new job, confronting death in old age, but it's almost always the same cause, the fear of the unknown.

"Let me tell you a story. During the last war against Hamas in Gaza, our commando unit was asked to go into one of their tunnels and follow it all the way into Gaza City. We had good intelligence that Hamas was storing rockets and other supplies in a house where the tunnel began. That house was almost a mile behind enemy lines.

"We had explosives, and we wanted to blow up the house with their weapons. We had night vision equipment and guns with silencers and knew we would probably encounter Hamas soldiers in the tunnel."

Lisa asked, "Were you afraid?"

"We were all scared to death; two guys threw up just before we went down into the tunnel, but we knew we had to do it. Anyway, we climbed down into that tunnel, and it was pitch black. About a mile in we saw two flashlights approaching us. We waited until they were almost at our position and then killed them. We got to the end of the tunnel and found their supplies. They had almost one-hundred rockets stored in that house. We blew it up, and we all made it back to our front lines.

"Here's the point; on the continuum of fear, that was about as bad as you can imagine. In the grand scheme of things this little adventure should generate much less fear, fear yes, but not extreme fear. Fear is a good thing; it makes us prepared for the unexpected. Will the Waqf be trying to stop us? Absolutely, but we have the advantage, because we know they'll be looking for us."

"You're right; I feel a little better already. What I do know is that I need to do this, and it's the right thing to do."

"At the end of the day my love, that's all that counts."

Lisa returned to her unfinished yogurt and began eating her breakfast. She smiled at Ari; he had helped resolve the conflict racing through her mind.

Uri returned and the three began placing the refrigerated supplies into the back of his pickup truck.

A man sitting in his car across the street had seen the truck being loaded with supplies and immediately checked in with the head of Waqf security. "Hakeem, this is Khalid. The man I've been following, Uri Shafer, he's been loading a truck in his garage with the American and the other Israeli. We have a transponder on his other car but not on the truck. It looks like they're planning to leave for a long time. What do you want me to do?"

"Khalid, I want you to follow them wherever they go, but at a safe distance. If you get a chance, place a transponder on the truck. I'll contact the others and have them get ready to follow the group if they leave Jerusalem."

Uri pulled into the Antiquities Authority parking lot a little before seven o'clock. Dalia was already there, and they all helped her transfer equipment into his Ford F150. After loading everything into Uri's truck, there was no extra space available. They even had to place some of the equipment in the backseat.

Dalia sat in the front with Uri, and Lisa and Ari squeezed into the backseat with the more delicate equipment between them. They set out a few minutes after seven o'clock. Uri headed west on Route 1. They were a little early for the rush-hour traffic and quickly left Jerusalem. An hour later they turned south on Route 6 and headed in the direction of Be'er Sheva.

Because Lisa lived in California, she was familiar with how the desert of eastern California had been transformed into some of the best farmland in the state with high-tech irrigation techniques. Israel had a similar climate, and the vast irrigated farmland west of Jerusalem shifted slowly into an arid landscape devoid of anything green as they drove southward into the Negev desert.

They stopped for lunch at a small roadside restaurant. They were making good time, and Uri thought they would reach the Timna Mountains in the late afternoon. They were all in good spirits as they ordered their food. None of them noticed the man place a magnetic transponder under the rear bumper of Uri's truck.

After lunch and bathroom stops they continued on, following Route 40 southeast into Route 90. They finally left the highway an hour north of Eliat at a small town named Elifoz. There wasn't really a road, just a well-worn path leading out into the desert. They moved slowly around the Timna Mountain Range in a counterclockwise direction. They all marveled at the unusual geological landscape: rocks looking like gigantic mushrooms, pockmarked areas looking like the surface of the moon, sheer cliffs rising vertically from the ground, and vast areas of sand; not the sandy dunes of the desert of North Africa, but barren sandy ground none the less.

A little after three o'clock, they reached the end of the dirt path. Uri checked his Google Earth map and headed in a northeasterly direction toward their goal. The Timna Mountains looked majestic, and their coppery color indicated riches in untapped mineral deposits.

As they rounded an outcropping of rocks, the Pillars of Solomon came into view. Uri stopped the car near the rock formations, and they all left the truck and looked upward at the towering columns of rock carved by nature into the face of the mountain. The pillars were actually the termination point of a mountain plateau, a butte to be more precise; a shear vertical cliff intersecting a flattened top that seemed to stretch for miles. Lisa wasn't a geologist, but she could imagine how millions of years in the past water slowly ate away at the rock forming the periodic convoluted sections of the cliff. The place indeed looked like columns carved into the side of the shear face of the mountainside. Uri said, "This is just the beginning. These formations extend for another twenty kilometers."

Lisa, followed by the others, walked up to the face of the cliff and felt a compelling need to touch the columns. The four walked around the area for a few minutes just checking things out. Lisa searched the surrounding foothills to the east looking for anything that might look like the Finger of God, but nothing seemed to fit the bill.

Uri said, "This is as good a place as any to set up camp. We've got about three hours until sunset. Let's set everything up before it gets dark."

The four helped lift the large orange nylon tent from the back of the truck. They found a relatively flat area, and with Uri's guidance, they were able to erect their large six meter by ten meter temporary accommodations. Uri checked all the stakes pounded into the ground to make sure the tent could withstand the worst sandstorm the Negev Desert might throw at them.

After setting up four cots inside the tent, and a table and four chairs in the shade of the cliff, they took a water break and sat down at the table for a much-needed rest. A slight breeze was sweeping the desert floor. It provided only partial relief to the never-ending heat of the desert.

After their break, Ari and Uri lifted a solar powered refrigerator from the back of the truck. Uri positioned the solar array in an almost horizontal position, and confirmed the unit was working properly.

Meanwhile, the girls moved the more sensitive equipment inside the tent. After the refrigerator had cooled down, Uri transferred food from a Styrofoam cooler. By six o'clock they had unloaded everything, and the campsite was organized.

Uri pulled out a bottle of wine from under the driver's seat. "Come on," he said, "this bottle is from the Tzora Kibbutz. I thought we should have a nice dinner and celebrate with a good bottle of wine on the first night."

Dalia laughed, "And what might you be offering us for our first night's banquet."

"Uri thought for a moment, "Well, you have a choice of chateaubriand, lobster, shish kabobs, or hamburgers."

Ari said, "Let's save the chateaubriand and lobster for when we find the treasure. I vote for the shish kabobs."

The others agreed, and with the menu selected, Uri walked over to his portable grill and turned on the propane tank. Ari took out his Swiss Army knife and used the wine opener attachment to remove the cork from the bottle of wine. He filled four paper cups with the red wine, and as they each took a glass, Dalia proposed a toast. "Here's to our future success. May the Lord shine his countenance upon us, and may he grant us the wisdom and good luck to find these hidden documents."

The four touched paper cups and said amen in unison and then drank the wine. Dinner was nothing exotic: lamb shish kabobs, a rye bread torn into four equal portions, potato chips, and some chocolate chip cookies for dessert.

By the time they had finished their dinner, the sun had already passed behind the Pillars of Solomon. Uri opened a second bottle of wine, and the four sat in their chairs watching the stars begin their journey across the night sky. It was a moonless night, and the stars lit up the sky with a dazzling display demonstrating the vastness of the universe. Dalia said, "The stars are never this bright in the city. Out here, in the middle of nowhere, it's easy to see why our ancestors all looked with wonder at these distant suns."

Lisa, the ancient history expert said, "The ancient Babylonians were the masters of the night sky. They were even able to predict solar and lunar eclipses."

Uri asked, "How do you know that?"

Lisa answered, "Because it's all written down in the Enūma Anu Enlil tablets from the Old Babylonian Period."

Ari said, "Yea, but they still thought the world was flat."

Lisa answered, "Perhaps my love, but they did the best they could with the information they had.

Dalia asked, "So what do we do tomorrow?"

Uri answered, "I think we should take my truck and drive along the cliffs until we see something that looks like The Finger of God. If we find something that looks promising, we can move the campsite close to the area and then begin to look for the hidden cave."

With the sun setting, the temperature began to drop, and Lisa opened her backpack and pulled out a windbreaker. Uri suddenly remembered, "We forgot one very important thing." He pulled a shovel from the back of the truck and handed it to Ari. "The honor is yours my friend. I think our latrine should be located over there behind that large rock."

Ari took the shovel from his buddy and headed off into the night. Uri said, "Make it at least a meter deep, and leave the shovel there."

Lisa asked, "Do we get toilet paper?"

Uri laughed, "Oh yes, this is a first-class expedition; there's a case in the truck. I'll move it into the tent. It probably hasn't rained here in a hundred years, but let's play it safe."

Ari returned, "Mission accomplished. It's done, and I even tested it."

The four relaxed in their chairs, mesmerized by the night sky. A meteor streaked through the upper atmosphere as it burned up.

"Is that a good or a bad omen?" Ari asked.

Lisa answered, "That depends on what culture you're from. The Persians thought it was the sign of evil foreboding things to come, but the Babylonians knew it was a sign of good luck."

Dalia said, "Let's hope the Babylonians were right."

At about ten o'clock they moved into the tent. Uri closed the flaps on the tent's windows to keep out the cold night air, and then zipped up the tent's entrance. "Uri said, "I forgot one very important thing; always keep the tent doorway shut. We don't want any scorpions in our sleeping bags."

Four cots, four sleeping bags, four people; Ari thought not much opportunity for a little late-night fun. It had been a long day, and the four hunters quickly fell asleep.

Meanwhile, four Waqf men watching from the protection of a nearby rock formation, waited for the reinforcements they had requested earlier in the afternoon. They waited patiently in their cars without anything to eat. The others were expected to arrive in another three hours, hopefully with food and supplies.

Chapter 20

Sunrise in the Timna Mountains is unlike any place on earth. The sun reflects off the rich mineral deposits creating a sparkling array of colors from crystals embedded in the mountain. The dominant color, however, is a reddish-orange, perhaps what the Martian landscape might look like at the beginning of a day on the fourth planet from the sun.

Lisa unzipped the door flap on their tent and looked out at the sun casting long shadows across the barren land. She was the first to wake up, and she took the opportunity to take a bathroom break. She grabbed a roll of toilet paper and headed out to their makeshift bathroom.

She analyzed Ari's excavation and longed for a port-a-potty. She squatted over the trench in the ground, fighting to keep her balance, and took care of business. She took the shovel left behind by Ari and threw a well-directed shovel-full of sand into the latrine.

Walking back to the tent, she noticed the sun reflecting off something at the base of a mushroom-shaped rock two kilometers to the west. At first she was just curious, but then as she thought more about it, she realized the reflection was most likely not from something natural but rather from a manmade object.

The sun's reflection stopped almost as quickly as it began. It didn't take her long to think of the Waqf, and by the time she reached the tent, she began searching for Uri's binoculars.

She found them in the corner of the tent on a small table and moved a chair just inside the tent's entrance. She sat down, raised the binoculars, and scanned the area where she had seen the momentary reflection. She set the optics on maximum zoom, adjusted the focus, and analyzed what came into view. It took a moment for her brain to confirm what her eyes were seeing, the back half of two cars parked at the base of the mushroom rock. She continued to look at the cars until she was startled by the pressure of a gentle hand on her shoulder. Her heart rate doubled in an instant.

She jerked around in her chair at the sudden intrusion. It was Ari, "What are you doing?" he asked.

"I think we have visitors. I saw a funny reflection of light when I was walking back from the latrine. There're a couple of cars parked at the base of that mushroom-shaped rock."

Ari took the binoculars from her and focused in on the objects of interest. He studied the area for a long time and then concluded, "I think you're right. That's very good news."

Lisa said, "How could that be good news?"

"It's good news because we know they're there, and they don't know that we know. That gives us the tactical advantage."

Lisa wasn't very good at the war game. She understood what Ari meant, but she still felt uncomfortable. Ari walked over to Uri's cot and shook his friend awake. Uri responded with some Hebrew profanity, and the noise was enough to wake Dalia.

"What's going on?" she said.

Ari answered, "We have visitors."

Uri and Dalia were instantly awake, and Ari explained what Lisa had discovered. After the others checked things out with the binoculars, the four huddled in the middle of the tent and Lisa asked, "What are we going to do?"

Uri said, "Let's have breakfast and talk about it. How about yogurt with some granola?"

Lisa couldn't understand how the others could be so calm. There were probably several armed men two kilometers away, and the others were acting like nothing was wrong. Uri walked out to the solar refrigerator and took out some yogurt. He never looked in the direction of the mushroom-shaped rock. They sat down at their small table.

"How can you guys stay so calm?" Lisa asked.

Dalia answered, "We've all been through several wars. You know even women serve in the Israeli Defense Force. We all fought in Lebanon and Gaza together. We've been trained to remain calm. If you don't stay calm, you wind up dead."

Lisa understood but nonetheless was scared to death. She watched the others eat seemingly without a care in the world.

Ari said, "They probably followed us from Jerusalem."

Uri said, "I was watching to see if we were followed. Once we got past Be'er Sheva the road was empty. If they were following us, I would have seen them. That means they probably placed a transponder on my truck. I'll check it out later."

Lisa asked, "Why haven't they attacked us?"

Dalia answered, "I think they know even less than we do about where the documents are hidden, so they've decided to follow us. They'll let us do all the work, and then when we find the documents, they'll attack."

Ari, who had been thinking said, "Today, let's go about our normal business. We'll take the car and slowly travel around the Pillars of Solomon looking for the Finger of God. If we find it, we'll pretend we haven't. Tonight, Uri and I will pay a little visit to their camp to see how many we're dealing with. That way we'll know where we stand."

Uri said, "If we need to, we can go back some night and take them all out."

Lisa was angry, "You mean you'd just go over there and kill them all?"

Uri looked her in the eyes. "Lisa, you're not from Israel; you don't understand; we're still at war with these fanatics; there was never peace, just one ceasefire after another. They've already killed two innocent people; and why? Just over a scroll, a dammed piece of paper threatening their so-called rights to the city of Jerusalem. I can tell you with absolute certainty, if they get hold of those hidden documents, they'll be trying to kill us for sure."

It was a rather sobering lecture from Uri. Dalia added, "Lisa, Americans haven't lived with suicide bombers and rockets raining down on their cities. There are many wonderful Palestinians; I work with some and consider many as good friends; but the radicals have taken over as their spokespersons, and Hamas and the Waqf are the worst of the worst. They don't want to see peace in the Middle East, because if there was peace, the people wouldn't need their organizations, so they constantly foment violence and call for the destruction of Israel.

"And don't get me wrong, some Israelis are just as bad, and many want to kill every Palestinian in Gaza and the West Bank. They think that would solve the problem, but they're wrong too. The problem is there aren't many moderates on both sides willing to speak out, and until the moderates take over the political dialog, there'll never be peace."

Lisa didn't really know how to respond. It was true; her life had been without witnessing much violence of any kind. She finally said, "I'm sorry but it's very hard for me to understand. It's beyond anything I can relate to. I've just become a creature of the nightly news and see only the stories the American media wish to portray."

They finished their breakfast and bagged up the disposable plates and utensils. Water was at a premium here in the desert and not to be wasted on cleaning dirty plates.

Ari warned, "The temptation will be to keep looking out in the desert to see where the Waqf are hiding, but we can't do that. They must believe we have no idea they are there. That's our one advantage, and we have to keep it."

Uri and Dalia made some salami sandwiches for lunch, while Ari and Lisa filled the pickup truck with bottles of water and some other equipment. It took all of Lisa's willpower to not look over at the mushroom-shaped rock.

The four left a little after eight o'clock. The temperature already registered ninety-five degrees, and a bright blue sky ensured even higher temperatures in the afternoon. Uri followed the area called the Pillars of Solomon slowly toward the southwest. To the Waqf soldiers they appeared to be looking out into the desert which was exactly what they were doing.

Lisa said, "If the Finger of God is indeed some rock structure and its shadow at sunrise is going to point the way, then the rock formation should be to the east of the Pillars of Solomon. That's where we need to focus our attention, in areas where the rock formations are to the east of the pillars."

Uri drove along with his foot off the accelerator, and the truck barely crept along. From time to time, in promising areas, he would stop the truck, and everyone would search the horizon for the Finger of God. Without seeing anything even close to a finger, they stopped for lunch a little before noon. Uri said, "We're almost to the end of the pillars area, maybe another six kilometers at most."

They ate their sandwiches and Jaffa Oranges in the shadow of a rock formation about half a kilometer from the cliffs. Ari had been thinking since the beginning of their trip about the search for the hidden cave, and he was constantly coming back to what the translation of the scroll said; the cave was hidden in the birthplace of the Pillars of Solomon.

The foolishness of their conclusion finally struck him. The Pillars of Solomon were basically limestone. Pure limestone could certainly be used to construct a beautiful column, but what if the pillars weren't made of limestone? What if they were made of marble or granite or even bronze? If that were the case, the pillars wouldn't have been born in this place. Ari ran his theory by the others. "Do any of you know what the columns at Solomon's temple were made of?"

With nobody prepared to answer yes, Dalia said, "Let me call Ellie Gold; she may know the answer."

Dalia tried her cellphone but there was no signal. It was the same with the other phones. Uri brought over the satellite phone and handed it to Dalia. She called her office and spoke to her secretary who transferred her to Dr. Gold's office. "Ellie, this is Dalia. I have a quick question; do you know the material the columns of the First Temple were made of?"

Dr. Gold answered, "Well of course there's no real proof, but the old texts refer to the columns being made of bronze."

Dalia told the others, and Ari immediately asked Dalia to find out where the ancient bronze foundries would have been located. Dalia asked Dr. Gold the question and she answered quickly, "The biggest ancient foundry was in the Timna Valley."

"Find out where," Ari said.

Dr. Gold said, "I have an old map of where the foundry was located. Let me overlay that map on a Google Map. I'll call you back with the GPS coordinates."

Dalia thanked her friend and then Ari smiled at the others. "A bronze column would have been born at a foundry, not out here. This area is rich in copper; you can tell from the color of the rocks. They would have mined the copper rich ore somewhere near here and then extracted the copper in a smelting plant somewhere near the copper ore deposit. It would make sense to cast those bronze columns in the same location where the smelting plant was located."

Lisa asked, "So do we abandon this area as soon as Dr. Gold gives us the location?"

Uri said, "I don't think we should go there yet. I think we have some unfinished business with the guys who've been following us."

Ari said, "You know what I'm thinking Uri? I'm thinking this spot is the perfect place for an ambush. See the way the rocks to the east sort of create a chokepoint for anyone wanting to attack us?"

Uri agreed and Ari continued. "Tonight we scout their camp just like we said we would. Then tomorrow, we break camp and move everything here. Tomorrow we'll make them think we've found the hidden cave. Then we'll set the trap, because once they think they don't need us anymore, they'll come to kill us for sure."

The satellite phone rang. It was Ellie Gold with the foundry's GPS coordinates. Dalia thanked her for the help.

Dalia wrote down the longitude and latitude numbers and handed the paper to Uri. "So," she said, "How do we feel about Ari's and Uri's plans?"

It wasn't like a formal vote or anything, just four heads nodding, but it was definitely a unanimous decision. Lisa couldn't believe that she was actually agreeing.

Lisa said, "Just in case the Finger of God is here, I think we should still continue on this afternoon until we explore the entire Pillars of Solomon area."

Again, everyone nodded their heads. So the four returned to their truck and once again began a slow search of the remaining Pillars of Solomon cliffs.

Chapter 21

Moshe Stern had become a difficult person to be with. The search of telephone numbers on Jamal Hashem's phone had taken too long. It was one excuse after another. There was a backlog of requests coming into the group responsible for completing the search.

Now, he was finally scanning the list of names and addresses associated with each telephone number. He and Elsi Fischer began searching police and Interpol databases for any names that came up. There was only one hit. It was the name of Hakeem Kassab, the head of Waqf security. "So Elsi, the plot thickens. It seems Mr. Hashem is definitely reporting into the Waqf."

"Should we pick him up for questioning?" Elsi asked.

"No, I have a better idea. I'm going to talk to the higher ups and get this number put on our intelligence watch list. The Americans can help us with this. With their help, we'll know everyone he calls on his cellphone and where he is when he makes the call."

Chapter 22

The afternoon search for the Finger of God proved unsuccessful. Two of the Waqf men had been following Uri's car at a safe distance. They had seen his pickup truck stop from time to time, and it was clear the group was searching for something. From what they had been told, the group was probably looking for some rock formation called the Finger of God. Late in the afternoon, Uri's car had turned around and seemed to be heading back to their campsite. The Waqf men repositioned their car behind a rock formation until Uri's car passed.

Uri said, "Ari, look at the tire tracks. We're being followed and they turned away from us as soon as we started heading back to the campsite."

Ari said, "I'm thinking they will have searched the tent while we were gone. I carefully placed some papers on the table. I'll know if they were disturbed."

Sure enough, a quick check of the table inside their tent verified the papers had been moved. Ari said, "Uri, I think you need to break out another bottle of red wine."

Uri smiled, "Yes, we need to ensure everything appears normal, and a little wine before our exciting dinner of either hamburgers or shish kabobs is perfectly normal."

Dalia, who was beginning to warm to Uri, laughed, "I vote for hamburgers; I can't take kabobs two nights in a row."

The four sat in the shade outside their tent sipping wine. Lisa was thinking about Professor Bornstein, but Ari and Uri had other things on their mind. Uri asked, "Where do you think they'll set up their sentries tonight?"

Ari considered the question. "I'm assuming they've set up camp behind that Mushroom-shaped rock. I'm guessing the large rock halfway between us and the mushroom rock would be the best place. That's what I'd do if I was making the decisions. The key question is whether they have night vision equipment, and if they do, whether it's visible light or infrared."

Uri sipped some more wine and said, "Tonight, we can wrap ourselves in the sleeping bags. That will counter the infrared, and we'll set up a large campfire to partially blind them."

Ari said, "We'll follow the pillars around to their left flank, and then we'll come up behind them. Lisa, have you ever shot a gun before?"

"No," she said, "and I can't shoot another person."

Uri ignoring her response said, "We'll give her the Glock. It packs less punch, but it's easier to aim. I've got TAR-21 rifles for the rest of us. I should have thought to bring some silencers, but we've got plenty of ammo."

Uri walked to his truck and took out the Glock. He showed Lisa how to hold the weapon with two hands, how the safety worked, how to chamber a round, and how to switch clips."

Dalia said, "Lisa, I know it's hard for you to consider killing another person, but when the time comes you'll have the courage to do it. These guys will shoot the men first and then rape us before they kill us. As long as you believe it's the only way to save your life, you'll pull the trigger."

Lisa heard the words of encouragement, but it seemed like an abstract discussion on the subject of murder. She knew the threat was very real, but still being able to kill another human being was almost beyond her capability.

Ari said, "Well on that happy note, let's fix the hamburgers."

Lisa tried to perk up. "I'll help you; it will take my mind off the subject."

Uri took out two compressed logs from his truck, and placed them strategically in front of the tent and in line with the path to the latrine. Lisa looked at how calm everyone seemed. "Why am I the only one who's scared shitless?" she asked.

Dalia laughed, "We all are, but when you let fear takeover your mind, bad things will happen. None of us are nonchalant about what's going to happen. We all know it's dangerous.

"After you guys reconnoiter, I'll call Uncle Moshe and let him know what's happening. Maybe the anti-terrorist group can send some people out to help us?"

Lisa thought it was the first sensible thing she had heard in the last couple of hours. Maybe Israeli troops would ride to the rescue like in the Old West movies, except they would be riding Humvees or Apache Helicopters, not horses. She busied herself by cooking the hamburgers on the portable grill, while the others set up the table for dinner.

During dinner she poked at her food while the others pushed down the calories. How can they be so calm and collected, she wondered? Perhaps it was the constant threat of war or maybe their army training. Whatever it was, she wished she could feel the same way.

Darkness at their campsite came in two phases. First, as the sun dropped behind the butte to their backs, a lingering twilight covered the landscape. Then an hour later the sun finally dropped below the horizon, and the stars and an almost quarter-moon were all they could see.

Ari said, "We should leave now. We need to see how many of them are there, and if we wait too long, they may all be asleep and difficult to find."

Uri lit the two logs and soon a pretty large fire was ablaze. Uri pulled three automatic assault rifles from his truck and handed one to Dalia and another to Ari. A second trip brought several ammo clips which he passed around.

Ari said, "If you hear shots, I want you both to fall back between two of the pillars and hide in one of the recesses in the cliff. The all clear password for tonight will be *scroll*. Don't come out if we say any other word."

Dalia retreated into the tent and checked out her weapon and then set it down on the table next to her chair. Lisa, feeling very uncomfortable held the

Glock in her lap. Meanwhile Ari, followed five minutes later by Uri, left for the latrine with sleeping bags wrapped around their bodies, and Uri was wearing night vision equipment. They then moved together slowly along the partial cover provided by the pillars and began a flanking maneuver in anticipation of coming in behind the Waqf force.

Dalia asked, "How long have you and Ari had a thing going?"

Lisa thought this was going to be a tell-all, girl to girl, discussion, and the imminent threat of death created a definite bond. It was sort of like the Band of Brothers thing, except this was a band of sisters. "I liked him when we first met at the dig, but he seemed aloof. We wound up working near each other, and the more time we spent together the more I fell for him. It was what happened in the catacombs that changed the relationship. From then on it was different. Before, I was too worried about what would happen when I went back to California, and afterward I just wanted to live for the moment."

Dalia confided, "I think I kind of like Uri. He's sort of like Ari, a very sensible sort of guy. He's not intimidated by my position or knowledge, and let me tell you, most men are; they're just too macho. After all, Israel is pretty close to Italy. Are the men in America intimidated by smart women?"

Lisa thought, "Most, but it's getting better. In another couple of generations maybe we'll actually be treated as equals."

Both women laughed and then began telling each other all about their lives, the good, the bad, and the ugly.

Lisa asked, "So how did you get interested in archeology?"

Dalia laughed, "Everyone who lives in Israel is an archeologist. The whole country is one big dig. For me it was a birthright. My father and his father both worked on different sites. It was in their blood. When I was little, they would tell me stories about what they had discovered, and I was fascinated. One day my father took me out on a dig and I found an old Roman coin. From then on, I was hooked."

Meanwhile, the men had walked about a kilometer to the left, and began moving behind the protection of an outcropping of rocks as they performed their flanking maneuver. Uri wore their only night-vision equipment, and Ari continued to stumble over small rocks as he struggled to keep up. It took them about an hour to circle behind the Waqf group hiding behind the mushroom-shaped rock.

After inspecting their camp, Uri passed his goggles to Ari. There were six cars parked behind the rock. Thirteen men were sitting in the back of trucks eating some food. Ari whispered, "We ate a lot better than these poor schmucks. They've got no tent and can't risk starting a fire. I count thirteen men; do you agree?"

"Yes, and that's not counting any sentries. We should stay here to see if they change the guards. Then we'll know the total count."

The temperature was starting to drop and both men decided to crawl into their sleeping bags to stay warm. The Waqf soldiers seemed very disciplined. They were very quiet. They knew their voices would easily carry a long distance in the desert at night.

After finishing their meals, one of the men began walking toward Ari's and Uri's position. What was he doing? Had they been spotted? Probably not; the guy wasn't carrying a gun. He stopped about ten meters from their hiding place and then pulled down his zipper and took a leak. After zipping up, he returned to the Waqf's campsite. Others soon followed the example of the first soldier.

It was ten o'clock on Ari's watch when three men headed out toward the pillars. It was time for a change of the guard. Sure enough, three other men returned twenty minutes later and started to eat dinner.

Ari said, "I think we've seen enough. There're a total of sixteen men here. It won't be a fair fight because we're going to have the element of surprise on our side."

Uri said, "We'll take them all out at that chokepoint we talked about. They'll all be bunched up together. We'll catch them in our cross-fire. Let's hope they don't have any night-vision equipment."

They slowly retreated from the Waqf campsite and then followed the reverse path back to their own camp. As they neared the latrine, they advanced more slowly and finally Ari said, "Scroll."

Dalia appeared from behind a rock. "You almost got yourselves shot. Another few meters without the password, and I might have fired."

The three returned to their campsite where Lisa was still sitting in her chair keeping the fire going. Ari said, "Okay, there're sixteen of them. They've got three guys keeping watch on us and guarding their own campsite. They've got six cars, and no real camping equipment. Our plan is going to work. We'll take them all out at that chokepoint."

Dalia went inside the tent and returned with the satellite phone. She turned it on and kept getting static. She couldn't make a call. "This happened to me once before. There must be too much solar interference right now. We'll try again in the morning."

Lisa thought, *so much for the Calvary coming to the rescue.*

The four drew lots to determine the order of standing guard during the night. Dalia drew first watch, and she sat on a chair behind the protection of a large rock. If anyone attempted to infiltrate their camp, they would be dead before they ever reached the tent.

Lisa lay on her cot next to Ari. She had forgotten to call her sister Ruth. She was just too wrapped up in her own world, and she felt ashamed at having failed to make the call. A tear dripped down her cheek as she thought about her older sister. Ruth had always been the stronger of the two, especially when both their parents died only months apart. Ruth had always taken care of her, and what if she died out here in this godforsaken spot? What then? She would have died without ever having had the chance to thank her sister for all those years of protection. The thought left Lisa heartbroken, and she cried herself to sleep.

Dalia shook her awake. Lisa wiped away the dried tears in her eyes; she had the second shift. Before Dalia left for a few hours' sleep, she explained how the night-vision equipment functioned. Lisa sat in a chair looking out into the desert. She kept scanning the terrain, hoping she never saw anything. She was under strict orders not to use her gun, but to wake the others if she saw anything. Not to worry; the gun sat in Lisa's lap, and she wasn't about to use it.

She sat in the chair, seeing only an eerie green glow through the night-vision goggles, and thought about killing another human being. Dalia said she would be able to do it if her life depended on it, but somehow she couldn't accept the fact that she could actually kill someone.

Then she thought about Ari. Could she pull the trigger and kill someone who was about to kill her first true love? Yes, she definitely could. The thought disturbed her, and she realized that killing another person depended on the circumstances. Maybe she couldn't do it to save her own life, but doing it to protect Ari or even her sister was a far-different matter. Yes, she would definitely do it to save them.

Then it finally hit her. That's how soldiers in war must approach the whole thing. They would definitely do it to save their comrades in arms. It was once again the Band of Brothers thing.

Chapter 23

The sun rising above the Timna Mountains to the east brought an end to a possible attack from the Waqf. Dalia tried to reach her uncle again, but the static on the phone prevented any calls from being made. She would keep on trying. After a quick breakfast, they began preparing to reposition their campsite. They took their time, wanting to give the Waqf people enough time to react to what they were doing.

An hour later they were on their way, traveling at a speed sufficient to leave a cloud of dust in the air, an unmistakable sign about the direction of their travels. It took about fifteen minutes to locate their new campsite. Ari had Uri slow his truck as they neared the area. He wanted to set up camp in the perfect position. He finally pointed and said, "Over there, just on this side of that large rock."

It took another hour to set up the tent and prepare the rest of their new campsite. Ari said, "If I was the Waqf, I'd set up their new monitoring point behind that large rock formation about two kilometers to the east."

They took a break and sat down at their table nursing bottles of water. Uri explained the strategy for the upcoming battle. "Those two hills create a natural chokepoint about 200 meters from our campsite. Ari and I will position ourselves behind some rocks on either side of the narrowest point. Dalia, you and Lisa can position yourselves behind the large rock just in front of the campsite. As soon as they get to the chokepoint, we'll open fire. It should be over quickly."

Dalia asked, "If we have to retreat, where should we go?"

Ari looked back at the pillars. "Somewhere inside the protection created by the pillars. We can find the perfect spot later today."

Lisa asked, "How are we going to get them to believe we've found the documents?"

Ari answered, "I've been thinking about that. Here's what I think we should do. We'll give the Waqf time to set up their surveillance. Then we'll take out the survey equipment and begin taking measurements. When they see that, they'll know something's up. We'll make them think we've located the cave back inside the pillars, and then we'll act like Houdini."

Uri laughed, "Houdini, what do you mean?"

Ari answered, "All we'll need are garbage bags and our sleeping bags to produce the illusion. I'll explain everything later."

Ari noticed a flash of reflected light near the rock he predicted would be used by the Waqf. "They're here," he said, "Right where we want them. Let's give them a few minutes to get organized, and then we'll begin our Oscar winning performance."

An hour later Ari began setting up the survey system in plain view of the Waqf men. Lisa took notes as Ari began measuring angles and distances to the east. Ari said, "See that pointed rock out by the horizon. I'm going to assume it's the Finger of God. So now, we take some measurements, something they will believe are being used to predict where the shadow of the Finger of God will fall, and now I'll move my surveying system to simulate the path of the shadow and there's the cave."

Ari pointed to an area that could easily have defined an entrance to a cave between two of the pillars cut into the cliff. "Okay he said, "Now let's all run over there and inspect the area. We need to look excited everyone. We think we've just found the cave."

The four ran at a frantic pace over to the pillars. Ari led the way into the void created by the space between the two huge pillars. The four disappeared into the darkness inside the mountainside. They were all laughing hard. It was difficult to stop. Finally Ari said, "Okay, now we go out and start jumping up and down and hugging each other. Then we'll go over to the truck and remove our lights and the pickaxe. We'll then go back to this place and take enough time so they think we're breaking into the cave's entrance with the pickaxe."

The four emerged from the protection of the pillars and began jumping up and down. Ari kissed Lisa, and Uri kissed Dalia, and that kiss lasted much longer than necessary. They huddled together and began dancing in celebration. They finally moved to the truck and removed the pickaxe and several high-powered lanterns; and then they returned to the dark area between the pillars.

They sat down on the ground and waited for almost two hours. After Uri kissed Dalia, Lisa noticed the two seemed to be sitting very close to each other. Lisa said nothing, but it was clear Ari's friend and Dalia had come to a new understanding of their relationship.

Ari finally broke the silence. "Okay, now for the best part of the plan. We go back out to the truck, and we each carry our sleeping bags back into the darkness between the pillars. I'm going to also bring back some of our plastic garbage bags, and then we'll create our illusion. And remember, everyone is very happy."

The four walked out from the darkness of the pillars in an ecstatic state. Ari had his arm around Lisa and Uri and Dalia held hands as they all walked to the truck. Ari slipped some black garbage bags under his shirt, and the four each held a sleeping bag as they walked back to the pillars. They disappeared into the darkness and then sat down on the ground. Ari took out four garbage bags and tightened the drawstrings on one until it was almost completely closed off. He then began blowing up the garbage bag until it was almost full, and then he tied a knot in the end of the bag to create a fairly large balloon. He placed the balloon inside the sleeping bag and held up his illusion.

"There it is my friends, a large urn protected from damage by the sleeping bag."

The others couldn't believe how perfect the illusion really looked. The others quickly duplicated Ari's balloon. "Okay," he said, "Uri and I will help carry these two very heavy urns back to our tent. Then we'll return for the final two urns, and then we'll open up a bottle of wine and celebrate."

Uri and Ari struggled to carefully carry their heavy precious urns to the tent, followed by Lisa and Dalia. They threw the fake urns into the back of the tent and then returned to the pillars where they removed the final two fake urns to the safety of the tent. Then, it was celebration time, but not before Ari did a surprising thing. He took an assault rifle from the truck and began shooting it into the air as he danced in circles.

"What are you doing?" asked Lisa.

Ari answered, "I'm celebrating in the traditional Arab way, and most importantly, they now know we are armed and won't risk attacking us until after dark."

Uri broke out a bottle of red wine, and the four sat in the shade of a large rock enjoying the drink.

Chapter 24

Samir Salib, the leader of the Waqf group, had been watching from the protection of a large rock formation. He had read the translation of the scroll. The scroll had been protected for all these centuries by an urn, and he saw no reason to believe the documents described in the scroll would not also be protected in urns. And for sure four urns protected in sleeping bags had been removed from the area between two massive pillars. And now those pathetic infidels were celebrating their victory, and one was actually shooting off a gun.

He walked back to his men hidden from view. He tried his satellite phone, but there was too much static. He walked up to Nizar Abboud and said, "I want you to drive back to an area where you can use your cellphone. Call Hakeem and tell him they found the documents and they're armed. It's too risky to attack them during the day. We'll wait until they're asleep and then kill them all and take possession of the urns holding the documents. Give him our GPS coordinates, and ask him what he wants us to do with the documents once we get them. And be sure you drive away very slowly so they can't see any sand being thrown up into the air."

Abboud immediately took one of the cars and drove slowly eastward for ten minutes before he increased speed. It took him almost two hours to reach the town of Be'er Ora, where a nearby cell tower provided a good signal. He then dialed Hakeem's private cellphone number, and conveyed the message from Samir.

An Israeli counter-terrorism intelligence group located in a suburb of Haifa was monitoring all calls to and from Hakeem Kassab's cellphone. A young lieutenant recognized the importance of the call and sent an e-mail message to the head of the department labelled urgent. Unfortunately, the head of the department was away at lunch and didn't see the message until after three o'clock. He immediately called General Simcus, the head of the Israeli Defense Force. Simcus had not been briefed on the existence of the scroll or its translation. It took almost an hour before he agreed to send out a counter-terrorist unit to rescue the group at the Pillars of Solomon.

His call went out to General Chaim Yidlan, the head of Yamam, an elite Israeli anti-terrorist unit within the IDF. It was a little after six o'clock before a group of ten soldiers had collected their equipment and left their command center located just outside of Haifa. The driver of the lead vehicle in the three-truck convoy wasn't able to reach maximum speed until he had cleared the rush-hour traffic near their military post. The lieutenant in charge of the group looked at his watch and estimated they wouldn't reach the GPS coordinates until after midnight. He hoped he was not too late.

Chapter 25

By reusing the sleeping bags and deflating and then inflating the garbage bags, it appeared as if a total of sixteen imaginary urns were transferred into their tent. They stopped working a little after four o'clock, convinced the Waqf believed they had found the hidden documents.

They tried to appear normal and celebrated as they ate another shish kabob dinner. Uri and Ari talked about their ideal positions to catch the Waqf in a deadly cross-fire. Lisa tried to block out their discussion. What if she had to fire her weapon? What if she had to kill another person? A lot of what ifs. There was only one reality; she was going to take part in an effort to kill sixteen humans. Were they bad people? Absolutely! The same people had already killed two innocent men, and for what; a lousy piece of ancient history.

Uri left the group and walked over to his truck. He fished out a rubber hose from the back of the truck and collected four empty wine bottles. He then opened the cap to the gasoline tank and syphoned gasoline into the glass bottles. He went into the tent and returned with four pieces of cloth from a torn undershirt. He then forced the cloth strips into the four bottles. He said, "We only have one piece of night-vision equipment. I'll have it, and as soon as those guys are in the right position, I'll light up the area with one of these. Ari, you use a second one to keep the area lit up. Dalia and Lisa, you save your bottles in case they're able to get close to you."

Lisa considered her new job. Now she would be throwing Molotov Cocktails; a new way to kill people. She doubted she would be able to light the wick let alone throw the thing at someone. She asked, "Are we going to light a fire again tonight?"

Ari and Uri considered the terrain. Ari said, "There's no need for a fire, we can all reach our positons without being seen; and besides a fire will just let them see us. The best thing is for Uri and me to cut a hole in the back of the tent and leave that way. It'll be dark about eight o'clock. We'll turn off the lights in the tent at nine and then we'll all get in position. They'll want to attack after they think we're asleep."

Uri agreed, and then walked out to his car and returned with a deck of cards. "So now a little game of cards to pass the time. I'm thinking strip poker. What do you all think?"

Dalia said, "Dream on Uri. Maybe another day when this is all over. You wouldn't want these guys to attack when you're not wearing any clothes?"

"Me?" he said, "You're talking to the best poker player in the IDF."

He reached down and picked up a handful of sand, placed it on the table and split it up into four equal piles. "Okay ladies and gentlemen, it's going to be Five Card Stud, and we'll see who ends up with the most grains of sand."

Salib, who was watching with binoculars from their protective rock, laughed. "Can you believe it, they're playing cards. Well it's going to be the last card game they ever play. Get everything ready. We're going to attack after they're asleep.

At nine o'clock they turned off the lights. Uri cut a slit in the back of the tent and he and Ari crawled out the back. Ten minutes after they left, Dalia and Lisa climbed out the back of the tent and took up their assigned positions; Lisa sat in the sand with clips of ammunition in her pocket, her Glock in her right hand, and a Molotov Cocktail sitting in the sand in front of her. She positioned herself on one side of the large rock while Dalia stationed herself at the other side.

Meanwhile, Ari and Uri had split up at the pillars and were moving in opposite directions. Ari, without the help of night vision equipment had to rely on moonlight to help him find his way to the chokepoint's right flank. He hoped the Waqf wouldn't strike before he arrived at his position, but he felt certain they would wait until they were sure their potential victims were asleep.

Ari moved slowly, trying to find a path to the chokepoint without being seen with any night vision equipment. It took him twenty minutes to reach his assigned station. He positioned himself behind a protective rock. From this perch, the quarter-moon gave him a clear view of the chokepoint, and the rock would protect him from any inadvertent friendly or enemy fire.

Just sitting there waiting for the action to begin, he thought about Lisa. He sensed her fear of the upcoming battle and had chosen not to say anything. She was an American after all, not used to war. Americans were funny. They hadn't seen a war on their own soil for over one-hundred years, and very few men or women served in their army. It wasn't that way in Israel. Everyone served, everyone had family or friends who had died in recent wars, and the entire country was always in a state of alert.

Perhaps he and his countrymen had become too accustomed to wars and death, but then again, Lisa seemed to be strong in so many other ways, and she was smart. If it hadn't been for her, he'd be dead in the catacombs of Jerusalem. When this was all over, they'd have the time to see if their love for each other was more than a relationship forged by circumstance.

The others were also lost in thought, each in their own way preparing for the upcoming battle, each thinking about new relationships and the ultimate inevitability of death.

Chapter 26

The first hint of the upcoming battle came when Uri saw movement near the mushroom-shaped rock. At first he wasn't sure if this was the beginning of the attack, but his night-vision equipment finally detected the unmistakable image of a large group of men moving slowly toward their camp. He immediately signaled the women and Ari with two quick pulses of light from a flashlight hidden from the advancing Waqf soldiers. The Waqf men were spread out in a straight line, but as they approached the chokepoint, they bunched up into a tight pack. Uri counted the men as they approached. There were fourteen of them. That meant either two were staying back at their campsite or were performing a flanking maneuver. He considered the latter the most likely, but sending only two men to attack from the flank seemed like a foolish thing to do.

Uri knew, when this was all over, body count was going to be critical. They needed to be absolutely certain they had taken care of all sixteen Waqf soldiers. Uri took one last count of the enemy. There were still fourteen of them, now only twenty meters away from where Uri wanted to throw his first Molotov Cocktail. He took out his lighter and when they had reached the three meter mark, he lit the cloth wick and tossed the gasoline-filled bottle high into the air toward the center of the group.

The bottle burst into flames as it struck the ground. The dark night was suddenly transformed into a yellowish twilight. The gasoline burst from the broken bottle and ignited three of the nearest fighters. The others, caught off guard, searched the area for the source of the thrown weapon. Ari began firing from his positon and Uri added to the conflagration. They both quickly emptied their first clips before the Waqf troops even understood what was happening. As the flames from the first cocktail began to dissipate, Ari threw the second bottle.

The Waqf soldiers had fallen to the ground after the first Molotov Cocktail burst into flames, and the second bottle spreading flames just behind them, created instant fear and panic. The men stood up and began firing in all directions

Ari and Uri, with their assault rifles on semi-automatic, began picking off the tightly bunched up soldiers one after the other. A stray bullet struck the rock in front of Ari, and rock chips sliced into his face, temporarily blinded him. He stopped firing and wiped blood and dust from both eyes.

The second bottle landing slightly behind the remaining group of men forced the soldiers forward toward the two girls. Ari and Uri were well into their second clip of ammo, and there were only two remaining fighters. Both men were running in the direction of the girls when Dalia threw the third bottle. The explosion of flames blocked their forward path. Both soldiers fell to the ground and were simultaneously hit from the fire of three assault rifles. The battle was over in less than two minutes. As Uri ran to check on the dead soldiers he shouted, "There're two more of them. Watch the flanks."

Ari ran back to the area where the two girls sat behind the large protective rock. He told Dalia to watch the right flank while he and Lisa were taking care of the left flank. Uri finally returned. "They're all dead," he said, "But there were only fourteen of them. We've still got two more. Maybe they stayed back at their campsite, but I doubt it."

The battlefield was perfectly silent, almost too quiet after the noise of the fight. The smell of gunpowder filled the air. Uri, with his night-vision equipment, was monitoring the left and right flanks and also checking the rear area along the pillars. Still nothing; just an uncomfortable quiet.

The attack came from an unexpected direction, the same chokepoint as the original attack. Beyond the surprise of the direction of the attack was the fact that there were another dozen men shooting at them. Ari screamed, "Lisa, throw the bottle."

Lisa's hand shook as she lit the wick, and taking aim, she hurtled it directly into the pack of men running toward them. The bottle burst into flames in the middle of the charging men. Terrified screams and the smell of burning flesh filled the night air. As the three others directed their fire at the charging men, more Waqf men advanced simultaneously from both of their flanks. Where had they all come from? How could sixteen suddenly turn into almost forty?

Without thinking, Lisa began firing her Glock at the moving targets rushing toward her. The others were emptying their assault rifles into the men charging from both sides. While the men were changing clips the charging men overran their positions. They hit Uri and Ari in the head with the butts of their rifles, knocking them unconscious and dragged the two women away from their positions.

Samir Salib looked over the battlefield. Twenty-six of his men lay dead, murdered by these infidels. He hurried into their tent and was shocked to find no urns. Where had they gone? He had seen them carried into the tent, and his men had been monitoring the campsite every minute. If they had been removed, he would have known. The sleeping bags used to protect the urns were there, but no urns. Then he saw an inflated garbage bag in the corner of the tent, and he immediately understood what had happened. There were no urns; there never had been; he'd been tricked into thinking there was so he would attack. Somehow they had known that he and his men were watching them.

In anger he walked out to where his men were holding the women and the still unconscious men. He stood in front of Dalia and slapped her across the face. "Where are the urns?" he screamed in Arabic. The man's veins were almost bursting from his forehead.

Dalia spit out blood from her cut lip and said, "We don't know. We stopped looking when we saw you were watching."

Samir walked away into the carnage on the battlefield. Kassab had insisted on sending additional forces to assist Salib, and Samir knew that without them, the battle would have been lost. He had been foolish to underestimate these cunning Israelis.

He tried calling Hakeem Kassab on the satellite telephone. There was still some static, but it was working now. At hearing the news, Kassab erupted, calling Salib the dirtiest of Arab names. He thought for a moment, and then asked, "Are you calling from the satellite phone?"

Samir answered, "Yes, it's working now."

"Do they have a satellite phone?"

Samir screamed at his men to check for a satellite phone, and Kassab continued. "If they have a satellite phone then they could have called for help. If you find a phone then get everyone out of there as soon as you can. I need to talk to the Grand Mufti before we tell you what to do."

One of Samir's men yelled. "They have a satellite phone, and it's working."

Samir relayed the information, and Kassab ordered him to reposition his remaining forces at basecamp sixteen and await further orders.

The sand leading to the Israeli campsite was littered with his friends. Using headlights from their cars, Samir's men placed their fallen comrades into the back of one of their trucks. They tied up the two women and both men. As Ari and Uri began to regain consciousness, they were both thrown into the back of another truck along with the two women. Two guards, with drawn AK-47 rifles, guarded them as the Waqf convoy left the area. Uri's truck was taken, but the Waqf soldiers left their tent and other belongings behind.

The convoy headed due west across the desert toward Highway 10. After reaching the highway, they drove northwest about ten miles and then left the road just as the moon fell below the horizon. The convoy headed southwest into the mountains just east of the Egyptian border.

Ari finally sat upright in the back of the truck and looked at his three friends. They each had the look of defeat written across their faces, and he could see blood still dripping from Dalia's swollen lip. Where had the additional Waqf soldiers come from? His only conclusion was that they had called in reinforcements. He knew he had been reckless in recommending standing and fighting. The smart move would have been to leave the area and seek outside help, and now he and his friends would pay the ultimate price for his macho bravado.

At dawn, the convoy slowed down as it approached a grouping of hills. The area was filled with cliffs, ravines, and canyons created millions of years ago by erosion from an ancient sea. The line of trucks weaved back and forth as they moved through a narrow ravine. Suddenly the vehicles entered a large clearing protected on all sides by vast overhanging cliffs. Under the protection of the limestone rocks, a dozen sand-colored tents were nestled together under the overhanging cliffs.

Ari quickly understood the natural protection afforded by the campsite. It was impossible to see from the desert, and the protection of the overhanging cliffs made detection from the air very difficult. The IDF needed to know about this place. Unfortunately, Ari knew it was unlikely he would ever be able to get the message out.

The trucks were parked under the cliffs, once again completely hidden from view. The soldiers dragged their prisoners out of the back of the truck and forced them to lie on the ground. Ten minutes later they were moved to one of the tents where an armed guard stood just outside and watched over them after they were each bound securely to chairs.

Chapter 27

General Yidlan received a copy of the conversation between Samir Salib and Hakeem Kassab. He immediately contacted the group trying to reach the campsite. "Colonel Weiss, this is General Yidlan. How long before you reach them?"

Weiss answered, "About ten minutes General Yidlan."

Yidlan then read the message that had been intercepted and said, "Try to find out where they took our people."

Ten minutes later the Yamam battle group reached the campsite and dispersed, searching for clues as to what had happened. Colonel Weiss contacted General Yidlan twenty minutes later with his report. "General, there's been a battle here. From the amount of blood in the sand, I'd say at least a couple dozen Waqf soldiers were killed or wounded. It looks like our people surprised them as they tried to sneak up on their camp. Their tent is still here but everything else has been swept clean. It looks like they left here heading due west. I recommend that we attempt to follow them."

General Yidlan approved of Weiss's plan. Yidlan then called his old friend Moshe Stern. "Moshe, it's

Chaim Yidlan. Listen, I probably shouldn't be calling you, but I wanted to let you know what's happening."

Stern listened with a lump in his throat as the general briefed him on the status of his favorite niece, and then the general asked what he knew about the other Israelis and the young American. Moshe Stern explained as much as he knew about three of them. When he was done, Yidlan sensed he was trying to save a group of people who definitely had the ability to take care of themselves, but now they were outgunned and probably in a fight for their lives.

Chapter 28

Samir Salib had received his orders directly from Sheikh Muhammad Hussein. Samir had never met the man, and his voice certainly commanded respect. Hakeem Kassab had also been on the conference call, but it was clear the Grand Mufti himself was in charge. Sitting in his tent, he privately questioned the wisdom of what he was being asked to do. He was, after all, merely a soldier, not a great political thinker, so he accepted his assignment without argument. If left to him, he would have tortured the two women until the men talked. That was always the way to get people to talk.

Samir, in a rare moment of thoughtfulness, thought about the epic battle between Islam and the rest of the world. The Temple Mount was sacred ground and Jerusalem itself was holy; it said so in the Koran. Palestine had been Islamic since the time of the Ottoman Empire. The imam at the mosque where he prayed said so, and who was he to question this learned man. His family had been driven out of Jerusalem during the 1948 war, and he had grown up in a refugee camp in Gaza. Why had the U.N. given his land to the Jews? Why couldn't the rest of the world understand the righteousness of the Palestinian's cause? This was his country, and he had a right to take it back from the infidels regardless of what the rest of the world thought. If he died in the process, then so be it. He would be martyred and receive the love of hundreds of virgins in heaven.

Enough of philosophy; he walked into the prisoner's tent and smashed Ari in the face with his fist. Ari's chair tipped over onto the floor of the tent as his three friends looked on.

Lisa knew their chances of survival were not looking very good. Why hadn't they all been killed already? It seemed clear to Lisa that the Waqf had no idea where these documents were hidden, and they thought her group did. That meant they wanted to keep them alive until the documents had been found.

Samir spoke to the group. "You're all lucky. I want to kill you right now, but instead a person will arrive tomorrow who's very good at getting information from people. So prepare yourselves for the worst imaginable day of your lives."

Samir walked out of the tent after telling the guard to shoot them if they tried to escape.

Uri said, "This isn't really a major base of operations. There's no infrastructure here. They probably just stock the place with provisions and only use it in case of an emergency."

Dalia said, "They're going to kill us, that's for sure."

Lisa disagreed. "Not until they find out where the documents are hidden. They think we know, and after they find out everything we know, then they'll kill us."

Ari looked around the tent, desperately seeking a means of escape. Except for a table and eight chairs, the tent was empty. The place must have been used for meetings and nothing more.

What did Ari know? For sure he knew they had been taken to an isolated out of the way hideout Israeli forces would never be able to locate. That was not good, and what it really meant was they were on their own and couldn't expect any help from the outside.

Dalia said, "We need to find out more about this place." She shouted in Arabic at the guard who seemed to be stationed just outside the tent. "I have to go to the bathroom."

The young guy with a shit-eating grin on his face looked at her and smiled. He shouted at someone out of sight, and a minute later another guard entered the tent and untied Dalai from her chair. With her hands still bound together behind her back she was led from the tent to a latrine a minute's walk away. The guard with a leer on his face pulled down her pants and watched as she peed into the shallow trench.

Back in the tent, bound to the chair and alone with her friends, Dalia said, "Three of the cars have left. The guy who took me to the latrine and the guard outside the tent are the only people I saw. There are four other tents, and the others may be inside sleeping."

Ari said, "The guy in charge said the Waqf was sending someone to question us. That means we have to escape tonight when everyone is sleeping."

"Easier said than done," Uri said. "The way we're bound to these chairs, we won't be able to use our hands to untie each other."

Lisa asked, "Can we break the chairs? Then maybe we can get close enough to each other to untie the ropes."

Ari considered that approach. "It might work, but we can't try to do that until tonight."

Chapter 29

Colonel Weiss's team followed the tracks of the convoy until it reached Highway 10. It appeared the Waqf men had headed northwest along the highway. They sped along the road hoping to catch sight of the missing people, but gave up all hope after they had reached Highway 174. It was just impossible to know which direction they had gone.

"General Yidlan, this is Colonel Weiss. We've lost all track of them. They headed northwest on Highway 10. We've traveled all the way up to Highway 174 without seeing them. Can you send up an unmanned drone to search for them?"

"Colonel, I'll set that up immediately. In the meantime, I want you to head back to our barracks in Eilat. From what I've been able to find out, the search for these ancient documents is going to center around the Timna Mountains area, and Eilat's our closest base. Check in with the base commander there and get some rest. As soon as we know something, I'll let you know."

Chapter 30

The morning passed without another visit from the leader of the Waqf team. Their guard periodically opened the tent's flap and looked inside to ensure his prisoners were still bound to their chairs.

The ropes binding Lisa were digging into her arms and the lack of blood circulating in her limbs created a numbness that had recently turned into a steady throbbing. She looked at her three friends, and the others seemed to be in a similar state of physical pain. Lisa said, "We won't have to wait for the torture guy to get here; we'll be dead from gangrene before he arrives."

Ari said, "Tell them you have to go to the bathroom, and when they tie you back to the chair again, force your arms outward so they can't tighten the rope as much."

Dalia called out in Arabic, "My friend has to go to the bathroom."

The guard yelled to one of his friends, and a man appeared with a pronounced smile on his face. He untied Lisa from her chair and led her outside to the latrine with her arms still tied behind her back. This time there was a group of soldiers gathered around the trench watching the guard pull down Lisa's cargo shorts. The young soldiers whistled as their comrade slowly pulled down her low-cut black underpants with a prolonged stoppage between her legs.

As Lisa squatted over the trench, the soldiers cheered and shouted out words she couldn't understand. Lisa closed her eyes, trying to block out the abusive intrusion into her privacy.

With the show finally over, the crowd dispersed and Lisa was led back to her prison. When the guard tied her once again to the chair, she tried to do what Ari had suggested, and after the guard finished tying her, the ropes were much less confining. She told the others, "I counted nine of them by the latrine, and another three were walking around the campsite. So with our two guards, that makes at least fourteen in the campsite.

In the afternoon they were given water and cans of what looked and smelled like dog food. Each was then walked out to the latrine and had a chance to provide feedback on just what they had seen. There were very few soldiers around. Most of the Waqf men must have been resting inside the other tents.

While the soldiers took turns standing guard outside their prison, the four captives tried to figure out how to break the chairs without being heard. The chairs were cheaply made but with strong hardwood. Uri finally said, "When the time comes, we should tip over one of the chairs. Then, I'll try to push my chair over onto the other chair. I'm the heaviest, so I'll have the best chance of breaking the chair."

"What if it doesn't break?" Lisa asked.

Uri answered, "Then each of us will keep on falling down onto the same chair until it breaks."

Nobody had a better idea, but they spent the better part of the day trying to think of one. They were fed the same food for dinner as they had for lunch. Dalia laughed. "Oh, how I long for one of Uri's shish kabobs."

Darkness finally fell on the campsite. They could hear the Waqf men outside eating dinner in the cool night air. There was very little laughter. They were probably all thinking about their comrades who had fallen in battle back at the Pillars of Solomon.

The Waqf camp had settled into a routine. Their guards were changed every two hours, and every ten minutes or so the single guard on duty would open the flap-door on the tent to check up on them. Their plan was simple; free themselves from the chairs without being heard and then wait until the guard checked up on them and take him out of action. There wasn't much of a plan after that, perhaps because they all seemed to understand that freeing themselves from the chairs without being heard probably wasn't going to happen.

The guards changed shifts about four hours after sundown. Ari said, "If they stay true to form, he'll check up on us again in ten minutes. When he goes back outside, Dalia will try to tip her chair over next to Uri."

Two minutes later their plan suddenly changed. A tall man dressed like Omar Sharif in Lawrence of Arabia lifted the flap of the tent and placed his finger over his lips. He spoke in Arabic, "I'm here to rescue you."

Dalia translated for Lisa who suddenly had a smile on her face. The man with a large black mustache took out his Khanjar, a short curved Arab knife, and quickly freed the four prisoners from their bindings. The man whispered to them. "Follow me and be very quiet. The others are sleeping."

The five, led by the Arab, emerged from the tent. Lisa saw their guard lying in the sand with a pool of blood under his neck. It didn't take much to figure out what had happened. The five moved quietly away from the camp and into the darkness. A quarter- moon allowed the group to move rapidly toward the entrance to the ravine that the trucks had used to enter their secret hideout. At the beginning of the entrance, the Arab man turned to them. "I am Saladin Abdul-Hamid. My brother and I were on our way to a nearby oasis when we saw your captors bring you here. They're Hamas; we know them; they cause us all kinds of problems. We're Bedouins from the Al-Tarabin tribe. We have four camels on the other side of the hill. Hurry, we must be away from here before they discover you have escaped."

Ari translated for Lisa as they followed the handsome Bedouin in the flowing long black robe. They were out of breath when they finally reached the safety of the next hill. Another man who looked like a younger Saladin and perhaps in his late teens, held the harnesses of four camels resting on the ground.

Saladin quickly arranged the pairings of people onto the camels to balance the weight. Lisa was helped onto the saddle of one of the beasts, who snorted at the intrusion. Ari sat behind her, and the others quickly mounted the two other animals. The fourth camel was loaded down with supplies. At a signal from Saladin, the four camels rose onto their feet and began a rapid trot toward the south and away from the Waqf campsite.

Lisa, who had never ridden a camel, was bouncing around until Ari told her to just relax and go with the flow of the animal's funny gate. She finally caught on and began to actually enjoy the thrill of the ride. After ten minutes, they slowed to a fast walk and Saladin introduced his younger brother Malik. Saladin said, "Our family is camped about ten kilometers from here. We will go there and then decide what to do next."

There were no arguments from the four, and they continued on their journey under a cloudless star-filled night sky. A brisk westerly wind began stirring up the desert sand. Malik passed out scarfs that they wrapped around their faces to ward off the microparticles of silica. It was good to be free, and Lisa leaned back against Ari feeling the comfort of his love. Perhaps Lisa's affection was the result of a mutually shared avoidance of a death sentence. At this point, she didn't much care why she felt the way she did. It had become just wanting to enjoy the moment.

The Bedouin camp came up suddenly. Some nearby palm trees suggested a source of water was close to the camp. In the partial moonlight, Lisa could make out about a dozen huge tents draped in a mixture of animal skins. Their arrival awakened the sleepy residents who left their tents to see what Saladin and Malik had brought to their makeshift camp.

At a voice command from Saladin, the camels knelt down on their front legs and then lay down on the sand. An elderly man, who Saladin introduced as the paternal leader of his family, welcomed them to his home. He and Saladin spoke in a Bedouin dialect which Dalia, the linguist in the group, recognized. "Saladin's father welcomes us all to his home, and we will be treated as a part of his family."

Uri thanked the elder, "Shalom Aleichem." He then greeted the Bedouin leader with a gesturing of his hand to his forehead and then his lips with the universal sign of Arab friendship to their host.

Saladin spoke in Hebrew, "Come, let us share food to celebrate your freedom, and you must tell us how you came to be captured by these terrible men."

As the four freed friends followed Saladin toward the largest tent, Dalia said, "Lisa, it is the Bedouin custom that the women eat in the back section of the tent. The men will stay in the front of the tent. I'm not sure how they'll handle sleeping, but try to follow my lead."

Upon entering the huge tent, Lisa and Dalia were led into the back area by an elderly woman who Lisa assumed might have been the elder's wife. Saladin, meanwhile, escorted Ari and Uri to a sitting area near the front. Saladin, along with his brother Malik and their father, arranged themselves on large cushions.

In spite of the late hour, the men were immediately served hot tea followed by stewed lamb with raisins and rice on pita bread. Ari and Uri raised their cups of tea in a toast to the Bedouins who had saved their lives. Saladin said, "Please my friends, eat first and then tell us your story."

For a last-minute meal, the food was excellent. The stewed lamb dish created a wonderful combination of sweetness and texture. They all ate in silence and Ari savored each bite he took. He knew how lucky they were to have been saved by these nomadic men of the desert.

Over tea, Saladin's father spoke and Saladin translated. "My father wishes to know how you came to be honored guests in his house."

Ari had been thinking about what he would say for some time, and had settled on limited truth. "The four of us were on an archeological expedition in the Timna Mountains area. The men who captured us are from the Waqf. They had been watching us for days. They wanted to steal whatever artifacts we found. They tried to attack us last night, and we were overwhelmed, but we killed many of their men in the fight. They dragged us to the place where you found us. They said they were waiting for someone from Jerusalem to come question us, but then they were going to kill us. If you hadn't risked your life to save us, we'd have been killed for sure."

Saladin translated Ari's story from Hebrew into the strange dialect. His father, who had been listening intently, nodded his understanding. He then spoke and Saladin translated. "My father said the Waqf are very bad people. They are supposed to protect and manage the sacred Muslim sites, but they have become too political. They support Hamas and other radical groups, and they are destroying our country. He also wants to know how he can help you."

Ari answered, "Tell your father that we thank him for his support, and that if possible, we would like to be taken to the nearest town where we can call the Israeli Government for help."

Saladin translated the request and after his father spoke, he translated back into Hebrew. "My father says you will rest tonight as his guests, and then in the morning you will be escorted to the nearest town."

Ari, almost as an afterthought, said, "Saladin, have you or your father ever heard of something called the Finger of God?"

Saladin said, "I have not, but let me ask my father."

Saladin's father thought for a long time about the question and then spoke to Saladin. "My father says he has not heard of the Finger of God, but he has heard of the Hand of God. It is a rock formation located in the Timna Valley. The ancients say it was a place where God pointed the way to the Promised Land for Moses, but he thinks those are just stories, and it is just a rock formation that looks like a hand."

Ari, trying not to look too excited, said, "We've been trying to find it. We believe there are some old documents hidden somewhere near there. Can you show us its location on a map?"

Saladin again translated the answer. "My father says that if this search for the ancient documents is important to you then you must let his two sons lead you to the location of the Hand of God."

Ari knew he couldn't deny the elder's offer of assistance after his sons had saved their lives. He said, "We would be eternally grateful for your help."

Meanwhile, the girls had also been treated like honored guests. The Bedouin women were impressed with Dalia's command of their language, and they had never met an American before, however, they had only a limited understanding of where or what America was.

With Dalia translating, Lisa surprised the women with her knowledge of Bedouin history dating back to before the Ottoman Empire. Ancient history was her specialty after all. Lisa explained the history of the Bedouin people, not meant as a lecture but rather to see if her knowledge matched that of her hosts. Surprisingly, the women indicated that such historical matters were only for the men of the community to consider.

The women wanted to know if Lisa and Dalia were married. Dalia explained they were both in love, but not yet committed. All of the older women laughed and offered advice to Dalia. Lisa just smiled, not understanding a word of the conversation.

A girl came up to the eldest woman and spoke to her. "Your tent is ready," the elderly woman said. "I will let my son Saladin know that your men can join you as they wish."

The young girl led Lisa and Dalia to a nearby tent. Dalia thanked the young girl who looked embarrassed and ran away. Ten minutes later Ari and Uri arrived at the tent door and entered their bedroom for the night.

Lisa kissed Ari and Dalia hugged Uri. "We have some great news, Ari said. "Saladin's father knows of a rock formation called the Hand of God. The Finger of God must be part of the same rock. And better than that, Saladin and Malik are going to take us there."

The girls described their dinner with the other women, but Dalia left out the part about being in love. Uri said, "Tomorrow morning at breakfast we'll plan our trip."

Ari looked at his watch. It was almost 2:00 a.m. "Let's get some sleep. We've been going non-stop for almost two days."

Large sleeping pads had been laid out at the back of the tent and the four quickly rearranged their mattresses; Lisa slept next to Ari, and Dalia snuggled up close to Uri.

Chapter 31

The dead guard was discovered by the Waqf soldier going on guard duty. He immediately awakened Salib who began taking his anger out on his men. At first he thought the four infidels had cut themselves free of their bonds and then killed the guard.

They began a rapid search of the area in their cars, believing the four had fled on foot. His understanding of the most likely scenario quickly changed, however, when his men found the tracks of four camels leading out into the desert. They began following the tracks, but a stiff wind from the west soon obliterated the tracks and made further pursuit impossible. The tracks had led around the next mountain and the ultimate direction of the fugitives could not be determined.

Samir arrived back at his campsite knowing he needed to contact Hakeem Kassab, but he also knew Kassab and the Grand Mufti would hold him personally accountable. His return to Jerusalem would almost certainly be met with a quick death sentence. He thought about what had just happened. The four prisoners were freed by a person or several people who had arrived by camel. Camels meant Bedouins. Some local Bedouins must have seen the captured infidels being treated roughly and imprisoned in the tent. They must have snuck into the campsite after dark and killed the guard. But where did they take his prisoners? That was the question.

Salib knew there were few options. The closest major town was at least sixty kilometers away. The more likely scenario was the group had fled to one of the small Bedouin villages or one of the temporary campsites the Bedouins were known to frequent in both the Negev and Sinai deserts. He finally settled on a plan. Tomorrow he would send his people out into the desert to look at the nearby Bedouin towns and the known Bedouin campsites. If he could reestablish contact with the infidels, then he could save his own life, and that was something he desperately wanted to do.

Salib gave new orders to his men and told them they would continue the search early the next morning.

Chapter 32

Dawn found Lisa sleeping in Ari's arms. She looked over at Dalia who was still pressed up against Uri. Lisa stood up from their shared mattress and opened the tent's flap-door. There were several dozen lambs and goats wandering about the campsite in search of something eatable. She had not noticed the animals last night or the fact that the campsite was located in an oasis in the middle of the desert. Several dozen date palms were scattered around the area.

She walked to the greenest area and found a freshwater spring and then wandered back to the main camp. There were about a dozen women and girls already up, and many were busy milking some goats near one of the tents. The women were friendly and greeted her with the Arab greeting of Shalom Aleichem, peace be unto you. She returned the greeting and smiled at everyone. A middle-aged lady motioned for her to sit down at her milking stool and try milking one of the goats.

Lisa sat down at the stool and tried her hand at extracting the white liquid. The goat recognized the inexperienced hand and protested loudly. Soon a half-dozen little girls were standing over Lisa laughing as she struggled to squeeze out the milk. With a little bit of guidance from the lady, she was soon up to speed and enjoying the sight of a full bucket of fresh warm milk.

Ari snuck up behind her and kissed her on the back of the neck. The outward sign of affection was foreign to the Bedouin women who stared in amazement at the two outsiders. "Look at what I've done Ari. We'll have it for breakfast."

Lisa stood up and relinquished her seat of honor beneath the goat to the woman who had been there before. Hand in hand, they walked back to their tent where they found Uri and Dalia both awake and ready to start their day. As the four left their tent, Saladin appeared and explained that breakfast would be served in the same large tent where they had dined the night before.

Once again the men sat in front, and the women were fed in the rear. Saladin said, "We must plan our adventure. What will you need to find the artifacts you seek?"

Ari said, "A survey instrument, ropes, and a pickaxe. We may need other things, but until we see the area, we won't know for sure. Do you have access to a satellite phone?"

Saladin answered, "The rope and the pickaxe we have here. My cousin may have access to a satellite phone. We're going to travel to a nearby town after breakfast. Many people from our tribe live there. My cousin has a truck that we use to trade our lambs for other things a couple times a year. We'll borrow it to find this Hand of God, and maybe someone in the town will have survey equipment."

Their breakfast consisted of pita bread, hummus, fresh yogurt with honey, and cold goat's milk. Uri asked, "Where do you have a refrigerator?"

Saladin laughed, "We try to carry on with our nomadic ways, but we couldn't resist trading a few of our lambs for a solar-powered refrigerator. Now, nobody ever gets sick drinking milk that's a few days' old."

Ari asked, "And where did you get the honey?"

Saladin answered, "Like I said, once a year we drive a few goats over to a kibbutz on the road to Haifa. They have an orange grove and bees there, and we trade the lambs for the honey and some fresh fruit. Our culture has a long history of trading with others for the luxuries of life."

After breakfast, the entire Abdul-Hamid clan gathered around a half-dozen camels and after thanking Saladin's father for his hospitality, the six explorers set off into the desert in the direction of the small Bedouin town of Zaramin, about twenty kilometers east of Ezuz. Lisa was riding her own camel, and had finally figured out how to match the syncopated rhythm of her ugly-looking beast.

Malik and Saladin took turns leading their caravan. The group moved in a southeasterly direction working their way across the open desert, through narrow ravines, and around the foothills of rocky mountains. They rested from time to time and drank water from what Lisa figured must be lamb or goat bladders encased in animal hides. The water was a little off in flavor but certainly drinkable.

After a three hour trek through the Negev Desert, Saladin pointed to a town below a hill just on the edge of the horizon. "That is the town of Zaramin my friends. We should be there in another thirty minutes."

As if sensing the end of their journey and the prospects of water and food, the camels seemed to increase their gate. Saladin's estimate was pretty close to the actual arrival time, and the caravan rode into the outskirts of the small town a little after eleven o'clock.

Their arrival caused only a minor commotion; several dogs barked at the heels of the six camels. Lisa thought the place looked more like a ghost town than a vibrant community. A few men were tending grazing lambs and goats just north of the village amid some green fields created by a vast irrigation system. There were only about fifty homes in the town, mostly made out of clay bricks probably trucked in from some other area. There were less than a dozen cars and a few trucks parked in the town, and the center of activity seemed to be a single-pump gas station in the center of the community. Adjacent to the gas station, the Bedouin equivalent of a 7-Eleven store seemed to be the only other commercial establishment.

Saladin's cousin's home was located on the edge of the small town. An olive tree and a large date palm provided some shade in the back of the house which faced the desert. Parking thirsty camels in a residential area wasn't a problem at all, because many of the animals seemed to be roaming the street unattended by their owners. Communal watering troughs positioned along the road were reason enough to stay in town if you were a camel.

Our arrival was heard within his cousin's home because a man in his thirties, looking a lot like Saladin, met the group as the camels knelt down to offload their human cargos. Saladin and Malik hugged their cousin, and the three began to speak rapidly. Dalia explained Saladin and Malik were filling their cousin in on the details of what had happened over the last twenty-four hours.

Looking a little suspicious, Saladin's cousin was escorted over to the others and Saladin introduced his cousin Aziz Abdul-Hamid. The man shook hands with Ari and Uri and bowed graciously to Lisa and Dalia. A Bedouin woman carrying a toddler in her arms emerged from the home. Aziz directed his wife to prepare their home for his cousins and their honored friends.

Luckily, Aziz spoke Hebrew, and over tea served in the main room of their small house, they discussed the possibility of acquiring Aziz's truck and supplies for their trip. He willingly offered his truck, and the nearby store could sell them food, but nobody in the town had surveying equipment. When asked about the possibility of a satellite phone, Aziz left the house and returned ten minutes later. "My friend says we can borrow the phone to make some calls, but you can't take it with you on your expedition."

Dalia spoke in the Bedouin dialect. "Your friend is very generous. We will only make a few calls and then you can return it to him."

Aziz was surprised to hear Dalia speak in his native tongue. Women were to be seen not heard. Aziz handed the phone to Saladin, who handed it to Uri, who handed it to Dalia. Equal rights for women would have to wait a few centuries in this Bedouin community.

Dalia immediately called her uncle. "Uncle Moshe, it's Dalia."

"Where are you? Are you safe? The IDF is searching for you. The Intelligence Service intercepted a call that you had been captured."

"We were Uncle Moshe, but we were rescued by Bedouins."

She then proceeded to provide the detective with a brief summary of their ordeal. She explained their Bedouin friends knew where the Finger of God was located and they were getting provisions in the

Bedouin town of Zaramin, a small town deep in the Negev desert.

When she explained they would be continuing on their quest to find the ancient documents, Moshe was angry. "My beautiful niece, you are crazy. I will call the IDF, and they will provide security for you."

Dalia replied, "Uncle Moshe, we're safe now. The Waqf people have no idea where we are or where we're going. We don't need any help. We'll be back in Jerusalem in a few days."

Moshe asked, "Where will you be going?"

"We're going into the Timna Valley. We believe the cave holding the documents is near an ancient foundry. Our Bedouin friend Saladin says the Finger of God is located near the old foundry."

Moshe pressed the issue. "Where exactly is this ancient factory?"

"Talk to Professor Ellie Gold. She has an ancient map showing the location. Listen uncle, I've got to go now. We're borrowing someone's satellite phone."

She hung up before Detective Stern could protest. His free-spirited niece was at it again, flaunting her own personal safety. She had no idea of the danger she was in. He was going to have to get personally involved, but first he needed to call his friend General Yidlan to update him on the status of Dalia and her friends.

Ari had been thinking about the lack of surveying equipment. He asked Aziz if anyone in town would have a protractor. Ari had to explain what a protractor was. Aziz thought the town's school teacher might have one. He left to ask the teacher and Ari said, "Lisa, you need to contact your friend back at UCLA. We need her to estimate the angular change between tomorrow morning and the Summer Solstice. We're not going to be able to call her from the site. She'll just have to make a guess."

Lisa looked at her watch. Carol would just be getting to work. She took the satellite phone and dialed her friend's number. "Carol, it's Lisa again. Listen, I can't talk for long. I need you to run your computer program right now and tell us the angular change in the direction of the sunrise between tomorrow morning and the Summer Solstice, and to also compensate for the time between 425 BC and today."

Carol Winslow said, "Don't be so pushy honey; I'm sitting down at my computer right now. Okay, the Summer Solstice was exactly seventy nine days ago, and 425 BC is 2439 years ago. Okay, the computer's thinking and here's the answer. You need to move your survey equipment exactly 11.6534 degrees to compensate for the change in position of the rising sun and the date. Remember, you owe me a dinner and say thank you please."

Lisa laughed, "Thank you Carol. I've written down the information, and we'll definitely go to dinner when I get back."

Ari considered the information. "It all depends on how far the Finger of God is from the cave. If it's nearby, we may get pretty close without precision survey equipment, but if it's far away, we could be way off. We'll just have to wait and see."

Aziz returned with a cheap plastic protractor and explained the teacher said they could keep it. Ari needed a wooden stake, some glue, a thread, a small weight, and a straight metal rod. Aziz left to find the material, and Uri asked what Ari was doing. "I'm going to make a poor-man's transit. If we're lucky we may be able to get pretty close with my crude survey system."

Saladin said, "Let's go over to the community store to get some supplies while Aziz collects the other things you need."

Two of Samir's men had arrived near Zaramin a little before noon. They had found a position on a hill overlooking the small town. They both knew if they entered the Bedouin town they would not be welcome, and if their prisoners were there, they would immediately be warned of the Waqf's arrival by the townspeople. Instead, they stayed hidden on the hill and used powerful binoculars to monitor activity within the town. They took turns scanning the place for the Israelis who had killed many of their friends.

They spotted the infidels as they left a small home on the edge of town and walked toward a store next to a gas station. The Waqf soldiers immediately called Samir on their satellite phone and gave him their GPS coordinates. Samir, suddenly with renewed hope, began calling his men to give them the GPS coordinates of the town.

The store alongside the gas station was run by an elderly man. He was missing half his teeth, but for some strange reason his smile was infectious. Dalia spoke to him about how they could pay for the supplies. The man took out his own satellite phone and showed Dalia a PayAnywhere app. Dalia explained that they had lost their credit cards, and the man said all he needed was the credit card number, and he could enter the number manually. Any friend of Aziz could be trusted.

With the method of payment settled, everyone split up and began buying supplies. By two o'clock all of the provisions had been loaded onto the bed of Aziz's truck. Uri drove with Saladin sitting in the front passenger seat. The others found comfortable positions in the back leaning up against the supplies.

The old truck smelled from lamb, and Aziz made no attempt to keep the bed of the truck clean. Lamb droppings were scattered everywhere and the odor was overpowering.

They headed southeast along Highway 10 and switched over onto Highway 12. Finally, when they were directly west of the Timna Valley, they left the safety of the highway and began moving at a much slower speed over the desolate barren ground.

This part of the Negev Desert was unlike the other areas Lisa had seen. She had been to Death Valley once when she was growing up. The family had taken one of those three-week car trips to the West Coast. If you took Death Valley, added a couple inches of loose sand, threw in a mixture of hills and mountains, and then topped it all off with a variety of bizarre-looking rock formations and large and small boulders strewn in random fashion, it would look a lot like this desolate place.

Uri was able to make a steady ten miles per hour, but with constant changes in direction to avoid the many obstacles in their path. Everyone in the back of the pickup truck was getting sick to their stomach.

Suddenly Lisa was shocked to hear Malik say in broken English, "I think I'm getting sick. This is worse than a ride on a bad camel."

Lisa was shocked, "Malik, where did you learn to speak English?"

"I worked at an archeological excavation in the Sinai a few years back. Everyone there spoke English because it was run by the University of Chicago. I picked up just enough to get by."

Lisa scolded him. "Malik, your English is perfect. I wish I could speak Hebrew as well as you speak

English. If I was here longer I'm sure I would, but I'm going back to California in a few weeks, and I won't get much practice speaking Hebrew there."

The truck continued on at a steady pace. The flat terrain eventually became hills and the hills slowly transformed into foothills; and finally they reached the Timna Mountains. They were massive, having been uplifted out of the ground by massive geological forces many millennia ago. This section of the mountains reminded Lisa of the Rocky Mountains; rocks void of any vegetation rising up with strange shapes; huge slabs of grey and sand-colored stone defying gravity.

With Saladin directing Uri, the truck wound its way through passes between the mountains. As they approached the Timna Valley, the mountains began to take on a cinnamon color, and as they passed through narrow ravines created by ancient rivers, Lisa could see many mineral-rich formations. This area would have been a source of many minerals and chemicals available to Bronze Age people who were just learning how to forge tools and weapons from the copper and tin hidden within the mountains.

Saladin guided Uri from his internal compass; maps or a GPS navigation system were not necessary. The general direction was due west, but navigation through the passes in the Timna Mountains didn't allow for movement in a straight line. Finally Saladin pointed to a narrow gap between two mountains. "The Timna Valley is just ahead between those two mountains"

Lisa had no idea of what to expect, but as they passed through the gap, a large open area stretching for many kilometers in all directions became visible. The geology of the valley was different. The larger massive boulders were missing, but scattered throughout the valley in their place as far as the eye could see were thousands of unusually shaped rock formations poking out of the ground.

Uri asked Saladin, "Where is the ancient foundry?"

Saladin pointed to the northeast. "See the flat-toped mountain straight ahead; the ancient foundry is close to that mountain. That's where the ancients used to make bronze. They built the foundry near the source of the copper."

"And where is the Hand of God?"

"Straight ahead my friend; halfway between here and the foundry."

Ten minutes later they had reached a very unusual rock formation. Uri slowly circled it from a distance of about one-hundred meters. Everyone's eyes were focused on the formation of stone standing about one-hundred meters in height. As they reached the south side of the formation, Uri stopped the car. Everyone jumped out and stared up at the pile of stone. From this angle, it did indeed look like a hand, and this Hand of God had one of its fingers, the Finger of God pointed straight up into the afternoon sky. Lisa could see why the ancients revered this rock formation. It would be a constant reminder to those standing beneath it that God was looking down at them from the heavens above.

Ari positioned his wooden stake directly west of the Finger of God near its base. While the others set up the campsite, he used the pickaxe as a hammer and pounded the wooden stake into the sandy ground, trying to keep it in a vertical position. He then glued the plastic protractor on the top of the stake with quick-setting epoxy Aziz had found at his neighbor's house. While the glue was curing, Ari attached some sewing thread to a nail, being careful to center the thread on the center of the nail head. He then attached the thread to the protractor about a half inch away from the stake, and used the nail hanging from the thread as a plumb bob. By making slight adjustments to the position of the stake, he was able to align the handmade instrument so the stake was in a perfectly vertical position. He now had a functional surveying instrument; not very accurate, but better than nothing.

After setting up the campsite, the others joined Ari and admired his handiwork. Ari explained, "We're going to be pretty far away from where the shadow of the finger hits the mountain behind the foundry, and there's a low hill blocking a view of the base of the mountain. Tomorrow, one of us will take the truck to a position near where we think the shadow will hit the mountain. When the rising sun is centered at the top of the finger that person will move the truck so it is just below the top of the shadow. I will then record that direction on the protractor using the straight metal rod resting on top of the protractor to determine a line of sight.

"Then, I'll rotate the directional rod 11.65 degrees to simulate the Summer Solstice. Each of you will be stationed along the way within sight of each other. I will give hand signals to move the closest person to be in line with the new direction. That person will pass along the signal to the next person until we're all aligned in the new direction and the truck is also positioned along that line. The person in the car will then mark the spot. Hopefully the cave will be in that location."

Back at the campsite, they took out their dinners. They opened cans of cooked meat and rice. Malik said it was lamb, seasoned with Turkish spices. They washed down the food with some warm orange juice. Lisa longed for one of Uri's shish kabobs, but given the circumstances, the meal was at least filling.

Saladin asked, "Tell us about how you came to believe there are ancient artifacts hidden in a cave."

It was a reasonable question given the assistance Saladin and Malik had given them, so they spent an hour telling them the full story. Saladin and Malik listened in silence, and when the story was finished, Saladin said, "The Waqf are pigs. Do they really believe the Jews have no legitimate rights to Jerusalem? My country has a history of all religions having lived here, certainly not in peace, but at least they have all lived here."

Ari replied, "Let me tell you a story that will help explain things. Once upon a time a scorpion was trying to cross the Jordan River. It came across a turtle that was going to swim across the river. The scorpion asked to be taken across the river on the turtle's back. The turtle asked why he should do that. You'll sting me when we're in the river and I'll die. The scorpion said he certainly wouldn't do that because then they would both die. The turtle thought about what the scorpion had said and finally agreed to carry the scorpion across the river. Halfway across the river the scorpion stung the turtle. As the turtle and scorpion sank into the river, the turtle asked the scorpion why he had stung him. The scorpion answered because this is the Middle East."

Everyone laughed at the truth behind the old parable.

Lisa asked, "Ari, I don't know anything about how to make bronze columns. How would they have done it? The columns must have been very heavy. How could they have possibly transported them all the way to Jerusalem?"

Ari took a drink from his half-empty juice container. "Well first, they would need to make the bronze, and to do that, they needed copper and tin. They made those metals over there at the foundry by smelting the raw ores. Then they mixed the pure copper and tin together to form the alloy bronze.

"Now comes the interesting process. I'm guessing now, but the columns certainly weren't made in one piece. As you pointed out, they would have been too heavy to move. So probably the column was designed to use large interlocking rings that were stacked one on top of the other.

"First, they would make a wax positive of the ring. Then they would encase the inside and outside of the wax ring in clay. When they fired the clay to harden it, the wax would melt and run out of a small hole in the bottom of the clay. So now they had a hardened clay mold, and they could pour the molten bronze into the hollow space.

"They could have then transported the large bronze rings to Jerusalem where they would have been assembled into the large column right at the temple."

Chapter 33

Samir and his men were watching the campsite from a distance of five kilometers protected by a large rock formation. He had not yet contacted Kassab. He wanted to have the ancient documents in his hands before risking the wrath of his boss.

He had exercised great caution as his men had followed the pickup truck across the desert. While on the highway, only one of his cars followed the infidels and Bedouins, and that car was instructed to stay far-back almost completely out of sight. When Aziz's truck left the highway and moved out into the Negev desert, his best tracker had followed the dust and sand cloud created by the truck. Samir was absolutely certain his group's presence had not been discovered.

Nonetheless, he had positioned a number of guards on his flanks to protect against an unexpected attack in the middle of the night. He had seen a translation of the ancient scroll and had observed the group circling a strange rock formation. He guessed it was something that must be the Finger of God because he could see a narrow spire rise in the center of the massive rock formation.

With his binoculars, he could see the man called Ari position some type of device near the rock formation, and then the group had settled down in their camp. Samir was certain they were in the right place, and soon the ancient documents would be in his hands.

Chapter 34

Both Bedouins awakened everyone an hour before dawn. They seemed to have built-in alarm clocks. Ari stayed at the makeshift survey instrument, and then in the greyness of the pre-dawn light, Uri headed on a westerly heading and dropped off others at one-kilometer intervals. He then proceeded to a position near the ruins of the ancient foundry.

The sun began rising behind a group of mountains far to the east, and as the sun peeked above the tip of the Finger of God, Ari checked and double-checked his survey transit. It was as close to level as he could get it. It took about twenty minutes for the sun to rise to a point where it was just centered at the tip of the Finger of God. Ari placed the long metal rod on top of the protractor and using his binoculars began following the shadow of the tip of the Finger of God as it slowly traversed the face of the mountain behind the ancient foundry.

Meanwhile, Uri moved closer to the mountain where he had a clear view of the finger's shadow. When the sun was centered behind the top of the Finger of God, he rushed to the mountain and threw a cushion on the ground directly below the shadow. He studied where the highpoint of the shadow hit the mountain. He knew this wasn't the location of the cave, but he knew the elevation was important for eventually being able to locate the cave's elevation.

While this was going on, Ari was making final adjustments to the position of the rod on top of the protractor. He located an unusual rock formation just above the top of the shadow, and adjusted the rod so it was aligned with this unusually shaped rock. He adjusted the rod ten times, and each time he recorded the angle on the protractor. He then calculated the average reading and wrote it down on a piece of paper.

He then moved the rod so it was rotated 11.65 degrees counter-clockwise, although the best he could really do with the crude instrument was somewhere between eleven and twelve degrees, but he did the best he could.

Now for the difficult part. Dalia was standing about a kilometer away from Ari's instrument. Using hand signals, he directed Dalia to move to her left. She had to walk about two-hundred meters before she was lined up with the position of the rod. The others had seen her walk to her left, and they followed her movements. Ari made some final corrections to Dalia's position. He then raised both of his hands into the air to signal that she was correctly positioned. Dalia then raised both arms into the air and the signal was passed along to the others.

Ari now began signaling Malik, the next person in line, and he too was finally standing in the correct position. The process was repeated over and over. By the time the third person was in position, Ari could no longer see the fourth person because of the small hill blocking his view. That's when Dalia took over and by sighting along the line established between Malik and Lisa, she was able to direct Saladin to the proper position.

Finally, Malik moved Uri in his car to a final position along the foot of the mountain. Uri dropped another cushion to mark the position and then drove back to the campsite, picking everyone up along the way. By the time they had picked up Ari, the group was in good spirits.

It took them an hour to break camp and reposition their campsite close to where Uri had dropped the second cushion. They took a breakfast break, and while dining on pita bread and juice, they all stared up at the mountain. Somewhere hidden from view was a cave, a place perhaps holding the key to understanding a period in time when there were very few written records.

Lisa thought about what the consequences of the information might be. Would it turn the Middle East upside-down? Only time would answer the question. As a student of history, she knew understanding ancient history far outweighed the concern for what the potential consequences of those historical records might create. She remembered the differences of opinion among the experts regarding what the Dead Sea Scrolls had revealed about those ancient times. It might take generations for historians to agree on what these ancient records might reveal.

She wondered if as a discoverer of the documents she would be afforded the opportunity to study them before they were released to the general public. If so, her career as a Historian would probably be guaranteed for life, but she knew these were just dreams. Her mission now was to help the team find the cave and then recover the artifacts.

Ari told the group. "We still don't know the elevation of the hidden cave. If you look back at the mountain where the sun rose, you can see it's not flat at the top. If we had done this on the morning of the Summer Solstice, the Finger of God would probably have pointed to a lower elevation, but without a more sophisticated survey instrument, it would be impossible to know the exact position."

Uri asked, "How far off could the cave be from this location?"

Ari answered, "It's difficult to say, but I'm sure my device could only get to plus or minus one degree. If you consider that the instrument is at least six kilometers away, that would mean we could expect the cave to be within maybe 100 meters in each direction. Then I'd add another 100 meters to account for other measurement errors. In total we're probably looking at a stretch of the mountain of about 500 meters."

Dalia looking at the mountain said, "We should consider the problem from the ancient Israeli's point of view. If this was a natural cave, then the entrance might be anywhere, but if it was an excavated cave, wouldn't they have wanted to cut it out at ground level?"

Lisa said, "But if they wanted to keep it hidden from people, why would they put it at ground level. I'd make sure it stayed hidden by putting it high up into the mountain, and if it's a natural cave, the entrance could be anywhere."

Uri said, "When I was marking the spot of where the shadow hit the mountain, I think it was about 100 meters above the ground. Ari, you said when you compensate for the differences between today and the Summer Solstice, the real shadow would have been somewhat lower."

Saladin added, "I know there are many natural caves in this area. Many of my ancestors found protection in these caves during sandstorms and other natural disasters."

Ari said, "Maybe the bigger question is how they would seal the cave to ensure it wasn't found by accident?"

Lisa said, "Remember how the alcove was hidden. We never would have seen it even if we were looking at it. We only found it because of the earthquake. So I think we should look for masonry work using natural rocks from the area. The rocks would fit together perfectly, just like in the catacombs."

Dalia said, "I agree with Lisa. Why do something different, and remember, they would eventually want to recover the documents, so why make it too difficult."

Ari suggested, "So let's divide up into two groups, one team will look from here and to the left about 300 meters. The second team will search from here to the right about 300 meters. Let's start at ground level and then work our way up the mountain."

Ari, Lisa, and Malik worked to the left. The mountain was far from a sheer cliff. In fact, it looked more like millions of years of erosion and geological uplifting had created thousands of landslides. The result was a gradual incline created by tens of thousands of rocks tumbling down the side of the mountain and piling up near the bottom.

Ari carried a pickaxe as the three carefully examined the base of the mountain. It took them almost an hour to move 300 meters to the left. Ari used the pickaxe as a crowbar to dislodge small rocks and then tapped face-rocks to see if there was a hollow sound indicating empty space behind the rock. It was hard work, and the three climbed over rocks and fit into small crannies to try to find the hidden cave. If they had known what the mountain would have looked like, they would have brought different tools, and if they weren't successful today, they might have to return at a later date with proper equipment to excavate the area.

Chapter 35

At sunrise Samir had been awakened by one of his men who had been observing the infidels' campsite. He hurried to the observation post and was handed the binoculars. He could see Ari standing next to a piece of equipment giving hand signals to another person a kilometer further away.

He watched with growing curiosity. What were these people doing? It took another twenty minutes before he figured out what was happening. They had probably observed where the Finger of God's shadow had struck the mountain and were using some crude survey equipment to determine where the shadow would have fallen on the morning of the Summer Solstice. When the infidels began to break camp, he gathered his men and explained what was happening.

He directed four of his best men to walk close to where the Israelis had repositioned their camp. Every hour he wanted one person to report back from the observation post, and they could take turns walking back and forth. As his men moved out, he thought about the big picture. He was certain the Zionists would find the ancient documents described in the scroll, and he was sure his men could easily take the artifacts from the poorly armed pigs.

So what then? He would contact Hakeem Kassab of course and explain how he had recovered the documents. What to do with the documents; that was the question?

He could destroy them immediately, but he guessed the Grand Mufti would probably want to analyze the ancient artifacts and then decide what to do with them. That meant they needed to be brought back to Jerusalem, but should they risk doing that immediately? He thought not. Instead he would recommend to Kassab that the documents be moved to a safe place for a couple of weeks until things had quieted down. For sure the police or even the IDF would be searching for these infidels, and of course they would soon all be dead. That would lead to a manhunt for his own group and perhaps the authorities might be following Kassab or the Grand Mufti as well. Yes, it would be better to hide the documents until things quieted down. He would make this suggestion to Kassab. He normally only took orders, but this time he felt it would be important to let Kassab know he wasn't just a yes man.

Chapter 36

Moshe Stern had talked to General Yidlan immediately after Dalia had called him. The general was relieved to hear the Israelis and the American girl had escaped from the Waqf, and he immediately contacted Colonel Weiss and apprised him of the situation. Weiss wanted to know whether he should return to his base and stand down from the mission. General Yidlan thought for a moment and then answered, "No Morty, Moshe Stern's niece Dalia sounds like a loose cannon. She's likely to get into trouble again. Stay in Eilat another day; have a swim in the Red Sea. I'll contact you if anything changes."

Moshe Stern had not slept the entire night. He arrived at the police station in a piss-poor mood. His partner knew him well enough to know something was definitely wrong. She brought him a cup of hot tea and sat down at his desk. "So Moshe, what's the problem; you look like death warmed over."

"Is it that obvious?"

"Does the scorpion live in the desert?"

"It's Dalia," he said, "she was captured by the Waqf, and some Bedouins helped her escape. She doesn't realize how dangerous these people are."

Stern gave her all the details. Elsi thought a moment. "Moshe, let's talk to this Professor Gold and find out where this foundry is located. Then let's take a drive out into the Negev and locate you niece. If nothing else you'll have the peace of mind to be guarding your niece."

Stern smiled at his long-time partner. "I should marry you Elsi. You always have the answer to every problem."

Elsi leaned over and kissed him on the cheek. "Maybe someday you'll follow through on your threat."

Chapter 37

The search for the hidden cave was not easy work, and when the sun was directly overhead, they decided to rest for lunch. Neither group had any luck along the base of the mountain. After lunch they would focus on the ten to thirty meter elevation.

"What if we don't find it?" Lisa said.

Ari answered, "There are two ifs; if the scroll is authentic, and if the Finger of God is what we've just found, then this is the place. If someone already recovered these documents, there wouldn't be a reason to cover up the cave. So, I'm betting it's here. If we can't find it, then we'll have to get some heavy construction equipment; but I think we're going to find it."

After lunch they continued where they had left off. The three climbed up the mountain. Lisa was at the ten meter level, Ari at twenty meters, and Malik, the youngest, scampered like a mountain goat up to a height of thirty meters. The three advanced slowly to the left, not one above the other; but staggered so that if a rock fell from Malik or Ari it wouldn't hit the person below.

Malik kept the pickaxe and passed it down on a rope to Ari or Lisa if they wanted to inspect a possible area with a little more thoroughness. Lisa was getting pretty good at looking at a particular area and quickly coming to a conclusion about the possibilities. If in doubt she called for the pickaxe and carefully removed some questionable rocks embedded in the side of the mountain.

Her hands were getting tired from gripping the mountainside as she moved further to the left. She found a long straight hairline crack in the face of a rock and asked for the pickaxe. Malik passed it down to Ari who then swung it back and forth as he lowered it to her. She grabbed it and steadied herself against a large rock as she swung the heavy tool at the crack in the rock. A piece of rock broke free. She swung the axe again and another larger chunk of rock was dislodged from the mountain. During the third swing, the pickaxe suddenly met no resistance and disappeared into the mountain all the way to its handle.

Lisa's heart began racing. She still didn't want to cause a false alarm, so she kept swinging the axe near the place in the mountain where there appeared to be a potential hollow spot. After five more swings and the appearance of a larger hole, she screamed at the top of her voice. "I think I've found it! No, I'm sure I've found it!"

Malik and Ari climbed down from higher up, and five minutes later everyone was gathered on the mountainside staring into the void behind the apparent entrance to the cave. Uri had brought a large flashlight, and when he shined it into the hole in the wall, he reported seeing nothing. "I'm just looking into a very large open space. Nothing's reflecting back that I can see."

The group took turns breaking down the entrance to the cave. Everyone wanted a turn with the pickaxe. Saladin and Malik shook their heads as the girls took a turn with the axe. Women using a pickaxe?

That was men's work; women should never have to do that kind of manual labor.

After fifteen minutes of hard work, the hole in the mountain was large enough for one person at a time to squeeze through the opening. Ari said, "Lisa, you found it; you should have the honor."

Lisa wasn't about to pass up the opportunity. She took the flashlight from Uri and squeezed through the hole. Inside the cave, she stood upright and began moving the flashlight. She hadn't really thought much about what she would find, but what she could see was something she certainly hadn't expected. For some reason she thought the cave would be rather small, but the space she was confronted with was far beyond anything she had expected to see.

The cave was immense. The chamber she had entered rose to a height of almost twenty meters, and the width of the chamber was at least 100 meters. More importantly, the cave stretched further than the light from her flashlight could reach. She just stared in disbelief at the immense size of the place.

She suddenly realized the others were yelling at her, wanting to know what she saw. She stuck her head outside the cave. "You're not going to believe this; the cave is larger than anything I expected. We're going to need more flashlights.

Uri and Saladin brought more flashlights from the truck. Dalia, followed by Malik, easily squeezed through the opening to the cave. The others were really too big, so they spent another ten minutes enlarging the hole. Finally they were all inside the cave. Each had a flashlight and they began walking around the inside of the cave, fascinated by the size of the cavern and wondering what lay beyond the limits of what their flashlights could allow them to see.

The smell of the place was something close to what an unused linen closet in your grandmother's house might smell like; not unpleasant, just musty. Dalia finally recovered from the euphoria of the discovery. "Come on guys," she said, "Let's find the ancient artifacts."

They first completed a systematic search of the main cavern. Lisa expected the documents, just like the scroll, would be packed in urns and the urns would just be sitting there in the middle of the entrance to the cave. Then she realized how foolish it would have been to just leave the urns out in the open. Whoever had planned the hiding place of the documents certainly didn't want some stranger who happened to discover the cave to also find the documents. No, the documents would be hidden from plain sight in a place known to the Hebrew priests who had put them here in the first place.

Lisa had once visited Mammoth Cave in Kentucky, and this cave reminded her of what that place had looked like. The walls of the cave were smooth, polished over millions of years from water reacting with the limestone. That was the nature of caves. There were stalactites and stalagmites suggesting the presence of a wet climate before the desert had dried everything out.

The six began following the cavern as it sloped gradually downward into the depths of the mountain. They moved slowly over the obstacle course on the floor of the cave and eventually came to a constriction. The cavern narrowed to a small opening about two meters across and ten meters high. They moved single-file through the gap, eventually entering into another large chamber.

Dalia finally broke the silence. "How far into the mountain do you think this place goes?"

Ari answered, "Who knows; the mountain seems to go on for many kilometers, so the cave may go that far."

Lisa said, "I've been in a large cave in Kentucky. It went on forever, and there were many different paths to take. The water eroded the limestone almost at random and in three dimensions, and there were even underground rivers."

Uri said, "There may have been rivers here millions of years ago, but I doubt there's any water here now."

The second immense chamber they had entered stretched on for hundreds of meters. They split up and began walking around the walls of the cavern. Dalia, who was walking with Uri, noticed it first; a red six-pointed star painted on the wall of the cave. She called the others over to see what she had discovered. Lisa said, "It's just like the mark in the catacombs where the scroll was hidden. Do you suppose the documents are hidden behind the wall just below the mark, just like in the catacombs?"

Ari said, "It makes sense. The priests who hid this had to make sure their descendants could find the documents. They would have passed down the story of how to recover the documents from generation to generation. The blood-marked star would have been an easy thing for the descendants of the priests to remember. Let's get a pickaxe and see if the documents are behind this wall."

Ari returned with a pickaxe a few minutes later, and they all gathered around the red star as Ari began swinging the axe at the space below the mark. They all took turns with the axe, not because Ari was tired, but because they all wanted to participate in the discovery of the documents. The wall began to give up its secret; slowly, but steadily, pieces of rock were dislodged. An opening appeared and grew larger with each swing of the axe.

Their expectations began to grow; smiles appeared on all their faces; they shined their lights into the dark void; they all demanded an opportunity to help break into the hidden area. It took ten minutes of hard work, but finally they had cleared enough rock to squeeze through into the hidden sanctuary.

They looked at each other. Who would have the honor of being first? Ari looked at Saladin. "Saladin, if it wasn't for you, none of us would be alive today. You must have the honor of being first."

Saladin smiled, his white teeth glistening in the dim light. "You do me a great honor my friends. I will never forget this day."

Saladin took a flashlight and squeezed through the opening into the darkness of the hidden space. The others waited anxiously for some word, some indication of what lay behind the opening. Finally Saladin stuck his head back outside. "There's a long passage leading back into the mountain. Let's all walk there together."

A minute later they had all entered a narrow tunnel. They began walking slowly with their lights dancing back and forth along the walls. The narrow shaft turned sharply to the right and suddenly their search for the documents ended. Thirty-three urns wrapped in protective fine linen sitting undisturbed for millennia were exposed from the light of six flashlights.

The six explorers stood in silence and admired their discovery. Tears came to Dalia's eyes. The others were too shocked to even talk. Finally Dalia approached the ancient relics. She cautiously touched an urn, caressing the fine linen cloth. As if in response, the ancient protective cloth fell from the urn at her touch, exposing the plain clay vessel it had been protecting for thousands of years.

The others began touching the other urns, as if they needed physical proof of the artifacts existence. Finally Dalia spoke. "This is going to become the most important archeological find of all time. Whatever's inside these urns will define our understanding of ancient times. The Dead Sea Scrolls will be insignificant in comparison to this find."

Uri laughed, "Let's hope there's something inside, otherwise we'll be laughed at by every archeologist."

Lisa said, "Come on Uri, of course there's something inside. Who would go to the trouble of hiding them if there was nothing inside?"

Everyone knew Lisa was right. Whatever was hidden inside these urns was important to these people, and if it was important to them, then it would be important to humanity.

Chapter 38

Salib waited impatiently, hidden behind a rock formation about two kilometers from the cave. He had seen them open the entrance and disappear inside. Twenty minutes later, the Israeli named Ari had walked out of the cave, picked up a pickaxe, and squeezed back through the opening to the cave's entrance. Had they found the ancient artifacts? Samir was not about to be fooled a second time. His men would wait until he was absolutely certain the hidden urns were found.

He kept looking at his watch. The minutes stretched into an hour; still no activity at the entrance to the cave. Where were these people? What were they doing? The lack of knowledge was almost beyond his ability to control.

Meanwhile the group inside the cave was busy enlarging the entrance to the hidden room. They wanted to make sure the urns could fit through the opening without being damaged. The opening was finally big enough to allow for the safe removal of the clay vessels. Their plan was simple; they would carefully move all the urns out of the hidden room and then carry them to the cave's entrance. They thought there would be enough room on the truck to hold all of the artifacts. If not, they would have to make two trips.

Dalia and Lisa stood outside of the entrance to the hidden chamber. The others made repeated trips to the back of the narrow passage and passed the urns through the opening to the girls. Dalia arranged the urns side by side. The protective fine linen cloth was breaking apart into small pieces, but the urns seemed in perfect condition.

Dalia knew she could have returned to Jerusalem without having touched the urns, and a group of professional archeologists could have been quickly assembled. They could have then returned to the cave with all of the necessary equipment needed to protect the linen cloth as well as the urns.

But Dalia also knew the Waqf would be looking for them, and they needed to protect the contents of the urns at all costs. It seemed like a sensible thing to do; get the urns back to the Antiquities Authority as soon as possible. If that meant destroying the linen cloth, then so be it.

Ari and Uri explored the hidden room after passing all of the urns out to the girls. They wanted to ensure there were no other hidden rooms or any other treasures. Other than the urns, the room appeared empty. The room and the cave could be explored more thoroughly by experts at a later date.

Once outside the hidden room, they each took an urn and carefully carried it to the entrance to the cave. The girls then handed the urns through the cave entrance to the men who carried them out to the truck and placed them carefully in the pickup truck's bed.

Samir, who had been carefully watching them as soon as they appeared in front of the cave, took note of the urns they were carrying. He had no intention of being fooled again. He had to be absolutely certain they had found the urns. He could just make out the shapes of the vessels. They were the same color as the urn that had contained the scroll. He was certain they had found the ancient documents.

As soon as the infidels returned to the cave, he quickly assembled his men and instructed them on his plan. They all ran to their hidden cars and began racing toward the entrance to the cave.

It took Lisa and the others another ten minutes to return to the cave's entrance with another six urns. Samir's men remained hidden behind a nearby rock, and as the twelfth urn was placed in the pickup truck, Samir gave the signal and his men quickly rushed toward the truck with their guns drawn.

Samir shouted at the girls in a loud voice. "Come out now or we'll start killing the others."

Dalia translated for Lisa, and the two women quickly squeezed through the cave entrance and out into the bright sunlight where they were confronted by a dozen of Samir's men.

Samir's men were laughing in delight. They knew their six prisoners would soon be dead, but the prospect of a little fun with the women before they were put to death was certainly something to look forward to. Samir ordered the six bound with their hands behind their backs, and he then ordered them to sit in the sand.

He ordered four of his men to look inside the cave to see if there were other urns. While he waited for their return he contemplated his next steps. The truth was he hadn't thought about his next steps. Now, with the ancient artifacts in his possession, he knew he could contact Hakeem. He would be viewed as a hero, not as an idiot who had lost his captives. But first, he would wait to see if there were any other artifacts hidden inside the cave. He wanted to know the exact number of urns first before he called Hakeem.

Of course the infidels would all have to be killed; they knew too much, and besides he viewed every Jew killed as a victory for Allah; and the Bedouins helped them, so they also deserved to die. First, however, he needed to find out who else knew about the urns, because he wanted to eliminate anyone who knew of their existence.

His men appeared with four additional urns and they told him there were still seventeen urns left inside the cave. They placed the urns in Saladin's truck and returned to the cave to remove the others.

Samir called Hakeem on his satellite phone. Hakeem didn't answer his cellphone, so Samir called the number of Hakeem's assistant. The man immediately left to find his boss, and a minute later they were talking. "Hakeem, this is Samir. I have the urns. There are thirty-three in all. We have the four infidels along with two Bedouins who were helping them. After we talk, I'm going to interrogate all of them to see who else knows about the urns. I'm assuming you want all of them killed."

Hakeem, with an unseen happiness in his voice said, "Well done Samir; I'll talk to the Grand Mufti to see what he wants done with the urns. We were wondering what happened to you. When our interrogator arrived at your hideout, everyone was gone."

"If I may make a suggestion Hakeem, I think it would be too dangerous to bring them back to Jerusalem right now. I recommend we hide them someplace until things quiet down; then we can bring them wherever the Grand Mufti wants them without any fear of their being captured."

"A good idea Samir; I think I know just the place, but I'll check with the Grand Mufti first. I'll call you back in a few minutes."

Samir had his men drag Ari to an area where he could not be seen by the others. "Zionist, of course you know you're going to die, but the question is whether it will be an easy death or the type of death that will take days, where your body is drained of blood slowly until you die. An easy death can be yours if you answer a question. I want to know who else knows of the urns."

Ari stared Samir in the eyes, "Whether I tell you or not, my death will be horrible. Do you really think I believe your promises? You will learn nothing from me."

Samir stood in front of Ari and suddenly kicked him repeatedly in the chest. Ari doubled over from the unexpected blow and lay in the sand.

When Lisa heard the sound of the gun echo through the mountains, she was horror-struck. Memories of Ari's face flashed in her mind. Had they actually killed her love? She looked at the others and began to cry. When Dalia tried to move to comfort her, she was hit across the face with the butt end of a gun. Her sunglasses sailed through the air and blood trickled down her chin and dripped onto the sand. Uri jumped to her defense and was kicked in the stomach. Saladin and Malik looked on with stoic faces. They had seen too much of this violence in their own lives to be surprised by the Waqf's men's actions.

Samir appeared from behind the rocks and grabbed hold of Lisa. He dragged her off behind a different set of rocks. Why not the same rock where they took Ari? If this guy wanted information, then why not show her Ari's body so she could see her own fate? As she was being pulled through the sand, she somehow focused on that question and then she knew. They weren't showing her Ari's body because he wasn't dead. That shot had been an attempt to scare her and the others into talking.

Hidden from the others, Samir spoke to her in Arabic. She didn't have a clue what he was saying. When he was done she said in English, "I'm an American and I don't speak Arabic only a little Hebrew."

Samir called to his men and one of the younger soldiers came over. Samir spoke to him and he translated into English. "He says he wants to know who else knows about the urns? If you don't tell him, he'll kill you just like he killed your friend."

Lisa said, "You can tell your boss that I'm not going to tell him anything."

Just then, Samir's satellite phone rang. He left Lisa with the other soldier and walked away while he talked to the person on the phone. He returned a few minutes later and spoke to the man guarding Lisa. He spoke in Arabic but Lisa was able to understand two words, *Kadesh Barnea*, the name of an ancient city in the Sinai Desert.

After talking to her guard, Samir left her and walked toward his men. Her guard pulled her through the sand back toward the others. The guard pushed her down onto the sand next to Dalia. Two other men were dragging Ari's lifeless body back to the group. At first, Lisa thought he was dead, but he began moving. She knelt down and kissed him on the lips.

Samir gave orders to his men in Arabic and they began herding Lisa and her friends toward the entrance to the cave. Dalia told Lisa, "They're going to put us back in the cave and then seal the entrance with explosives."

Lisa looked up at the rocks above the cave's entrance. She could see that a well-placed charge would dislodge enough rocks to easily block the opening. She guessed being alive in the cave was better than being shot immediately. The Waqf's men pushed Ari through the entrance, and then at gunpoint, the others were forced into the cave.

Lisa and the others stumbled in the partial light as they moved away from the entrance and back into the second chamber. They wanted to move far enough away from the entrance to ensure they survived the blast, and they quickly helped each other untie the ropes still binding their hands behind them. With no light to guide him, Malik moved his hands along the cave's wall until he finally located the small chamber that had held the urns and found four flashlights they had left behind.

They waited in silence. Ari was slowly recovering from his beating and trying to speak to the others, but his speech was slurred, and finally he just gave up and sat against Lisa in silence.

Samir's men placed the explosive charge in a cluster of large rocks overhanging the entrance to the cave. The truck containing all thirty-three urns was moved away from the entrance after Samir's explosive expert signaled that the charges were set.

The explosion started as a sharp high-pitched sound carried through the dense rock more quickly than through the air. That blast was followed by a noisy rumbling as rocks braking free from the blast slid down the side of the mountain and buried the entrance to the cave. The landslide was over in less than a minute, but Lisa and the others knew the entrance to the cave was most certainly blocked, and any chance of escape through the cave's entrance would be impossible.

The noise of the rock-slide suddenly ceased and was replaced with an eerie silence. Lisa said to the others, "We should only be using one flashlight at a time. We need to conserve the batteries."

Ari, who was finally able to sit up and talk said, "We need to look for another way out of here."

Dalia said, "Let's get going. We need to do it now."

While the others gathered up any useful equipment, Saladin checked out the entrance to the cave; there was no chance of escape through the main entrance. Other than the four flashlights there was nothing of use except for one pickaxe and a long rope. The Waqf's men had removed all of the urns and the hidden chamber was now totally empty.

With Uri helping Ari, the six began walking slowly into the heart of the cave, into areas they had not as yet explored. Dalia estimated they had about an hour left on each flashlight. That meant four hours of light, four hours to find another way out of this place.

They finally reached what appeared to be the end of the cave's second chamber. There was a small opening in the wall at the end of the chamber. Lisa could feel a cool breeze flowing through the opening. She said, "When I was visiting Mammoth Cave, I remember there were several openings to the outside. If there's a breeze blowing, that means there must be air circulating in the cave, and that means there must be at least two more entrances to the cave. Uri peeked into the hole in the wall. "I think there's another chamber behind this hole."

Saladin said, "Let's find out, unless someone has a better idea."

Everyone except Ari took turns with the pickaxe. By the time the opening was large enough for everyone to squeeze through, their first flashlight was out of power and they had turned on the second flashlight. It took all of their combined efforts to pull Ari through the narrow opening, but he finally squeezed through to the other side.

The newly discovered chamber seemed larger and quite different than the first or second. Hundreds of stalactites hanging from the ceiling and stalagmites reaching up from the floor told of thousands of years of water seeping down into this chamber from the ground above. It was hard to imagine a time when water was plentiful in this now arid land, but the existence of these formations confirmed the existence of a bountiful supply of ground-water.

With their second flashlight showing the way, they looked around the immense chamber. In the far distance, three tunnels led off from the main chamber in different directions. The group made their way across the uneven floor, skirting around the many stalagmites. Saladin asked, "Should we divide up into three groups to explore each tunnel?"

Lisa said, "I have a better idea."

At the entrance to the first tunnel, she reached down and gathered a handful of dust. She threw it up into the air and the six watched the dust as it settled back onto the floor of the cave. They then walked to the second tunnel and Lisa threw up a second handful of dust. This time the breeze flowing through the cave caught the dust and pushed it into the second tunnel. Hopefully the dust would be leading them to freedom. To be certain the second tunnel was the one to follow, Lisa repeated the dust toss at the third tunnel.

After confirming only the second tunnel offered any hope of escape, they began slowly walking down the narrow corridor. As they moved through the tunnel, the height of the ceiling began to drop. Soon the tunnel was only three meters wide and only one meter high. The six began crawling in the confined space.

The breeze picked up and everyone was excited about the possibility of finding freedom.

Just as suddenly as the tunnel had narrowed, it quickly opened up into another vast chamber. Lisa kept throwing dust into the air and the group followed its trail. They had lost all sense of direction; not just the directions of the compass, but also whether they had been going deeper into the ground or rising up into the mountain.

The dust led them to a far corner of the chamber, where it suddenly changed directions and shot upward toward the ceiling of the cave. Uri shined the light from the flashlight upward following the dust particles as they disappeared through a narrow gap in the roof of the cave. Dalia said, "Turn off the flashlight; I think I see daylight."

Uri turned off the light and Dalia was right. The ceiling was a little over five meters in height, and a hint of blue sky appeared about twenty meters above the ceiling. They had come so far, and were so close to freedom and yet these last thirty meters were an insurmountable barrier to overcome. The gap in the rock leading to freedom was just too narrow.

The six explorers just stared at the path to freedom they would never be able to use. Ari brought them out of their misery. "If there's air circulating in the cave, then there must be more openings. The fresh air leaves the cave here, but it must come into the cave through another opening, and it can't be the main entrance, because it's been sealed off. There's still a chance if we can find the other opening."

The others agreed, and with renewed hope they began walking back to the constriction between the two chambers where Lisa had first noticed the fresh air. By periodically tossing dust into the air, they were able to trace the origin of the fresh air. Their search finally led them to a small recess in the first chamber's wall just as the battery in the second flashlight failed. Dalia dropped the second flashlight on the ground and turned on their third flashlight.

Malik squeezed his small body into the opening and found a circular vertical shaft leading upward toward the surface. The tortuous path leading to freedom was narrow, less than one meter in places, but a faint glimmer of sunlight filtered down from above. "I can see light," he said.

Exhausted, the six just took turns looking up at their last chance at escape, pondering how they would be able to reach the surface. Finally Malik said, "I can climb that. I know I can. If you can help me reach the vent, I'll be able to brace myself against the sides of the shaft. When I reach the top, I'll lower a rope to pull you all up. I know I can do this. You must let me try."

They uncoiled their rope and it looked like it just might be long enough to reach the top, but it was just an estimate. There wasn't a better plan, so they all agreed to let Malik try the climb.

With Ari still hurting, Saladin and Uri stood side by side and lifted Malik onto their shoulders. With the rope coiled around Malik's arm, he reached up to the vertical shaft's entrance. He was just able to touch the ceiling but was still a little short of being able to reach a section of the vent that might allow him to pull himself up into the confined space.

He explained the situation to Uri and his brother. They agreed to push him upward with their hands. It would be a one-shot try, because if they were unsuccessful, he would probably fall to the floor of the cave. On the count of three Malik was lifted up as far as the two men could extend their arms. He grabbed onto a protruding rock extending inside the vent and pulled himself inside the fissure in the ceiling.

The others looked on with their two remaining flashlights providing Malik with as much light as possible. The vertical vent was only about a meter wide. Malik wedged his back against the side of the shaft, and by moving one foot at a time, he was able to slowly advance toward the top of the vent. It took him almost ten minutes of hard work to reach the halfway point, and then fatigue forced him to rest. It wasn't really rest because he still had to expend energy to just stay wedged against the side of the vent.

The others offered encouragement, and after a few minutes, he continued on his slow relentless journey toward freedom. Malik's hands and feet began to shake, almost out of control. It took his last ounce of resolve to climb the last meter, but the sight of the dazzling blue sky above his head, allowed him to summon up the last bit of strength left in his tired muscles.

His hand finally left the vent and searched for something above ground to hold. He finally found a place to grab onto, and he pulled himself up out of the hole. He cut his chest on a sharp rock while pulling his body out of the vent and then collapsed onto the ground. He was at the top of the mountain. He examined his cut chest and pressed his bloody shirt against his body to stop the bleeding. Then he yelled down to the others. "I've made it; I'll lower the rope now."

The order of ascent had been worked out before Malik left. Dalia, the lightest would be pulled up first. Then she and Malik could pull up Lisa and then the three would lift Uri. Ari would be next, and with four people lifting, it was hoped they could manage to pull his beaten body to freedom. Saladin would be the last one up.

Malik lowered his rope into the vent. Dalia tied the end around her waist. She positioned her body under the vertical shaft as Malik began lifting her upward. Once in the vent, she managed to assist Malik by trying to wedge her feet against the vent and lifting her shoulders a little at a time.

It took Malik almost five minutes to lift her to the top. She collapsed onto the ground and then managed to stand up and thanked Malik with a kiss on his lips that he would never forget.

Lisa was next, and with two people lifting, she arrived at the top in less than two minutes. Next came Uri; he was a lot heavier, and with three people lifting, they still needed five minutes to haul him to the surface. They all rested for a few minutes, and then Malik lowered the rope to Ari. Saladin helped tie the rope under his arms. His ribs were hurting and a dull continuous pain hinted at some broken bones.

With four people now lifting, Ari was carefully hoisted up into the vent and then upward at a slow steady pace. Upon reaching the top, he tried to lift himself out of the vent but needed help from the others.

With Ari recovering from the intense pain in his chest, the others quickly lifted Saladin to the surface. He said, "I tied the pickaxe and the flashlights to the end of the rope."

Malik lifted their equipment out of the vent. Everyone patted Malik on the back except for Saladin, the proud brother, who kissed him on both cheeks. Dalia was the first to stand up and actually look around at their new surroundings. They seemed to be on a plateau on top of the mountain. She walked to the edge of the butte and looked down at the base of the mountain. Off to her left, she could see the tracks in the sand left by the Waqf's cars and trucks that had been parked by the entrance. She couldn't make out the entrance to the cave, but she could see the many rocks that had fallen down the mountainside during the explosion.

Off in the other direction, the plateau seemed to gradually descend to the floor of the valley. At best it was a five kilometer trek, and it seemed like the easiest way to reach civilization. She returned to the others and explained what she had seen.

Uri said, "I'm going to find these assholes and kill them all. There's not going to be a trial, because there won't be anyone left to bring to justice."

Lisa said, "I think I know where they took the urns."

Dalia looked on in disbelief. "How do you know that?"

When they were questioning me, their leader got a call from someone. I didn't understand much of what they said because they were speaking in Arabic, but I did hear the words *Kadesh Barnea*. It's an ancient city located in the Sinai Desert."

Ari said, "That's in Egypt. The border with Egypt is pretty unprotected in this area. I'm sure they could easily get there without being spotted by an Israeli border patrol."

Uri said, "First let's figure out how to get back to civilization. We don't have water. We're not going to be able to just walk the eighty kilometers to the nearest city."

Saladin said, "There is an old small oasis fifteen kilometers from here. We can get water there. If we're lucky, there may even be some dates for us to eat. We need to leave now if we're going to make it by sundown."

With Saladin leading the group, the six set off along the descending plateau leading to ground level. Ari was now able to walk under his own power, but with a considerable amount of discomfort. Luckily the plateau was relatively flat as they descended into the valley. Ari found a large stick out in the middle of nowhere and it made a perfect walking cane. Since the walk was mostly downhill, they made the trip to the valley in a little less than one hour.

Saladin took his bearings from the different mountains and began walking northeast along the floor of the valley. He kept the group marching in the shade of the mountains. They stopped for short rests every hour, and as the afternoon sun began to descend behind the peaks of the tallest mountains, he indicated they were within an hour of the oasis. The others could see nothing but mountains and desert; however they put their full trust in their Bedouin friend.

Saladin suddenly stopped and pointed to the western horizon. "A sandstorm is approaching. We need to hurry."

Lisa looked at the horizon and saw a dark band in the sky, and it was slowly bearing down on their position. She thought it looked a lot like a storm front, but she knew that type of weather was unlikely to occur in this desert.

They all studied the approaching sandstorm. With Saladin leading the group, they began jogging directly north toward the protection of a nearby mountain. Ari was clearly struggling and Uri helped support him while they moved quickly ahead.

The band of darkness was moving quickly and extended all the way back to the horizon. It was like a vail of darkness being pulled across the blue sky. Saladin stopped and ordered all of them to hold onto the rope and not to let go under any circumstances. He said the sandstorm would arrive in less than five minutes and they wouldn't be able to see once the storm arrived.

They were all running toward the protection of the nearest mountain, but it was clear to Lisa that the storm would arrive long before they reached their goal. As she ran, she looked to her left and saw the band of sand almost directly overhead.

The full fury of the storm arrived suddenly and with a vengeance unlike anything Lisa had ever experienced. Sand endlessly pelted her body and stung her face. She held her left hand over her face to protect her skin, but she couldn't protect her entire face without letting go of the rope. She knew the wisdom of Saladin's order. She couldn't even see Dalia who was only two meters in front of her. If she let go of the rope, she might be lost from the group.

Lisa couldn't understand how Saladin was able to lead them toward the protection of the mountain. He certainly couldn't see anything. Then she realized he was moving at right angles to the storm, and as long as the sandstorm didn't change directions they could continue on the correct path.

She tried to yell something to the others, but as soon as she opened her mouth, it filled with sand. She spit out the small grains and just tried to concentrate on protecting her face as they continued on.

It took almost ten minutes for the group to reach the protection of the mountain. Saladin led them to an outcropping of rocks. With the sand striking the western side of the large boulder, the six huddled together on the opposite side.

Ari asked, "Saladin, how long will this last?"

"It's hard to tell. At this time of year they usually last a couple of hours, but it could go on for days. It all depends on the will of Allah."

The two women had their backs against the leeward side of the rock, and the men huddled in a semicircle facing the girls. By staying close together, they protected one another against nature's onslaught. Lisa kept her head down in her lap. The position offered the most protection against the sand whipping around the large rock which was blocking out only a majority of the airborne sand.

Time passed slowly as the sandstorm continued to transform the desert landscape. There was time for Lisa to reflect on many things, but most of all she thought of Ari and wondered how this would all work out in the end. It seemed hopeless; she would leave for California in a few weeks. Of course she would have some wonderful memories of Ari and her many new friends, and of course there was this adventure after all. How could she minimize what had happened in the last week? Her life had changed in so many ways. She wondered if they would ever make it back to civilization. It seemed they were plagued by one catastrophe after another. If it wasn't the Waqf trying to kill them, it was Mother Nature.

Saladin spoke above the roar of the wind. "It's starting to end."

Lisa couldn't really hear a difference in the sound of the sandstorm. How could Saladin know the storm was coming to an end? She listened carefully, trying to detect a change in the velocity of the wind. Maybe Saladin was right; the longer she listened the more her mind seemed to sense an easing back of the fury of the wind.

Just as suddenly as the storm had arrived, it faded into an unpleasant memory. They all stood up, shook the sand out of their hair, and brushed the sand from their clothes. It was almost dark when Saladin began once again to lead them to his hidden oasis.

Chapter 39

Uncle Moshe and Elsi had been fighting traffic for most of the morning. They finally reached an open stretch of highway just south of Be'er Sheva. They had a rough Google map of the location of the foundry faxed to them by Professor Gold.

As they left the highway and began driving east across the desert, Moshe thought of his young niece. He loved her as much as his own children, but he hated her head-strong approach to her profession. She was known in the Antiquities Authority as a person who got things done regardless of which bureaucrat stood in her way.

This time, however, she had gone too far. She underestimated the violence these Waqf people were capable of exercising. Two people were already dead, and now his precious niece was once again pushing the limits. He hoped he would find her busy at work searching for those ancient documents, but an inner voice told her she was in trouble, and his inner voice was rarely wrong.

They arrived at the location of the foundry in the late afternoon. The desert sun was beating unmercifully down on them as they left their air-conditioned car and walked amongst the ruins of the ancient manufacturing site. Stern turned to his partner, "The scroll said something called the Finger of God would point the way to the hidden cave."

Elsi said, "I have no idea of what the Finger of God is, but if the cave is near the foundry, and if a shadow pointed the way to the cave, then the finger of God must be east of here, and the hidden cave must be due west of here."

Stern pointed his binoculars toward the west. He followed the valley floor until it reached the Timna Mountains. Some trick of ancient geology had forced these magnificent mountains up out of the desert. Another day he might have taken the time to marvel at their beauty, but he was here today on a different mission, to protect his headstrong niece. If Dalia was somewhere out here, he certainly couldn't see her. "Okay Elsi, lets head over to those mountains and see if we can find my adventurous niece."

They returned to the comfort of their cool car and headed slowly west across the flat valley. Stern maneuvered his car around random rock formations seemingly pushed out of the ground by supernatural forces throughout the valley. As they approached the Mountains to the west of the foundry, Elsi could spot a variety of tire tracks. Fresh tire tracks indicated a large number of vehicles had recently been in the area.

Detective Stern suddenly veered his car sharply to the left and headed for something that had caught his eye. A collapsed Bedouin tent lay on the ground about one-hundred meters away from the mountain. He and Elsi left the car and began walking around the trashed campsite. Stern said, "They were here; I can feel it in my bones. This is a crime scene Elsi, so let's play detective and figure out what happened here."

The campsite was littered with empty cans of food and bottles of water. Elsi walked toward the mountain while Moshe searched the area around the tent.

Elsi could smell a hint of cordite, an explosive chemical that had a characteristic odor. She looked up at the mountain and could see that a rockslide had created a pile of rubble at the foot of the mountain. Perhaps a geologist could say how recently the rockslide had occurred, but she certainly wasn't a geologist. Her curiosity finally got the better of her, and she began carefully climbing up the massive pile of rocks. If an explosion had created this pile of rock then the charge would have probably been set off about fifty meters above the ground in what once might have been an overhanging rock formation. There were certainly plenty of them around as she scanned the cliffs around her. Luckily she had changed shoes before they left Jerusalem, but even with her gym shoes, she still found it difficult to scale the rubble.

It took her almost thirty minutes to reach a place where she thought an explosive charge might have been set. She began searching for physical evidence, something that might prove the rockslide was manmade. She stumbled as rocks slide down toward the ground below, but she continued to explore the entire area. She finally found what she was looking for, a severely dented small metal box with two scorched wires leading off toward a recess in the cliff.

Like any good detective, she kept a plastic evidence bag in one of her pockets. She picked up the wires and carefully deposited the remote detonation device in the bag. She yelled down at Moshe. "I've found something. The smell of cordite is recent, and I've found a remote detonation device. I'll bet that hidden cave entrance is right here, and the Waqf people blew up the mountain to block off the entrance."

She took her time descending the mountain and found Moshe crying at the campsite. Elsi had never seen her partner express much emotion. He was always pure business, so she was shocked to see him wiping away a torrent of tears. He held an evidence bag with a pair of designer sunglasses inside. "These are Dalia's. She just bought them a month ago. She told me they were the latest design and hard to get."

Elsi asked, "Did you find anything else?"

He pointed to his left. "There's some blood in the sand behind that rock. I didn't find any sign of a battle, no shell casings, just the sunglasses and the blood."

Elsi, who seemed able to think clearly said, "Okay, so what happened here? Maybe your niece and her friends found the cave. Then they were surprised by the Waqf people who captured them and took them prisoner. Maybe there was a fight behind that rock or maybe someone was shot. Then the Waqf created the landslide to hide the entrance to the cave."

Moshe Stern wiping away tears said, "So what did these evil people do to my niece? They could have taken her away along with her friends or they might have been left inside the cave. But why blow up the entrance to the cave if they already removed the artifacts? Why would they care if others found the empty cave? There's no reason for the Waqf to keep them alive if they found the documents. They probably want to kill anyone who knows they have the ancient artifacts. Elsi, I know I'm just rambling, but I think they're in that cave and hopefully they're still alive."

What Elsi didn't say was that they were probably in the cave because they didn't find any bodies near the entrance to the cave. Instead she said, "I agree with you; there're probably in the cave, but if they didn't find the artifacts, then maybe the Waqf is keeping them alive thinking your niece and her friends might still be able to lead them to the hidden treasure, but if that's the case, then they didn't need to blow up the entrance to the cave."

"Elsi, I hope you're right. Right now I need to call my friend General Yidlan"

He took out his satellite phone and punched in the general's number. "Chaimy, it's Moshe. I'm in the Timna Valley with my partner. We believe my niece and her friends may be trapped in a cave that was holding the hidden artifacts. I'm hoping they're still alive, but the Waqf people sealed off the cave's entrance with a rockslide. I need your help my friend. Can you get some of your people here quickly with some equipment to open up the cave's entrance?"

"Moshe, I've got my men at the base in Eilat. I'll have them take a helicopter over there as soon as they can. Give me your GPS coordinates."

After telling Yedlin their location, he and Elsi returned to their car where they could wait in air-conditioned comfort.

The sandstorm caught them by surprise, but they were able to move their car behind a large rock. At least they were inside the protection of Stern's car. As they waited for the storm to end, and with nothing better to do, the partners began recounting many of their shared exploits. It made for some good-natured fun as they each recounted the many blunders of the other. They had been a good team, and the two took comfort in the fact that working together they had solved many crimes.

After two hours, the sandstorm finally ended as abruptly as it had started, and now it was just a matter of time before the IDF would arrive. Moshe hoped they weren't too late.

Chapter 40

The oasis was hidden in a canyon in the Timna Mountains. Lisa had read about these ancient sources of water, but she had no real idea what these places might actually look like.

Saladin said his tribe had been using this place for centuries. From the moment they entered the protection of the hidden canyon, the temperature dropped and they found dozens of date palms surrounding an ancient watering hole. A plastic jug sat next to the water. Saladin said, "We need to drink from the center of the water source. That area will be free of bad things."

He waded slowly into the water, being sure not to disturb the sediment along the edge of the spring. He dipped the jug into the water and sipped the life-giving liquid. "It's good," he said with a grin.

He took a long drink and then passed the plastic bottle to the others. The water tasted of the desert, but Lisa drank without thinking about the biological consequences. After drinking their fill, Saladin left a full jug of water under a date palm. Malik climbed the nearest tree and tossed down the sweet fruit to the others.

An hour later they were all resting under palm trees, quietly absorbing everything they had been through.

Uri suddenly burst into uncontrollable laughter. The others looked at him waiting for an explanation. He finally said in English, "This place made me think of a joke an American friend once told me. Why do Arabs make such good lovers?"

He looked at the others waiting for the answer he knew would never come. "Because they sit under their palm trees eating their dates."

Everyone laughed except for Saladin who understood no English and Malik who obviously didn't understand the joke. Malik said, "I don't understand."

Uri told Dalia to explain the joke in the Bedouin language so both Saladin and Malik could understand. Dalia with a beet-red face tried to explain and once they understood the English word date had two meanings, they too broke out in laughter.

What followed, as they relaxed, were countless camel jokes from both Saladin and Malik. Lisa tried to understand the compelling need to act this way in an environment that might claim their lives at any moment, but finally gave up trying and just enjoyed the moment.

Finally Ari asked, "Saladin, how far is the nearest town where we can call the authorities?"

Saladin thought for a moment. "The closest town is Elifaz. It's a day's walk from here. If we leave in a few hours, the temperature will be better, but if everyone needs to rest, then we can spend the night here. What do you think?"

Lisa thought about her body. She was tired; almost too tired to continue on, but the thought of trying to make the one-day hike in the heat of the day seemed far worse. She said, "I vote for resting here a few hours and then continuing on tonight, but Ari, you're in the worst shape. Can you continue?"

Ari laughed, "Either way, the only thing keeping me going is thinking about getting those guys. Don't worry about me, that one goal is all I need."

The vote was unanimous. They would leave after a few hours rest. They all continued to munch on the sweet tasting dates as they rested against the trees. Dalia slept in Uri's arms and Lisa cuddled Ari in her arms as he slept. Malik looked completely rested and continued throwing down dates to his brother who was storing them in a pile on his Shemagh head scarf placed under a tree.

They left the sanctuary of the oasis as soon as the moon rose in the night sky. Their pockets were filled with dates, and Saladin had used his head scarf to create a makeshift backpack to hold the plastic jug full of water. The temperature had dropped as soon as the sun set, and it was a comfortable seventy degrees. In another two hours the heat stored in the desert sand would no longer be able to warm the air and the temperature would drop another ten degrees.

A desire for revenge consumed them all as they followed Saladin northeast in the direction of the town of Elifaz.

Chapter 41

It took three hours for the IDF Special Forces helicopter to land near Stern's car. Colonel Weiss introduced himself and the rest of his six-man force. Moshe Stern spent ten minutes explaining the situation. Weiss's team followed Moshe and Elsi to the rockslide covering the entrance to the cave. One of Weiss's team, probably the explosives expert, analyzed the situation. "This rockslide happened in the last few days. I can open the entrance by using a few shaped charges. I'll have the entrance cleared in a few minutes."

Weiss's explosives expert ran to the helicopter and returned with a satchel containing everything he needed. He placed the first charge about five feet above the ground behind a very large rock. A minute later the blast broke the silence of the late afternoon. Rocks flew out from the pile of rubble. After the dust cleared, Weiss's expert studied the results and said, "One more should do it."

He set the next charge in a hole behind another large rock, and when that charge detonated, a majority of the rocks covering the entrance were blown out into the desert. Weiss's men quickly began removing the remaining rubble covering the opening, and after a few minutes the cave's entrance was large enough for everyone to squeeze through.

Weiss's men brought flashlights and night vision equipment from the helicopter and the rescue party entered the cave. Stern had no idea of what to expect, but he feared the worst. The group had called out to anyone inside the cave, but there weren't any responses. Still, he hoped for the best.

Weiss led his men through the cave. They found the chamber that had held the ancient artifacts. They followed footprints in the dust-laden floor of the cave, and they eventually squeezed through the small gap in the wall leading into the third chamber. As they moved along, Uncle Moshe's hopes increased as he saw evidence of his niece and her friends trying to find a way out of the cave.

The group eventually reached the last chamber and found the mass of footprints directly under the vent leading upward to the outside world. Weiss stated the obvious. "There are footprints all around here. They thought about escaping up this vertical shaft, but the opening was too small."

Elsi spotted the footprints leading back in the opposite direction. "They left and walked back toward the front entrance to the cave."

The rescue team followed the footprints. They all squeezed back into the first chamber and eventually found the recess in the wall and the vertical shaft leading up to the surface. A dead flashlight on the ground confirmed they had been here. Weiss looked up into the vent. "They must have escaped up the shaft. Otherwise we would have found them by now. We've explored the whole cave and the footprints stop here. They definitely climbed up to the surface. That's the only explanation."

He looked at his men who were looking up into the vent. Sammy, do you feel like climbing up there?

After you climb to the surface, we'll find you with the helicopter."

It was more of an order than a request, but nonetheless Sammy quickly agreed. His buddies lifted him up into the shaft and he was soon making his way toward the surface. Although older than Malik, Sammy was in much better shape, and he was able to reach the surface in less than ten minutes. He called to Colonel Weiss on his communication system. "I'm on the top of the mountain. It's mostly flat, and it gradually descends to the valley floor." Sammy turned on his flashlight and looked around. "I see some fresh blood at the top of the vent. It looks like one of them is bleeding."

Weiss's team, along with Moshe and Elsi, left the cave's entrance and boarded the helicopter. The sun had set while they were in the cave. They picked up Sammy and flew slowly along the plateau scanning the area searching for any clues as to the whereabouts of Moshe Stern's niece and her friends. With the noise of the chopper drowning out voices, Weiss pulled out a map and yelled at Stern, "You said she was rescued by some Bedouins, right."

Stern nodded his head, and Weiss said, "If they're still with the Bedouins, they know this part of the desert like the back of their hands. They'll probably head for the nearest town, and that would be Elifaz. Weiss moved his finger along a path tracing the route Saladin had taken the group earlier. He moved up to the front of the helicopter and showed the pilot the course he wanted followed. The pilot nodded his head in agreement and Weiss left the map for the copilot to use.

The chopper moved slowly, staying about fifty meters above the ground. Weiss's men were using infrared night vision equipment to study the terrain, hoping to see some sign of the missing explorers. They passed to the east of the hidden oasis but never noticed the place where Dalia and her friends had found refuge.

Weiss did some calculating in his mind. If the group had escaped in the early afternoon, and immediately started their hike to safety, how far would they have gone? Maybe they could manage eight kilometers an hour at best, most likely four per hour. Weiss looked at his watch. It's been no more than ten hours since the explosion went off. At most they could have gone fifty kilometers, more likely forty, and that's without any rest stops. Bottom line is they probably are within forty kilometers of the cave, fifty at most. He looked at their airspeed and estimated they would spot them in the next ten minutes. He yelled at his men. "Keep a sharp lookout; if they came this way, we can expect to see them in the next few minutes.

The unmistakable thumping of the blades of a helicopter resonated along the valley as it approached from behind. Malik was the first to hear the sound. He looked back over his shoulder and tried to spot the aircraft. The others heard it as well. They all stopped and began scanning the horizon. Dalia was the first to spot the dark speck as it passed in front of the moon. The six quickly moved out into the open desert. They began waving their arms and shining their flashlights at the approaching helicopter, trying to catch the attention of the pilot.

One of Weiss's men with infrared night-vision equipment spotted the group waving in the desert. He yelled eight o'clock low to the pilot who saw them and immediately changed course. He increased his groundspeed and reached them in less than a minute. The chopper hovered near the six and slowly descended to the ground.

As the chopper's blades wound down, the soldiers climbed out of the back of the twin bladed aircraft. The Israeli soldiers were followed by a person all too familiar to Dalia. "Uncle Moshe," she screamed and ran up to him.

He grabbed her and held her in the air as he kissed her on both cheeks. "You little renegade; what have you gotten yourself into? Don't bother to answer; you're well; that's all that matters."

Weiss's medic examined Ari and agreed with Ari's self-diagnosis of possible broken ribs. Dalia said, "We found the documents. There were thirty-three urns hidden in the cave. The Waqf captured us and took the urns. Then they left us in the cave and blocked the entrance with an explosion."

Weiss said, "We know; we were in the cave looking for you. We followed your footprints in the cave and then guessed you'd be heading for Elifaz. We're going to take you back to our base in Eilat."

Moshe and Elsi quickly conferred. Moshe said, "I'm going with you; there's been a crime here. Drop Detective Fischer off at our car. She'll drive back to Jerusalem."

Lieutenant Weiss wasn't about to argue. He just wanted to get everyone back to the base at Eilat as quickly as possible. They all piled into the chopper and the pilot started the blades spinning. As brave as Malik was on his home turf, he was scared to death at his first ever ride in any kind of aircraft. Both he and Saladin were wide-eyed as the chopper lifted up off the ground and banked sharply back in the direction of the entrance to the cave.

The team medic passed out water to everyone. Lisa handed him a couple of dates. "They're fresh," she said with a smile on her face. "We stopped at an oasis for a snack."

The medic tossed one into his mouth and smiled. He gave her a thumbs up and began checking out Ari's vitals as the chopper flew quickly back to the entrance to the cave.

After dropping off Elsi with their one satellite phone in her hands and the keys to Moshe's car, the helicopter rose again into the night sky and headed for the safety of the Eilat military base.

Chapter 42

The Israeli Defense Force base in Eilat was asleep for the night, but Weiss had radioed ahead, and a doctor and the base commander met the chopper as it set down near one of the larger hangers servicing variable wing aircraft.

The doctor took one look at Ari, and after talking to the medic, whisked him off to the base hospital for x-rays. The base commander, General Feinberg, looked at Saladin and Malik, who were both dressed in traditional Bedouin clothes, with a significant amount of suspicion.

Weiss spoke with the general. "Sir, I need to talk to General Yidlan immediately. He's going to want to know that we rescued these people, and I'm sure we'll need guidance on what to do next."

Feinberg said, "I'll have Sergeant Lister take them to get some food. They look like they've been through hell."

"They have Sir, and things are likely to get a whole lot worse."

Colonel Weiss saluted the base commander and left to make his call. Feinberg turned to a sergeant walking by his side. "Sergeant, why don't you take our guests to get some food; they look starved. If any of you need anything, just ask the sergeant."

Feinberg then walked off the tarmac, probably heading back to his home to catch up on his sleep.

Meanwhile, Weiss had finally made contact with General Yidlan. "General, it's Colonel Weiss. I'm happy to report that we have completed our mission successfully. The three Israelis, the American woman, and two Bedouins are all safe and back at the Eilat base. They found the ancient artifacts. The group was then attacked by the Waqf. To make a long story short, the Waqf trapped them in a cave and then left with thirty-three urns containing the old documents."

General Yidlan, who had been awakened, was now fully alert. "Congratulations Morty. Begin questioning them immediately. Find out what happened to them. Intelligence intercepted a call from the Grand Mufti's top security guy. The urns are being taken to Base Aladdin, wherever that is. See if they know where that might be located. We need to recover those documents. The Prime Minister found out about the scroll yesterday, and I got a call from him today. I briefed him on the whole thing. He made it quite clear that this was very important; it's going to be a political hot potato. If these documents are what we think they are, it will be the proof we need to lay absolute claim to Jerusalem and all of Israel; but we've got to find them quickly, because the Waqf will probably destroy them all once they have a chance to look at them."

Lisa and the others were driven across the tarmac in jeeps. They left the airfield and headed to a large building in the residential section of the base. The sergeant said, "It's almost five o'clock, so they'll be serving breakfast. Just take what you want from the buffet line, and let's sit over in the corner.

Lisa grabbed an assortment of fruits and cheeses along with a large helping of scrambled eggs. The smell of hot coffee and freshly baked sweet rolls awakened her appetite, long dormant from the stress of their ordeal. She sat down at the corner table and looked at the others. There were smiles enough to go around, except for Malik, who was already stuffing food into his mouth from a pile of assorted treats on his tray.

Dalia lifted her glass of orange juice in a toast. "To our good friends Saladin and Malik who saved us twice from certain death."

Uri gave his own toast, "And may we recover the urns and extract our revenge."

The sergeant looked at the group; he had no idea what they were talking about, but Uri's statement of hoped for revenge provoked a certain degree of discomfort. Malik asked if he could go back for seconds. They all laughed, and the sergeant gave his approval.

Ari finally arrived, escorted by one of the medical staff. "What, you couldn't wait for me? What kind of friends are you?"

Lisa stood up and gave him a kiss. "I'm this kind of friend." She said.

"Nothing's broken. The doctor said it's just going to hurt like hell for a few weeks."

Ari left to get some food, and when he returned, Colonel Weiss was sitting at the table. "As soon as you guys finish eating, we need to debrief you. We need to recover the urns."

Ari ate quickly, and Colonel Weiss ordered coffee and tea to be brought to a nearby conference room. Weiss asked the sergeant to arrange accommodations for their guests, and he left to carry out his new orders.

Weiss led the group down a hallway to a small conference room. A chef from the kitchen followed them into the room rolling a cart with sweet rolls, coffee, and tea. Everyone gathered around the cart, choosing their beverage, and sat down at the round conference table.

Weiss looked at them, and after they had all settled in, he turned on a microphone in the middle of the table. "I'm not very good at taking notes," he said. "This way we'll have a permanent record. I want to hear the entire story. Start at the very beginning. Don't leave anything out. Even the smallest detail might be important. Who wants to begin?"

Ari began with the invitation by Professor Bornstein to visit the catacombs near the Temple Mount. Over the course of two hours they were able to tell their story. Everyone contributed to their epic tale. Even Malik explained how he climbed the vent in the cave and helped pull the others to safety.

Weiss sat in total silence; it was a story worthy of an Indiana Jones movie. Finally, when they had finished their epic tale, he asked, "Israeli Intelligence intercepted a call from the Waqf. The group who captured you and took possession of the urns were ordered to bring them to a place they called Base Aladdin. Do any of you know where that is?"

There was prolonged silence. Lisa looked at the others. It was a staring contest. Weiss finally sighed in desperation. "So I guess that means you know where their secret base is located. We need to recover those urns. If you have information regarding where they were taken, we need to know everything."

Ari looked at the others and spoke for the group. "Colonel Weiss, We think we know where the urns were taken, but here's the deal. We want to be involved in finding the urns. I'm sure you can appreciate our interest after having heard our story. We have all discussed this, and we're ready to trade that information."

Weiss stared daggers at Ari. "And what might you want in exchange for that information?"

"We'll tell you the location if you promise to let all of us participate in recovering the urns."

"That's impossible! This is a military operation now."

Moshe Stern spoke for the first time. "No Colonel Weiss, this is a criminal investigation. Professor Bornstein and another man were murdered; Antiquity Authority property has been stolen; people are guilty of attempted murder. Justice must be served. This is a criminal matter not a military affair."

Weiss placed his hand on his chin, and pushed his lips around while he thought about this dilemma. Then, like all good soldiers, he decided to call his superior officer. He told the others he would return shortly and left them alone in the conference room.

After he left, Moshe turned off the recording system and turned to his niece. "Dalia, are you crazy. After all that has happened, you want to risk your life again?"

Dalia answered, "It's because of all that we've been through that we want to see this through to the end. And don't forget, these are precious artifacts. Those urns may hold the key to establishing our people's claim to Jerusalem. What do these military types know about protecting fragile artifacts?"

Stern rose from his chair and walked over to his niece. She stood up and he embraced her. "You're as stubborn as your mother. When she was a little girl she never listened. She always had to do it her way." He shrugged his shoulders. "So if that's what you want to do, then I'm forced to come along as your protector."

Dalia kissed her uncle on his cheek, and he returned the kiss.

It took Colonel Weiss some time to reach General Yidlan. He was taking his morning shower. He finally came to the phone. Weiss got quickly to the point. "General, they know where Base Aladdin is, but they won't tell us unless they can all participate in the recovery."

"The General screamed at his Colonel, "They're in no position to make such a demand. Can't Moshe Stern talk some sense into them?"

"Detective Stern explained this was a civil matter, not a military affair. There are charges of murder and attempted murder to be filed against the Waqf, and he wants them brought to justice."

"Colonel, we're not dealing with a group of thugs here. These Waqf people are organized, well-armed, and dangerous. The police aren't going to be able to get those urns back. This is a military matter now. The Prime Minister made this my problem. He said to do whatever it took to get those artifacts."

Yidlan's anger finally subsided, "Let me understand; we're going to have to set up a secret recovery mission with your team along with five Israelis, one American and two Bedouins. I thought as an old fart I'd seen everything, but this tops them all.

"Okay, here's what I want you to do. Tell them they've got an agreement, but it depends on their information being vetted. We need to be sure they really know where this secret base is located. I'll be in the office in an hour. Call me when you have the information."

Weiss returned to the conference room and sat down at the table. He noticed that the microphone had been turned off and smiled. He turned it back on and said, "I've just spoken to General Yidlan. He agrees to your terms, but only under the condition that your information is correct.

Ari looked at Lisa. That was her signal to spill the beans. "We left out a part of the story. When the Waqf soldiers were questioning me, their leader got a call on his satellite phone. From the tone of the conversation it sounded like his boss. After he hung up, he told his men they were going to Kadesh Barnea."

Weiss smiled, "But they must have been speaking in Arabic. You don't understand Arabic, do you?"

"No, but I'm a historian specializing in ancient history, and I know a lot about Kadesh Barnea. It's an ancient town in the Sinai Desert. It has great historical significance. It was from Kadesh Barnea that Moses sent out the spies into the land of Canaan. Moses's brother Aaron was buried near there. It was from there that Moses sent envoys to the King of Edom, asking for permission to pass through his land. So you see Colonel, I know a great deal about Kadesh Barnea, and it's a very unusual name, one that stands out in English, Hebrew, or Arabic. In any language it's always pronounced the same."

Weiss felt like a little boy who had been scolded by his teacher. He frowned, "Kadesh Barnea is in Egypt in the Sinai Desert. That creates obvious complications."

Uri pointed out, "Our agreement didn't consider if there were complications, only that the information was correct. Actually, it might be easier for us to go there as citizens than for the military to mount an expedition."

Weiss said, "I'm going to need to confer with General Yidlan. He won't be at his office for another hour. Why don't you all get cleaned up in your guest quarters? We'll get you some clean clothes to wear while we clean the clothes you're wearing. Try to get some rest while I push this information up to a higher level."

Weiss made a phone call and two soldiers quickly appeared at the door to the conference room, one male and one female. The soldiers led the group toward the guest quarters, a single-story well-aged brick building overlooking a park where they were each given private rooms. They were issued plastic laundry bags and told to place their dirty clothes in the bags, and fresh clothing would be brought to their rooms while they showered.

Lisa hadn't showered since leaving Jerusalem. She had gotten past the bad smell stage along with the others somewhere back around the time of the first gunfight with the Waqf soldiers. She stripped and placed her clothes inside the bag. She then stepped inside the military version of a private bathroom which was nothing more than a toilet, a small sink with a mirror, and a prefabricated shower capable of barely holding a single person.

She turned on the water and adjusted the temperature to just below her pain threshold. As she stood under the stream of hot water, the true color of her skin finally emerged. She spent almost twenty minutes trying to wash away too many bad memories. She was lucky to be alive. Twice she and her friends had avoided death, not so much by their wits as by the grace of

God. She wasn't a particularly religious person, but some deeply embedded memory attributed her escapes to some type of divine intervention.

She wrapped a towel around her hair and another around her body and left the bathroom where she discovered her bag of dirty clothes had been taken and a stack of fresh military type clothing was now sitting on her bed.

The slightly grey underwear was four steps below Victoria's Secret, but the all-cotton undergarments were functional and did fit. The olive drab pants and blouse were a little long, but she rolled up the sleeves and pants. Her army issue boots were new and stiff. She finally looked in the mirror and put on her military hat. She saluted herself and laughed at the way she looked. Actually, she thought she looked kind of sexy. She hoped Ari would like her new look.

Lisa yawned; the endorphins were wearing off and fatigue was setting in. She lay down on her bed and immediately fell asleep.

Chapter 43

"Kadesh Barnea?" General Yidlan said, "That's hard to believe. I'll get a drone in the air. I want to check for recent activity. Morty, remember that old bunker we covered with sand and left vacant after we gave back the Sinai to the Egyptians? It's just a few kilometers north of Kadesh Barnea. I'm thinking they may have discovered the place and are using it. What do you think?"

Weiss answered, "That makes more sense than the old ruins of the ancient city. From what I remember, there's hardly anything left of the old city. The sand has consumed everything. If they got into that old bunker, it would be a good place to hide."

"I agree. I'll order the drone out immediately, and assuming it's the place, I'll have the blueprints of the bunker e-mailed to you. Assume that's where they're hiding until we know otherwise. Plan to go in there tonight. I'll talk to General Feinberg and have him give you all the support you need."

"So we're actually going to go into Egypt. We'll use Night Hawk helicopters; they're the stealthiest. Including my men and the civilians, we'll have over a dozen going in. I'll need three choppers for everyone and space for the cargo we plan on bringing back."

"Morty, I don't want any of you guys getting caught. You can't leave anyone behind; we can't risk a political problem with Egypt. Call me with your plan as soon as it's finalized, and if you need anything special, just give my staff a call."

"Roger that General; you can count on me."

Colonel Weiss had a problem; going into a neutral country was bad enough, but trying to get inside a reinforced bunker was a major complication. He got on his computer and pulled up a military map of the Sinai Desert. He expanded the area around Kadesh Barnea and sent the file to a color printer capable of printing a full one meter by one meter copy of the map. Meanwhile, he studied the map on his computer. The picture was taken from twenty-thousand meters with a high resolution camera. The picture was over twenty years old, but the new pictures from the drone would allow him to observe any changes in the terrain; and in the desert, there were always changes, some manmade, but mostly from natural causes.

He weighed crossing the border with trucks and jeeps, but the risk of being observed by an Egyptian Border Patrol was too great. The nice thing about the Night Hawk helicopters was that they were almost silent, and because of that, they were the favored method of ingress into enemy territory on a clandestine mission.

He checked his e-mail, and the blueprints for the old bunker had been sent by one of the general's staff. He knew the guy's name, and he remembered the general always relied on him to get things done immediately. He sent the electronic file to the same printer and then walked over to the computer services room to pick up his prints.

On the way over, he toyed with the idea of asking Ari, the architect, for help in analyzing the blueprints of the bunker. With his knowledge, he might be able to find some weak spots in the bunker's design. By the time he had the prints in his hand, he had decided to ask for Ari's help. Of course that meant getting the other civilians involved as well, but what the hell, they were now all part of his team. He could count on his own men to follow orders without asking questions. Civilians, on the other hand, had a habit of wanting to know what they were getting into; and even though all four Israelis had served in the IDF, they were still civilians.

His own team was asleep, and he wanted them to get some rest, because if things worked out, they'd be going into the Sinai tonight, and they all needed to be in tiptop shape.

Weiss knocked on all of his guest's doors and told them to meet out at the picnic table on the side of the building in ten minutes. Within five minutes they were all assembled, and each was wearing the latest in military fashion. Ari smiled and gave Lisa a thumbs up when he saw her outfit.

They all sat around the picnic table looking at the prints on the table. As far as Lisa was concerned, the only interesting thing on the table was a detailed map of what she correctly assumed was Kadesh Barnea.

Weiss placed the map of the Sinai in front of everyone and explained the situation. "In the 1967 war with Egypt, we captured the Sinai Desert. Immediately after the war we were concerned about being able to move our tanks into the desert quickly if there was another war with Egypt, so we built a number of large hidden bunkers to store our tanks. One of these bunkers is located just a few kilometers north of Kadesh Barnea."

He pointed to an area on the map identified with the codename Valliant. "This is the bunker, and near it you can see the telltale signs of the ancient town of Kadesh Barnea."

Lisa examined the area on the map closely, and she could indeed see some signs of the hidden bunker.

"General Yidlan has requested an immediate flyover with a drone to take pictures of the area. We believe your Waqf friends may have found this old bunker and are using it as a place to hide the ancient urns. They probably believe they're safe in Egypt.

"I have the blueprints of the bunker. If we confirm that's the place they brought the urns, we're going to try to enter the bunker tonight and recover the artifacts. Needless to say, this is a dangerous mission. I understand Ari is an architect. I want him to study the plans. We need to find a way of entering the bunker. I'm guessing we'll have the pictures from the drone in the early afternoon. That will give us the latest intelligence on where they may be hiding. We're going to go in by helicopter, probably sometime after midnight. I'm going to check on equipment with the commander of the base. I'll be back in an hour. Any questions?"

As Weiss walked away, the others looked at Ari who was already studying the plans. There were a total of six prints: exterior views of the bunker that were now deliberately covered with sand, a drawing of the bunker's interior layout, an electrical schematic, a drawing showing all of the HVAC equipment, a detailed drawing of the water storage system and plumbing, and a series of small drawings of the various permanent special pieces of mechanical equipment inside the bunker.

Ari said to the others, "I need to concentrate on this. Can you guys go sit over by that tree until I've studied everything?"

While Ari analyzed the blueprints, the others sat down under a palm tree and relaxed. Dalia asked, "Saladin, what can we do to make everything right for you? Of course we'll get your cousin a new truck, but what can we do for you?"

Saladin thought for a long time, and then he surprised the others with a difficult request. "Dalia, for years our tribe has been trying to resolve a dispute with the Israeli Government. As you know, we have lived in the Negev and Sinai for thousands of years. We are nomads by nature, but we have also remained in some areas for hundreds of years. My people have a claim to these lands but the government has said that there are no written records to verify these claims.

"Instead the government is trying to resettle us into small communities. My cousin lives in one of these. But many of us want to have legal rights to the lands where we graze our livestock and erect our tents. You can see the problem is a difficult one to solve because it's political, but that is my request; that you help my people resolve this problem."

Dalia was at first shocked that Saladin had asked for such a thing, but if it wasn't for him, they would all be dead. "Saladin, what you ask is beyond what I can give you, but I agree to bring your request to the authorities, and I'll do everything in my power to help your people achieve their goal."

Saladin smiled in appreciation. "May Allah help you in your mission."

Dalia then asked, "Malik, what can we do to repay you for helping us leave the cave?"

Malik ran his hand through the grass as if he were trying to capture the answer to the question. "You know," he said, "I am like my brother, and my father, and my father before him, a person of the desert. I pass by many ancient ruins as my lambs search for grass to graze upon. Before this week, I didn't take much notice of any of them, but trying to find these ancient urns and the documents inside them has given me a new appreciation for my ancestors. I think I want to go to school and become an archeologist?

Dalia smiled, "This is something I can help make happen. Each year the Antiquities Authority gives out ten scholarships to the Ben-Gurion University in Haifa. There is an Arab study curriculum that I think I can get you into. It will mean leaving home for several years. Are you prepared to do that?"

Malik looked at his brother who was smiling at his sibling. "Yes, as Allah is my witness, I am prepared to do this."

Uri piped in, "What about me? I lost my truck and all my equipment."

Dalia, who was sitting next to him, surprised everyone by giving him a passionate kiss on his lips. "Isn't that payment enough?" she asked.

Uri laughed, "One more should do it."

He wrapped his arms around Dalia and slowly placed his mouth over hers. The kiss lasted much too long for Moshe. "Enough of this nonsense; you're making an old man feel even older. For my generation a kiss like that one meant you were already married, at least in the first year of marriage anyway."

Ari finally called them back to the picnic table. "Here's what I've found out. The front door of the bunker is camouflaged with a screen that looks like sand. The side and roof are then buried in the sand. It looks like the tanks and other equipment were stored inside the bunker, and the front door is built like a bank vault. In fact the front door requires a specially designed key to open it."

Uri asked, "So where is it vulnerable?"

Ari answered, "Possibly in two places. First, fresh air is drawn in from four different vents located in the top of the bunker. Each vent is large enough to enter the bunker, but we'll need a way to cut through the air duct."

Lisa asked, "What's the second way to break in?"

"Well through the backdoor of course. They designed a small escape door in the back of the bunker. Normally the stairs leading up to the ground are covered with a screen and then a layer of sand to act as camouflage. The backdoor requires the same type of special key to open it from the outside, but it can easily be opened from the inside."

Uri said, "So we can get in the backdoor if we can find the key. It's just like my apartment."

The group continued with small talk while they waited for the Colonel to return.

Chapter 44

Colonel Weiss arrived on schedule with his entire team. They moved two picnic tables together and the eleven men and two women sat down around the table. Ari explained the layout and construction of the bunker to Weiss and his men. He showed them the location of the roof vents and the backdoor. "If General Yidlan can get us the key to the backdoor, that's the easiest way in. If he can't, then we can drop down through the ventilation system with ropes, but that will mean we have to cut through some ducts."

Weiss continued, "They must have found a way to break into the bunker's front door, and that entrance will be heavily guarded for sure. Let's hope we can find that key."

Weiss immediately called a number on his cellphone and was connected to a Lieutenant Davis. "Lieutenant Davis, this is Colonel Weiss. I know General Yidlan has kept you up to date on my team's mission. We need to try to get the special key used to open the backdoor to the bunker. If you can't find the key for us, we'll have to go in another way, but that key will make things a lot easier for us."

After ending the call, Weiss said, "He'll get back to us. Let's assume he can't find the key. How do we cut through the ventilation ducts without making any noise?"

It was Moshe Stern who finally suggested, "Let's give them the Auschwitz treatment. We can add some sleeping gas into the air intake system. That will put them all to sleep. Then we don't care how much noise we make."

Dalia asked, "Do you have a sleeping gas in your military arsenal?"

Weiss answered, "I would think so, but let me check."

Once again he called the general's staff assistant, and once again got the same response. He would call back with an answer.

Weiss addressed his expanded team. "We're going to talk through the mission plan now. All of this assumes the drone pictures confirm the Waqf are hiding in this bunker. We'll be taking three H60 Night Hawk helicopters. I will be in Chopper One, along with Sammy, Ari and Uri. Abe, Jacob, Simon, and Josh will be in Chopper Two. Saladin, Malik, Moshe, Dalia, and Lisa will ride in Chopper Three.

"These helicopters are designed for silent flight. We will fly in at an altitude of fifty meters to the landing site. I'll have the GPS coordinates in a few hours. We'll land about two kilometers east of the bunker and walk in from there.

"Saladin, Malik, and Moshe will guard the helicopters along with the flight crews. I want you to set up a perimeter a kilometer out from the chopper. You'll all have communications systems and will contact each other on Channel One. The assault team will communicate on Channel Two.

"The assault team will approach the bunker from the east. We will set up an extraction point for the urns about one-hundred meters from the back of the bunker. We'll define the exact position once we get the drone pictures. Dalia and Lisa will wait at the extraction point. The rest of us will proceed to the back of the bunker. Assuming we can't find the key to the backdoor, Sammy and Abe will then move to the top of the bunker and dispense the sleeping gas into the ventilation system."

Sammy interrupted, "Will they send the gas masks down from Haifa?"

"Yes, our Haifa base will send down gas masks. After waiting the appropriate time for the gas to take effect, Sammy will be lowered down into the duct with a portable acetylene torch. Ari says the duct is just made from galvanized steel so it should be easy to cut."

Sammy asked, "Ari, where should I make the cuts?"

Ari pointed to the vent closest to the back of the bunker. "I'd use this duct and make the cuts at the bottom of the vertical shaft just where it turns to become horizontal. That way, we can all just drop down into the bunker. It should be a ten meter drop to the concrete floor."

Weiss continued, "After Sammy does his thing, you'll drop down into the bunker and confirm that everyone is asleep."

Josh asked, "What do we do if people are still awake?"

"Weiss answered, "We have authorization to use all necessary force. These people are terrorists.

Shoot to kill; we're not taking any prisoners. There won't be room on the choppers for prisoners."

Moshe was about to complain but then thought of something else. Colonel, these people will all probably be alive, ready to strike again. I want them arrested. Would it be possible to upload all of their cellphone data? That way we can keep track of where they are and arrest them when we want."

Weiss smiled, "Detective Stern, you are one crafty policeman. Abe that will be your job; you upload all of their phone data. You have everything to do it, right?"

Abe answered, "No problem Colonel; consider it done."

"Ari has indicated the backdoor to the bunker can be opened from the inside without the special key. If he's right, then we collect the urns and bring them out the backdoor. Dalia, you and Lisa will move from our extraction point to the backdoor as soon as we have the bunker under our control. We will reposition all of the urns behind the bunker and then bring them to the choppers.

"Now, if we can't open the backdoor, then we'll have to hoist the urns up through the ventilation shaft. Dalia, you and Josh figure out what you need to protect the urns while they're being lifted. What have I missed?"

Lisa said, "There are thirty-three urns. Each one weighs about ten kilos. They're too bulky to carry more than one at a time. That means we'll have to make three trips back to the helicopter. Can we bring a cart or something else with us to transport the urns back to the helicopter?"

Ari said, "Why not just reposition one of the choppers to the back of the bunker."

Weiss said, "That will work better than dragging carts through the desert. We'll reposition Chopper Three once we are ready to leave the bunker. Dalia, you and Lisa work with Abe to get everything you need to protect the urns during transport."

Weiss looked around the table and checked his watch. "We all know our assignments. Let's all meet back here at 1800 hours."

The meeting broke up and everyone began preparing for the mission.

Chapter 45

The pictures from the drone arrived a little after four o'clock. Weiss downloaded the file and printed the pictures. He placed the new pictures alongside the old picture of the bunker. Weiss focused in on the fresh photos. Just as he suspected, there were tire tracks leading to the front of the bunker. The bunker was still hidden under the sand, but the photographic evidence was clear; someone was using the bunker.

Working on his computer, Weiss zoomed in on the bunker. The optics on the drone's camera system allowed him to analyze the area as if he were looking down on the site from fifteen meters. He systematically scanned the area surrounding the bunker looking for guards and found four stationed along the perimeter of the bunker out about one-hundred meters.

He zoomed in on the top of the bunker and located the ventilation ducts. The backdoor of the bunker still appeared camouflaged with sand. Next, he zoomed back out and located a proposed landing zone for the choppers. The area was hidden from the bunker by a few rolling mounds of sand. In contrast to the Negev, the Sinai desert looked more like the desert of North Africa where towering hills of sand shifted over the land on a weekly basis.

He immediately sent the files to the printer, and as he walked to the coffee pot located in the computer room, his phone rang. It was Lieutenant Davis with some good and bad news. The location of the special key to unlock the bunker's backdoor could not be found. However, two canisters of a special short acting sleeping gas and gas masks were being flown down from the military base at Haifa along with the instructions for use.

It was time to call General Yidlan and brief him on the mission, or to put it another way, to get his approval. The call lasted a good half-hour. The general liked the plan, especially the use of the sleeping gas. He too mentioned Auschwitz. Weiss thought there must be something about Stern and Yidlan having similar backgrounds.

Weiss rode his jeep out to a remote hanger in the corner of the airfield and inspected his choppers. The aircrews were busy prepping their aircraft for the upcoming mission. He gathered them around a nearby table, spread out the drone's pictures, and provided the GPS coordinates of his desired landing zone. The senior pilot looked at the pictures and nodded his head. "I'll plan a flight path into the area. We'll want to avoid a few Egyptian radar installations, but if we go in at fifty meters, we should be okay."

Weiss said, "We're having a final meeting at 1800 hours on the side of the guest barracks. Join us and I'll introduce the team."

The lead pilot said, "Rumor has it that there are some civilians on the team."

"That's correct; they argued their way onto the mission. Don't worry, I can vouch for all of them; they won't screw up."

Chapter 46

Mission supplies had been gathered and piled onto one of the picnic tables. Weiss introduced the flight crews to the team. Ari knew one of the pilots; they had worked together on a commando raid on the Golan Heights.

Weiss spread out the pictures from the drone on the empty table, everyone gathered around. "These latest pictures were taken five hours ago. As you can see, there are fresh tire tracks at the front of the bunker." He pointed to four circled areas. "They've got four sentries posted in these locations. They're out about one-hundred meters from the bunker. Abe, Simon, Josh, and Sammy you'll need to take these guys out. You can work out the details after the meeting.

"We'll plan on initiating the attack at 01:05 hours. Nobody ever changes their sentries on the quarter-hour, so that will give us almost fifteen minutes to disperse the gas, which by the way, is being flown down here as we speak. Sammy, you read the instructions for use. You are now the team's official gas man."

Sammy interrupted, "Colonel, Josh always has the gas problem, so he should be the gas man."

Amid laughter, Weiss said, "Thank you Sammy for your advice, but I think you're the best man for the job. Captain Morgan, why don't you brief us on you flight plan."

Captain Morgan placed another map on the table. "I've placed black circles around the Egyptian radar installations. Our flight path will take us northwest from the airfield for forty-three kilometers. From there we will enter Egyptian airspace at an altitude of fifty meters. As you can see from the red line, we will be making three course changes to avoid known Egyptian border security stations as well as their radar. Actually as far as missions go, this is pretty straight forward."

Lisa thought *pretty straight forward* was probably more of a hope than an impartial risk assessment.

Weiss continued on. "Thanks Captain. After leaving the choppers, the assault team will move to this mark on the map. The GPS coordinates of the mark were written on the map. It's behind a sand dune and should provide pretty good protection. From this point we will send you four guys out to take care of the sentries. After confirming they have all been taken care of, we will all meet at the back of the bunker.

Lisa understood that taken care of was a euphemism for killing. Had she really degenerated into a person capable of indirectly being involved in the killing of other persons? This wasn't a war after all. Then she finally realized this was a war, a war that had gone on for decades with no peace, just perpetual cease fires. And besides, these Waqf assholes had already tried to kill them twice, and in a sense, she too wanted revenge.

Weiss continued, "Abe and Sammy will then climb to the top of the bunker and disperse the gas into this fresh-air intake duct. Sammy you'll let us know how long we have to wait before they're all asleep."

Ari interrupted. "I can help Sammy with that. I'll do some calculations for the air handling system to see how quickly the gas will diffuse throughout the entire bunker."

Weiss continued, "Thanks Ari. Someone tell me about the stuff on the table."

Dalia said, "We've got blankets to protect the urns during transport and a net to lift the urns up through the ceiling if we can't open the backdoor."

Sammy added, "I've got the portable torch to cut the duct and a couple of ropes for the descent into the bunker and enough gas masks for everyone."

Weiss said, "Okay; Captain Morgan can you and your men bring these supplies into Chopper Three. Everyone else, let's get to the armory for our weapons."

Lisa hated guns and now she would be packing heat. This hadn't really been part of the plan as far as she was concerned. The chopper pilots headed back to the airfield while the rest of the team drove jeeps over to the armory.

Weiss asked Lisa if she had ever fired a gun. Lisa reluctantly answered, "Yes, at the gunfight with the Waqf, but I really had no idea what I was doing."

He talked to the soldier behind a counter, and suddenly an Uzi pistol appeared in front of her. She knew this because it said so right on the box.

Lisa opened the black plastic case and looked inside; she could at least do that much. Dalia looked at her and immediately understood the problem.

"You're afraid of guns aren't you?" Lisa nodded her head. "Listen, after I get my gun, we'll go over to the practice range. You probably won't have to use this, but if you do, you'll want to know what to do."

Weiss filled out paperwork and guns kept appearing on the counter. The Uzi Submachine guns were for Dalia and the rest of the assault team. Moshe, Saladin, and Malik were issued M 89SR sniper rifles fitted out with night-vision scopes and silencers. Boxes of ammunition clips were placed on the counter, and everyone, except for Lisa, seemed to know what to do. Dalia asked Weiss to order a holster for Lisa's pistol, and a box with a picture of a black leather holster was placed in front of her.

Dalia asked Weiss. "Where's the practice range. I need to teach Lisa how to shoot."

Weiss gave her directions and told the women to pick up their field gear after practicing at the range. The two women left the armory; Dalia had her Uzi slung over her shoulder and a pack holding a dozen ammunition clips tied around her waist. Lisa, on the other hand, was still carrying her gun in its case, afraid that it might accidently fire.

The practice range was located near the armory. That seemed like the right place for it. Dalia spoke to the sergeant running the place, and he assigned them to Station One. The place was empty. Lisa imagined it got pretty busy as the prospects for the next war increased.

Dalia had Lisa put on her waist holster. Lisa had seen enough movies to know where everything should go. Dalia then placed a half-dozen clips in the belt. Lisa said, "You all seem so casual around guns."

"We've all been to war. Everyone except for Saladin and Malik. The Bedouins are not required to serve in the army. They can if they want to, but it's not mandatory."

Dalia opened the case containing the Uzi pistol. It was all black; mostly metal but with a plastic grip. She handed the gun to Lisa. "It's not loaded yet." She said.

"It looks terrifying just the same."

Dalia showed Lisa the pistol's safety and explained how it worked. She snapped a clip into the Uzi and chambered a round. She then emptied the gun into the target at the far end of the practice range. She showed Lisa how to hold the gun and how to position her body.

It was finally time for Lisa to fire her instrument of death. She loaded a fresh clip and pointed the gun at the target. Dalia corrected her stance and had her hold her arms a little straighter. Then it was time; she pulled the trigger, and the gun fired. The bullet totally missed the target. Dalia said, "Squeeze the trigger, don't pull it."

Lisa's heart was racing, and this was only shooting at a target. How could she ever actually point the gun at someone and pull the trigger? Her shooting in the desert had been in the dark and she never even pointed the gun at anyone. She began to understand why guns were so important to some people. They were the great equalizer. You could be a ninety-eight pound weakling and still easily kill another person twice your size. She put those thoughts out of her mind as she concentrated on hitting the target.

Three ammunition clips later, Lisa had actually hit the target a few times; nothing close to the bull's-eye, but close enough to be lethal. Lisa said, "Hitting a target in a practice range isn't the same as aiming at someone you're trying to kill."

Dalia answered, "You're right, and no amount of practice can prepare you for that moment. You may panic or you may be able to do it. I think it all depends on the circumstances. I think if you believe your own life is threatened and there are no alternatives then you'll do it, but you won't know how you'll react until you're in the line of fire."

Dalia signed for some new ammunition and showed Lisa how to load the bullets into the clips. As they were leaving the firing range, Malik and Saladin arrived with Uri. They were going to get some instructions on the use of their night-vision sniper rifles. Both were smiling at being able to play with their new big-boy toys. Men will be men after all.

The two women then walked over to a nearby building. Dalia said it was the supply unit for the military base. She asked to speak to the quartermaster. The private behind the counter disappeared into the warehouse, and returned a minute later with a middle-aged bald sergeant who had a well-chewed cigar pressed between his teeth. The guy looked a little like Telly Savalis in one of those World War II movies.

Colonel Weiss had already talked to the sergeant. He pulled a piece of paper from his pocket and instructed the private behind the counter to pull the list of clothes on Weiss's list. The sergeant looked Dalia and Lisa over with a keen eye, and yelled some clothing size instructions back to the guy pulling the gear.

Five minutes later the clerk appeared with two duffel bags filled with everything on the list. Dalia showed Lisa how to adjust the straps to allow her to slip it on like a backpack. The two girls then walked back to their quarters loaded down with the heavy duffle bags on their backs.

Chapter 47

Lisa sat on the bed in her room and stared at the pile of clothing next to her. She began to rethink her desire to participate on this military mission. What was she thinking? It was not an easy question to answer. She had always been an achievement oriented person, and once she started something, whatever it was, she had to finish the job. But this was more than that. Lisa suspected it had something to do with seeking revenge for what the Waqf people had done; killing Professor Bornstein, trying to kill them, subjecting Ari to a vicious beating. Maybe it was the beating to her new-found love that had triggered the response.

As she was contemplating the situation, there was a knock at the door. It was Ari with a smile on his face. "So how's my little GI Jane doing?"

"Oh, I'm a regular Annie Oakley."

"Who's Annie Oakley?" Ari asked.

She was a famous sharpshooter in the Old West, and let me tell you, if I don't shoot myself in the foot, I'll be lucky; and look at all these things: a bulletproof vest, night vision equipment, an Uzi pistol, a metal helmet. I'm trying to understand it all and it's hard. I just can't figure out why I'm doing this."

Ari surrounded Lisa in his arms and kissed her on her forehead. "I wish I could help you process all of this, but you Americans live a very insulated life. Israelis on the other hand see death and the effects of war on a daily basis. Military service is part of our lives. Every couple of years our men and women drop what they're doing and put on their uniforms to fight these people. Not all Muslims you understand, just these radical terrorists who truly believe the State of Israel should not exist, and it's their sacred duty to kill every Jew they can find."

She lifted her head from his shoulder and kissed him on the lips. It wasn't a kiss of passion or friendship; rather, it was a simple statement of her love for this man who had suddenly entered into her life. "Ari, help me put on all of these things. I have no idea how they all fit together."

"I'll certainly help, but first I have to help you undress."

"Oh really; you think I can't do that myself?"

"Well I don't know, but I do have some very special talents to offer."

Lisa smiled as Ari began removing her clothes. He laughed when he saw her military issued grey cotton briefs. "I liked the Victoria's Secret underwear better."

"I'll bet you did," she said, as she began unbuttoning his shirt.

It was her turn to laugh at his olive drab boxer shorts. "And you my love are no GQ model."

"Well in that case I'll take them off so you won't be disappointed."

When they were done and relaxing, Lisa wondered whether this was the first time anyone had ever enjoyed sex on this military procured bed. Probably not, she thought; not with all these young female soldiers around.

Ari helped Lisa dress in her combat-ready military clothes. He adjusted the bullet-proof vest. When she asked what the large camouflaged cloth was for, he folded it into a square and attached it to the top of her helmet. "It's there to protect you when you're trying to hide in the sand. You can cover yourself with the cloth and hope for the best."

Lisa tightened her ammunition belt and holster around her waist and then placed her Uzi pistol in its holster. She did the pirouette thing in front of Ari, and he approved. They both then moved to Ari's room where he also dressed for the upcoming battle.

Chapter 48

The expanded mission team arrived at the airfield at eleven o'clock. The choppers were in final-prep by the maintenance crew. Mechanical problems on this mission would be a disaster.

Weiss supervised the loading of all of the equipment. Then it was time for a final meeting to ensure everyone knew their assignments. They reviewed the sequence of events and what to do under certain situations. Lisa listened carefully, but Ari knew if they ran into any problems, all bets were off, and they would be adapting to unforeseen threats on the fly.

Weiss was pleased with his team's awareness of the mission details. He checked with Captain Morgan, who confirmed they were ready to go, and they would lift off in seventeen minutes in order to meet their time schedule. Weiss took the time to explain how the night-vision equipment worked to Lisa, Saladin, and Malik. He then passed out the individual communication systems to everyone, and after they confirmed their systems were operational, he and his team boarded the choppers.

As the three choppers spooled up their engines, Lisa leaned back against a front bulkhead and stretched her feet out on the floor of Chopper Three.

With all of the gear in her helicopter, everyone was squeezed into the remaining space.

Moshe Stern had his game-face on. He had already served in three wars and knew, perhaps better than anyone else that this wasn't going to be a cake-walk by any stretch of the imagination. Malik was fidgeting next to Saladin, and it was apparent his youthful bravado had now turned to pre-battle jitters. Welcome to the club Lisa thought. Saladin sat with his eyes closed. He might be asleep, but Lisa thought he was probably just deep in some personal thoughts.

As the choppers lifted off the tarmac, Lisa checked her watch. They were right on schedule. The three choppers climbed slowly into the moonlit night and leveled out at 100 meters heading northeast. The three choppers flew in a tight formation, sending out the smallest possible radar signal to any Egyptian radar units.

The almost silent thumping produced by the chopper's blades created a rhythmic beat that under normal circumstance might have put Lisa to sleep, but the endorphins surging through her blood prevented any chance of sleep. Seventeen minutes into the flight the choppers suddenly veered to the left, dropped down to fifty meters, and began their run into Egyptian airspace.

Lisa looked out the open side doors where two of the flight crew were manning machine guns. She hoped they wouldn't be firing their weapons tonight. The lights of the outskirts of Eilat were replaced with total darkness as they entered the Sinai Desert. The choppers seemed to be flying a lot closer than fifty meters above ground, but she trusted the pilots and figured it was just her fear of the mission at work.

Right on schedule the helicopters changed course and headed directly to the GPS coordinates of the landing zone. Thirty-three minutes into the flight, the choppers began to reduce their groundspeed. The three H-60 Night Hawks nestled down behind the protection provided by a group of rolling sand dunes. As her chopper approached the ground, sand was blown everywhere including into the chopper. Lisa had an unexpected gift of sand in her mouth which she spit out on the cabin floor.

As soon as the engines had stopped, the helicopter's gunners, along with Moshe, Saladin, and Malik, jumped out of the plane and set up defensive positions around the perimeter of the landing site.

Chapter 49

Two Egyptian Border Patrol jeeps on a routine search for terrorists operating in the area heard the thumping of the helicopters as they flew over their position. They couldn't actually see the choppers, but they didn't sound like any helicopters they had ever heard before. They radioed their base, and after a ten-minute wait, the base confirmed that no Egyptian aircraft were operating in the area. They were ordered to investigate.

The Egyptian soldiers agreed on the direction the choppers were traveling, and the two jeeps set out ten meters abreast in the general direction of the thumping.

These soldiers had never been in combat. Once, six months ago, they had intercepted some Hamas fighters who were trying to sneak some rockets into the Gaza Strip. The terrorists had been detained and their weapons confiscated.

The patrol's leader knew these helicopters had all the earmarks of being Israeli, but what would Israeli aircraft be doing in the Sinai? Egypt and Israel had pretty good relations, at least as far as the soldiers knew. What was clear to the lieutenant in one of the jeeps was that he had no idea how far away the helicopters were. They might just be over the next sand dune or they might still be heading toward the Suez Canal.

He contacted his base again and asked if any unknown aircraft were being observed on radar? His contact at the base indicated no radar contacts had been observed, and he questioned if the lieutenant was certain he had heard the helicopters. Could the sounds have come from something on the ground? The lieutenant was adamant, they had all heard helicopters.

Chapter 50

After the perimeter of the landing zone was secure, the assault team unloaded their equipment. Following a final communications check, the team set out with Colonel Weiss in the lead. Dalia and Lisa were in the middle of the single file of soldiers as they wound their way through the desert. A bright moon along with the night-vision equipment provided an eerie green glow to the surroundings. Lisa thought it was like a surreal video game, except for the fact that deadly bullets could be flying at any moment.

The column of assault troops moved quietly around the sand dunes. Weiss kept the group moving at a steady pace with two of his men about fifty meters ahead of the column scouting each flank. The two scouts were in constant communication with Weiss on Channel Two.

Weiss announced the team would reach their first objective in about two minutes. Weiss halted the column and pointed to a hill just off to their left. We'll set up the first camp on this side of the hill. After everyone had placed their backpacks on the sand, Weiss sent out four of his men to eliminate the sentries.

Lisa thought to herself. Here she was participating in the deaths of four men. Not directly, but certainly indirectly. Granted, these were not nice people, but an objective person would consider it murder. Where was Moshe Stern the detective? Why wasn't he concerned about the murder of these men? The same answer finally came to her; it was always the same. Her friends had been at constant war with one Arab country or another since 1947. The only peace treaty ever signed was with Egypt. For everyone else it was just temporary ceasefires. And the rules of war were different than what was tolerated in reasonable societies during times of peace.

She looked at her watch. The appointed time for the elimination of the sentries was at hand. She heard no sounds, nothing unusual to suggest anything was happening, but of course it was. She sat on her backpack waiting for word. Then they all began checking in, not with voices but with clicks on their radios. A single click from each assassin confirming each was in position. At exactly the appointed time, Weiss whispered the code word *execute* into the radio, and almost immediately Lisa could hear the very faint popping of four silenced guns.

The sounds were followed by four more single clicks confirming the sentries had been eliminated. The team waited silently for the others to return. They were all back safely in five minutes.

No congratulations from Weiss. All he said was proceed with Phase Two. Sammy and Abe picked up their equipment and headed for the roof of the bunker. Then, just as everything was going like clockwork, they heard shouting in the distance. The bodies of the dead sentries had evidently been discovered.

Weiss spoke calmly into his headset. "Sammy get that gas into the vent as soon as possible. Let's get out there and take care of business. Dalia, you and Lisa stay here."

And just like that the others were gone, and Lisa saw their green glows disappear into the night. Dalia and Lisa were now mere spectators, not with front-row seats because the bunker was out of sight, but observers nonetheless. Sammy suddenly reported in. "The gas is going in now. Abe and I are going to move to the front of the bunker. We'll stay on top of the bunker. That will give us the high ground.

Amidst the crackling sound of automatic gunfire, Weiss checked in. "We're on the east side of the bunker behind a sand dune. It looks like a fresh group of soldiers just arrived in a truck. They must have found the bodies. About six of them are trying to perform a flanking maneuver and attack us from the rear."

Dalia interrupted the dialog. "Lisa and I will move to prevent the flanking maneuver."

After a moment of silence, Weiss said one word, "Understood."

Lisa followed Dalia as she moved forward and to the right. Lisa didn't understand the tactical language, but she did know she was going into combat. Even with the benefit of their night-vision equipment, Lisa still lost footing in the loose sand as they rushed forward.

As the two women approached the bunker, they could see green flashes of small-arms fire up ahead. Dalia stopped and scanned the area. She pointed up ahead and to her right. "I see them; we're going to move in behind a sand dune and when they finish their flanking maneuver, we'll be in position to catch them before they reach you."

Weiss answered, "Roger that Dalia and good luck."

Dalia led Lisa to a defensive position behind a low sand dune. She turned off her communication system and said to Lisa, "Take your gun off safety and stay behind the sand dune. Whatever you do, don't stand up. Six guys should emerge about ten meters in front of us. Then, they're going to turn back toward the bunker and catch our people from behind. Fire into the group as soon as I start to fire. Keep reloading clips. Don't stop firing until I tell you."

Lisa took her gun out of her holster and disengaged the safety. Her hands were shaking as she positioned herself near the top of the sand dune. How could she kill another person? It was against everything she believed in, and yet Ari and the others were in trouble. In her mind, she was beginning to understand all too well the concept of a Band of Brothers. The gunfight at the bunker continued off to their left, and then just as Dalia had predicted, the green glow from six soldiers appeared. They were crouched down low and moving along the edge of a sand dune.

The six Waqf soldiers crept to within ten meters of the sand dune the women were hiding behind and then turned to their right back toward the bunker. Just as they completed their turn, Dalia began to open fire with her Uzi Submachine gun. Lisa, shaking throughout her body began pulling the trigger on her pistol. She quickly emptied one clip and struggled to replace it with a full clip.

Meanwhile, Dalia continued to fire quick bursts into the remaining soldiers who were now seeking cover behind a sand dune. Three of them were already down, and the others were hiding, not really certain where the shots had come from. Dalia whispered to Lisa, "Count to fifty and then start firing at ten-second intervals. I'm going to move in behind them and finish them off."

Lisa waited as instructed and began slowly counting while Dalia began crawling off to her right. Lisa understood what Dalia was trying to do. What she didn't understand was how cool under fire this Israeli female warrior seemed to be. Was Lisa just a wimp, or was Dalia more like Wonder Woman?

Lisa completed her count and began firing in the direction of where the three remaining soldiers had taken refuge. Strangely, her hands were no longer shaking. Had the shock of the initial firefight overcome her jitters? At ten second intervals she continued to fire at the men. After her fourth shot, she heard a burst of gunfire and a few seconds later Dalia said over the communication system. "This is Dalia; all six soldiers have been eliminated. What are your orders?"

Weiss answered, "Good work. Can you work your way toward the front of the bunker? I just want you to observe what's happening."

Dalia answered, "Will do."

Lisa realized the night-vision equipment gave her team an enormous advantage. As the two women moved cautiously toward the front of the bunker, sporadic gunfire filled the night air.

Suddenly a skyrocket shot into the night sky. Dalia screamed, "Close your eyes; it's a flare to allow them to see us. Take off your night vision goggles. Lisa did as she was told. When she pulled off her goggles, it took several seconds for her eyes to adjust to the twilight conditions created by the burning flare descending on a parachute. Finally she could see the front of the bunker. There were about a half dozen Waqf men hiding behind a sand embankment facing the rest of Lisa's team. Lisa could see Sammy and Abe on top of the bunker. Dalia spoke to Weiss, "There're seven Waqf men hiding in the sand near the front east side of the bunker. If Sammy and Abe drop down on the west side of the bunker, they can sneak up behind them. The rest of the area seems to be clear of any men."

Weiss answered, "Sammy and Abe, execute Dalia's plan."

Sammy and Abe answered in the affirmative and three minutes later, they were sneaking in front of the bunker. Standing side by side, they rounded the corner of the bunker and began firing at the remaining Waqf soldiers.

Except for Sammy reporting that all threats had been eliminated, the sound of silence suddenly overwhelmed the battlefield. Weiss asked, "Injury report."

Josh reported a bullet wound to his left arm, but other than that, thankfully everyone else was untouched. Weiss changed channels on his communications system and talked to Captain Morgan. Morgan asked, "We heard gunshots. Are you okay?"

Weiss gave a brief description of the encounter and then told the captain to remain extra vigilant because the flare might have alerted anyone near the area.

Weiss switched back to Channel Two and ordered everyone to reassemble at the original meeting point. Five minutes later they had all collected their gear and were heading toward the back of the bunker. Sammy confirmed that according to the directions for use, the gas must have already put everyone to sleep inside the bunker, and they would have about two hours of time before the Waqf people began to awaken.

Chapter 51

Lieutenant Muhammad and his men could see the flare off in the distance. He radioed the information into his base commander who ordered him to investigate. His two jeeps began moving in the direction of where the flare had for a short time lit up the night sky.

The terrain was anything but suitable for a jeep to navigate. Hills and sand dunes made the going difficult. He guessed it would take almost thirty minutes to reach the area.

None of his men had ever been in a war, let alone a battle. They were all on edge. They had no idea of what they would find when they finally arrived at the location of the flare, but they all thought it must have something to do with the helicopters they had heard earlier that night.

Lieutenant Muhammad on the other hand was certain Israelis would be at the center of whatever problem lay ahead. He knew the Egyptian military didn't have silent helicopters like the ones he had heard.

Chapter 52

Lisa and the rest of the team were back on track. Sammy, with Abe's help, was cutting through the ventilation system and most of the others were clearing sand away from the back of the bunker. By the time Sammy, Abe, Josh, and Uri had slid down the rope into the bunker, the backdoor area was almost completely cleared of sand.

Inside, a power generator was providing enough electricity to light up the entire bunker. With their gas masks on, the four split into two groups. Uri and Josh moved to the backdoor of the bunker while Abe and Sammy checked on the sleeping Waqf soldiers.

Just as Ari had said, the backdoor was very similar to a bank vault door. A large wheel controlling locking lugs was turned counterclockwise. Slowly the lugs were disengaged from the steel doorframe. They then pulled the backdoor open and found the stairs leading up to ground level. Uri pulled on a long rope to release a screen keeping the sand away from the stairs. The screen fell down, and his friends suddenly were staring down at him.

Weiss said, "Okay guys, let's find the urns."

Lisa adjusted her gas mask and entered the bunker. Finding the urns took less time than she thought possible. As they were walking through the backdoor, Sammy radioed in. He had found the urns in a room near the front of the bunker. About twenty Waqf soldiers were scattered around the floor, mostly half-dressed, and on their way toward the front of the bunker. They had probably been awakened by the gunfight and were attempting to get dressed and help their comrades before they were overcome by the gas.

As they walked toward the front of the bunker, Lisa was captivated by the sight of men half undressed in a deep sleep lying on the floor in awkward positions. It looked like some type of zombie horror movie.

Sammy led them to the room containing the thirty-three urns. Behind her mask, Lisa smiled at the sight. They all looked intact, and none of the wax seals had been broken. Weiss switched his radio over to Channel One. "Captain Morgan, we've got the urns. Reposition Chopper Three to the back of the bunker. Have the rest of the security force remain with you."

"Roger that Colonel. We're spinning up Chopper Three as we speak."

Abe began collecting cellphones from the sleeping soldier's pockets and uploading their information into his small computer. Moshe Stern was going to get information that would keep him happy for years to come.

Each member of the assault team picked up an urn and they began the process of moving them all to the back of the bunker. Lisa and Dalia remained at the backdoor, and when Dalia heard Chopper Three approach, she lit a green landing flare and threw it on the ground where she wanted the helicopter to land.

The chopper approached the marked landing zone, hovered, and then settled down onto the sandy ground. The right gunner opened the side door and jumped down onto the ground.

Dalia and Lisa removed their masks and climbed through the side door. They began removing blankets from the pile in the back of the chopper. The rest of their team carried the urns out of the bunker and passed them up to Dalia who placed them on a blanket. Lisa then wrapped the urns in the blanket and placed them in the rear of the aircraft.

Moshe Stern was the first to see the faint green glow of the two jeeps. He immediately reported into Morgan. Morgan called Weiss on Channel Two. "Colonel, we've got two jeeps out about 1000 meters from our position. They're heading in your direction and we expect them to arrive there in about ten minutes."

Weiss considered the situation. He needed about twenty minutes to remove the remaining urns. The jeeps would arrive at the bunker by then. "Captain Morgan, I think they saw the flare and are investigating. They may be an Egyptian Border Security patrol. I want you to take your two choppers up into the air and move slowly to the east. Try to get them to follow you, but under no circumstances should you engage them or stay within range of their small arms. Let's hope they don't have any surface to air missiles."

Morgan answered, "Roger that Colonel. We'll be airborne shortly."

Morgan switched over to Channel One and ordered everyone back into the helicopters. The blades began to spin as the sentries jumped back into the chopper. After completing a headcount, the two choppers lifted off and began moving slowly to the east at an altitude of twenty meters.

Lieutenant Muhammad heard the choppers engines and saw the faint outline of the two helicopters as they rose slowly into the moonlit sky. What were they doing? They were just moving slowly off to the east. Had they seen his two jeeps? They probably had plenty of night-vision equipment on board those aircraft. Muhammad ordered his driver to follow the choppers, and the two jeeps moved in pursuit of the two Israeli aircraft.

It took about ten minutes for Lieutenant Muhammad to realize that something was wrong. The helicopters were just trying to get him to follow them. Why? He was quick to understand the reason. They didn't want him to continue on his old heading, and the reason was obvious. There was something out there the Israelis didn't want him to find.

He immediately ordered his driver to head back on their original heading. He radioed into his base and explained the situation. The base commander indicated that the Egyptian air force had been alerted, and several planes were being scrambled to investigate.

Morgan radioed Weiss on Channel Two. "The jeeps have stopped following us and are heading back toward you."

Weiss answered, "We need about five more minutes here. I want you to head back to Eilat on the planned exit route. We'll follow as soon as we can. I'll call you as soon as we're airborne."

"Roger that Colonel; good luck."

Weiss ordered his team to get back to the chopper with the last load of urns as quickly as possible. He ordered the pilot of Chopper Three to start his engine. He needed to save every second he could. With the urns all stuffed into the helicopter, it was going to be a very tight fit for everyone, but they'd have to make due. As the helicopter's blades began to spin faster and faster, the team members brought the last of the urns to the chopper's door. There was no time to wrap the last of the artifacts. Dalia and Lisa just placed them carefully on top of the bundled urns already in the back of the aircraft.

With the last urns wedged into place the team piled into the chopper. It was a tight fit, but at least the powerful helicopter could easily manage the weight. As the engine approached flight speed, the helicopter strained to lift off, and finally managed to break away from the ground and head north, away from the oncoming jeeps.

Lieutenant Muhammad heard the chopper's engines revving up and then saw the massive bird lift up into the sky and head off to the north. He immediately called into his base and spoke to the base commander. The commander ordered Muhammad to investigate the area where the helicopter had taken off from.

The two jeeps continued onto the area of interest. As they approached the bunker, they could see a light coming from the ground. Upon closer inspection, they realized the light was from an underground bunker. Muhammad called in his findings to the base. He then descended the stairs into the back of the bunker, and what he and his men found would haunt them for the rest of their lives.

Chapter 53

Chopper Three caught up with the rest of the flight near the Egyptian Israeli border. Inside Chopper Three, everyone was in good spirits. Josh's wound was only superficial, and he had a tourniquet tied off to stop the bleeding. Lisa was just thankful to be alive. She would have liked to slip into Ari's arms, but he was stuck in a corner near the co-pilot's seat.

They landed at the Eilat military airfield a little after three o'clock. The maintenance crew towed Chopper Three inside the hanger while the other two helicopters remained outside. General Feinberg greeted them as the assault team emerged from Chopper Three. He had no idea what the assault team had recovered, but knew it must be important.

Colonel Weiss saluted him and then the general gave him a hug; very non-military Lisa thought. Ari gave Lisa much more than a hug, and Dalia and Uri seemed bound together.

Weiss asked General Feinberg to set up guards around the hanger to protect the mysterious cargo, and Feinberg immediately made a call to his MPs.

Weiss took a much needed bathroom break and then found a private office. He dialed General Yidlan's private number and woke the general from a deep sleep. He was fully alert, however, when Weiss told him who was on the phone. "The mission was a total success General. We have the thirty-three urns, and they're safe inside a protected hanger on the Eilat military base."

He then briefed the general on the mission. There would be many more briefings for both Weiss and his men, however the one with the general was the most important.

Yidlan was delighted. "Morty, Congratulations; I need to talk to the Prime Minister to see what he wants done with the urns. You and your team need to get some much-needed rest. Call me later after you've had a chance to unwind. We'll let you know what to do with the treasure."

Weiss said, "One more thing General Yidlan. I know Stern's niece and the American are going to want to be the first to see what's inside the urns. I owe them both a lot. They probably saved our lives out there in the desert. Try to make sure they get that chance."

Yidlan said, "So Morty, a Sabre and an American saved your ass. What happened to that macho man I know?"

"Well General, it was a valuable lesson."

"I want to hear the full story of their heroics over dinner as soon as you can break away, and please give my congratulations to your entire team."

Weiss's team was decompressing in the hanger. He gathered them all around him and relayed the general's congratulations. "We'll debrief everyone tomorrow. Right now, let's all get some sleep."

As the gathering broke up, Weiss took Dalia aside. "I just want to thank you for what you did out there. It took a lot of guts to put yourself in harm's way. We were pinned down, and if those guys had gotten behind us, I think we would have all been killed."

Dalia said, "Lisa was there too."

"I know she was, and she did help, but you were the one who took the initiative and did exactly what was required. By the way, I asked the general to make sure you and Lisa are the first ones to take a look inside those urns. I think I know how much that would mean to both of you."

"Thank you Colonel; you're right, it would mean a lot to both of us."

The team found their way to some jeeps and a convoy of happy warriors was driven back to their barracks.

Ari followed Lisa into her room. He wasn't about to lose sight of her. They both desperately needed to get some sleep, but they also needed to decompress from the stress of the mission. After shedding their combat gear, Lisa jumped into his waiting arms. "I can't believe it's over," she said.

"Not just over, but we have the artifacts. After all our troubles, I hope it's worth it."

Ari just held her quietly in his arms as they rested on Lisa's bed. They were both thinking about everything that had happened to them in the last few days. Finally Ari said, "You and Dalia saved our lives out there. We were all pinned down against the side of the bunker behind a small sand dune. If those Waqf soldiers had been able to flank our position, we would have been toast."

"Lisa laughed, "I did very little; it was Dalia who figured out what we needed be done. She was the one who told me what to do. I wasn't much help at all."

"But you shot your weapon. You did something you found totally against your principles. That was a very brave thing you did."

"All I did was stick my gun above the sand dune and fired to create a diversion."

"Yes, but if you had been unable to do that, then Dalia might have failed in her mission, and we all might have died."

Lisa stopped the conversation by kissing Ari on the lips. It was the kind of kiss that left little room for doubt: tender and filled with love. Ari wanted it to never end. He placed his muscular arms around her and drew her into the comfort of his body. They both finally fell asleep with Lisa nestled in Ari's arms.

Chapter 54

At seven o'clock, General Yidlan called the Prime Minister. His personal secretary connected the general with the head of the Israeli Government. The General immediately cut to the chase. "Prime Minister, I have some good news; we've recovered all of the urns. They're sitting in a hanger in the Eilat military base with enough guards to ensure their safe keeping."

"Congratulations Chaimy. I guess you'll be giving out some medals."

General Yidlan hated his nickname, but he wasn't about to argue with the Prime Minister, and besides Chaim Weizmann, the first President of Israel, was also nicknamed Chaimy. "Mr. Prime Minister, the reason I'm calling is to ask you what you want done with the urns?"

"Chaimy, that's an interesting question. It seems to me there are three things to be considered. Of course there's the historical significance and scholars will need to study whatever is inside. But in addition, there're serious religious and political questions.

"The religious zealots in my coalition will want to use the information to their advantage, and of course if what's inside proves the Jewish people have a legal right to the city of Jerusalem as their capital, well that will open up a whole new can of political worms."

"Mr. Prime Minister, let me propose that we do two things in secret. First let me move the urns to the military base outside of Haifa. We'll be able to protect them there from any ideas the Waqf or anyone else has. Second, let's open the urns up and see what's inside. For all we know they may be empty. Once we know what's inside, you can decide how best to deal with the information."

The Prime Minister thought about the general's suggestion; it was reasonable and probably had no downside risk; the kind of decision the Prime Minster liked. "Do it Chaimy; move the urns to Haifa and find out what's inside, but remember, I don't want this to leak to the press or anyone else. Whoever you get to open these artifacts needs to sign a pledge of secrecy."

After the call, General Yidlan asked his aide to arrange a helicopter ride to the Eilat military base. While his aide was arranging for the flight, the general's phone rang. It was General Abdulla, his counterpart in the Egyptian Army. "Good morning General Abdulla, it's been a long time since we've talked. How are your wife and children?"

"They're doing very well General Yidlan. Thank you for asking. My oldest boy is ready to go to the University. He says he wants to be an engineer. That's a much better profession than ours, don't you think?"

"A wise choice for the young man. Every country can always use good engineers."

"General Yidlan, the reason I'm calling is that last night there was a little incident in the Sinai Desert. It seems one of our Border Patrol units heard several helicopters. They were an unusual type; he believes they were Night Hawk choppers. I'm sure you're familiar with the type. I assured him they couldn't be Israeli because that would mean they had invaded our country. Anyway, he investigated and found an old buried bunker filled with sleeping men and sixteen dead bodies just outside the bunker. It seems the unlucky ones outside the bunker were killed in a gunfight."

"That's very interesting General Abdulla."

"Yes it is General Yidlan, and here's the most unusual part; it seems the men inside the bunker were put to sleep with some type of short-acting sleeping gas."

"Yes, that is very strange indeed."

"The reason I'm calling is just to give you a heads up. We've arrested all of the men in the bunker on terrorism charges. It seems they had some nasty weapons inside that place. They'll be behind bars for a very long time."

"Where was this bunker located General Abdulla?"

"Near Kadesh Barnea."

"Ah yes, you know that's probably one of our old bunkers that we built after the 1967 war. We just left it there when we turned back the Sinai to you in 1979 after we signed the peace treaty."

"Well General Yidlan, I just wanted to let you know that we are as interested in getting rid of these Hamas terrorists and other no-goods as you are. Good day and I hope you had a chance to get some rest last night."

"Thank you General Abdulla; I slept like a baby."

General Yidlan smiled after the call. He actually had a pretty good relationship with Abdulla. They both had a common interest in ridding the Middle East of terrorists; for different reasons perhaps, but their goals were the same.

Chapter 55

It was almost noon when Lisa and Ari awoke, and after showering and dressing in their non-military clothes, they headed for the mess hall. The rest of their friends were eating in the corner of the building in a quiet spot. Malik's plate was piled high with food and everyone was enjoying themselves. With a grin on his face, Uri said, "Well it's about time Ari. You didn't answer your door this morning, so naturally I assumed you were already here."

Lisa smiled and said, "He was on a special secret mission; that's why he wasn't available this morning."

Uncle Moshe almost spit out his tea, and everyone laughed. Dalia said, "I talked to Colonel Weiss this morning. They're going to fly Saladin and Malik back to their cousin's house after lunch. I've already talked to my boss, and he's agreed to get Saladin's cousin a new truck. There's a dealer in Be'er Sheva that he can order it from."

Saladin said, "My cousin will be very happy. He has dreamed of a new truck for more than five years."

Dalia continued, "Getting Malik into university and Saladin his tribe's land rights will take some time, but I'm committed to making both happen."

Weiss and his team suddenly appeared with food trays and sat down at their table. Lisa guessed they had all passed whatever test new soldiers needed to pass, and they were now considered part of Weiss's team. Weiss said, "I just got a call from General Yidlan's aide. The general will be here in a few minutes. We've all got to meet with him at one o'clock in the conference room we used yesterday."

Dalia asked, "What's he want?"

Weiss answered, "I'm not really sure. I think it may be about what we do with the urns now that we have them."

Saladin asked, "Are Malik and I supposed to be there too?"

"Yes, the General's aide said we should all be there."

Weiss and his men finished their lunch and then the entire group moved to the conference room a little before one o'clock. Just as everyone was getting settled, General Yidlan walked in alongside General Feinberg, with Feinberg's aide trailing behind. Weiss introduced his team and the civilians to General Yidlan, and then the general asked them to sit down. Moshe, who needed no introduction, received a hug of close friendship instead.

Generals Yidlan and Feinberg remained standing and moved to the front of the room. Yidlan addressed the group. "Colonel Weiss, you and your team, including these civilians, are to be congratulated. I've just spoken to the Prime Minister. Needless to say, he is very excited about being able to look into our past by examining the contents of these ancient urns.

"First, however, it is my honor to award each of you a medal to recognize the extraordinary efforts you all made in finding and subsequently recovering these precious artifacts. The civilians here are being awarded the President's Award, the highest recognition for a civilian. When I call your name please come forward to accept the award."

The general called each of their names. Each civilian received a beautiful cedar-wood box containing a round gold medal with a gold menorah over a blue circular background. General Yidlan kissed his good friend Moshe Stern on both cheeks. Lisa was embarrassed to receive her medal, but accepted it graciously, as did the others.

"Next for the IDF soldiers here today, I have the honor of presenting the Medal of Valor. This special award is given to those soldiers who have shown courage in the face of the enemies of Israel."

Weiss and his team then marched up one by one as their names were called and took possession of their medals.

The two generals and their aide then sat down and Yidlan continued to speak. "The Prime Minister wants us to move the urns to the military base at Haifa where we can protect them from any outside threats. He also wants us to open the urns and assess what's inside. Doctor Herbst, you have the greatest understanding of what we need to do to accomplish this; what do you suggest?"

Dalia considered the question. "General, the scroll inside the first urn seemed to be well preserved; I'm hoping the contents of these other urns will also be in good shape. Any scrolls inside these urns will have been rolled up. This means they may be very brittle. The urns must be opened in a controlled humidity environment. Also, the first scroll was written in an ancient form of Hebrew. We're going to need an expert on this ancient writing to help with the translations. I recommend Professor Andre Braverman. He translated the first scroll, and I'm sure he would be willing to help out."

The general said, "We have a temperature and humidity controlled room on the base. I'll have the computer equipment stored inside moved to another location. We have one more problem to discuss. Colonel Weiss has indicated that some of you would like to be there when the urns are opened, and you have certainly earned that right. The Prime Minister has insisted on one rule. Anyone viewing the contents of the urns must sign a pledge of secrecy. I have brought these forms with me, so if any of you would like to see the contents, you'll need to sign the forms."

Dalia stood up and addressed General Yidlan. "General, these urns are not the property of the military. They are the property of the Antiquities Authority. These artifacts need to be analyzed by scholars, and the information contained in them made available to historians throughout the world. I object to this secrecy. There is no need for secrecy."

"Oh, on the contrary Doctor Herbst, this is very much a political problem. I am sure you can appreciate the political overtones surrounding these urns. Why do you think the Waqf were interested in retrieving them; they killed people to get their hands on the contents? They fear whatever is in the urns. The information hidden inside those simple clay pots may solve the Jerusalem problem once and for all. These urns must be treated as a political unknown until we understand their contents. The Prime Minister is the head of the Israeli Government and as such has the right to use the information in the urns to the advantage of the State. The military is now the custodian of these urns, and anyone wishing to see the contents will sign these documents. Do I make myself clear?"

Dalia said, "Perfectly clear General Yidlan. I don't wish to participate in the opening of the urns under those conditions. In fact, I will consult with the Antiquities Authority and will recommend that we release a statement to the scientific community regarding the existence of the urns, and that the IDF has taken possession of all thirty-three of them. She stood up, placed the box containing her medal in front of General Yidlan, and left the conference room.

Lisa had been shocked at the General's position. Historians throughout the world had a right to inspect the contents of the urns. The world should immediately be told about the find and participate in the analysis. She followed Dalia's example; pushed her medal across the table, stood up, and left the room.

Ari and Uri had trouble understanding the two women they both loved, but they also stood, and after returning the medals, left the room. Surprisingly, Malik joined his new friends in the act of defiance. Then Saladin, following Malik's lead, also pushed his medal across the table and left the room.

Moshe Stern laughed after the others had left. "Chaimy, she's one headstrong woman, but in this case she's right. You and I both know there's no downside risk in making the existence of the urns known to the world. At best, the contents will prove our legal right to Jerusalem, and at worst the contents will only be of importance to a few historians. The Prime Minister wants to use the contents to his own political advantage. I personally have no intention of looking at the scrolls, but I agree with the others."

He pushed the medal across the table and left to join his niece. General Yidlan was not pleased. He admired Moshe Stern's niece for her action, but now he was faced with a real problem. He hated these academic types. They were always positioning themselves on the side of righteousness.

304 The Proof

The meeting broke up and General Yidlan left with General Feinberg. He needed to talk to the Prime Minister. Meanwhile, Colonel Weiss left his men and sought out Dalia. She was with her friends outside the guest barracks. Uncharacteristically, he snapped to attention and saluted the group. "I knew as soon as the medals were being distributed that the general had a reason for the theatrics. I just wanted to tell you that I admire people who stand up for what's right. I was proud to witness what you did, and so were my men."

The Colonel saluted them again and walked away.

A jeep drove up to the group. A soldier had come to pick up Saladin and Malik. Both were embraced by the group, and Dalia spent a long time talking to Malik about how she would contact him about the scholarship she hoped to get for him. Much to his surprise, she kissed him on both cheeks and gave him a final hug.

As they drove off to their helicopter ride back to the desert, Dalia said, "We'll have to figure out a way to help Saladin with his tribe's land claim."

Moshe said, "I think it's time to return to our homes, don't you think?"

The others all agreed. Ari said, "We could ask the General for a helicopter ride, but I prefer renting a car from the car rental place on the base and driving back to Jerusalem."

They didn't need to pack anything; they just came with the clothes on their backs. They walked over to the Enterprise rental dealer, and rented a SUV with enough space for the five of them. Moshe was the only one with a driver's license and credit card, so he rented the car. The drive back to the city was rather quiet, and most everyone but Moshe caught up on their sleep.

As they neared the city, they all agreed to meet the next day in Dalia's office. Moshe dropped Lisa and Ari off at Ari's apartment, and Uri decided to be dropped off with Dalia. Moshe looked at his niece with that special look that indicated his approval. Dalia laughed and kissed her uncle on the top of his bald head.

Lisa reluctantly agreed to stay in Ari's apartment. There was still the very real threat of another Waqf attempt on their lives, but both agreed they couldn't continue to always live in continuous fear.

Ari placed his two commando knives on his nightstand just in case the Waqf tried to break in, and the two took turns in Ari's small bathroom preparing for bed. They were still exhausted from their adventures, and with Lisa surrounded in his arms, they both quickly fell asleep.

Chapter 56

It seemed like they had been involved in this thing for months, but in reality it had all happened in just a few days. They had been the most stressful days in Lisa's life since her parents had died but also the most rewarding. She had been involved in a great quest, had almost been killed three times, had become good friends with some amazing people; and most importantly of all, she had fallen in love with Ari Waldstein.

As she showered the next morning, all of these thoughts played over and over like a stuck record in her mind, and the one question she could not answer was the future of her relationship with Ari. She had only a couple of weeks before she needed to leave for California. Her heart wanted to stay in Israel, but her brain knew it wasn't possible. She needed a job, and the university was still paying her rent. She loved her work, and her adventures in the Holy Land had given her a renewed sense of purpose. She had always wanted to write a historical textbook, and the germ of an idea based upon her adventures held the promise of a great story.

Ari stood behind the kitchen sink fixing their breakfast. She put her arms around him and nibbled on his right ear. "My you're frisky this morning," he said, "What's gotten into you?"

"I've been thinking about us Ari. I've been trying to work out our future and I don't have an answer."

He turned around and gave her a kiss. "I've been thinking too, and you're right; we're both caught between our love and our careers, but sometimes these things have a way of working out."

"I hope you're right," she said with tears in her eyes.

Dalia had started out her day in her boss's office. He had listened intently to her story and was finally able to grasp the significance of what had happened. She explained what General Yidlan had said, the ultimatum he had delivered, and that's when the Director of the Antiquities Authority lost it. "He said what?"

Dalia explained the rules again. "That's absolutely unacceptable Dalia, absolutely unacceptable!" The Director thought about the problem and suddenly smiled. "What's the Prime Minister going to do if he can't get anyone to agree to translate the scrolls?"

Dalia smiled, "There're only a half-dozen people in Israel who could translate the ancient writing."

Director Becker said, "I know who they are. I'll call them all and explain the situation. After I explain the facts, none of them will agree to the Prime Minister's condition."

"After that what will the Prime Minister do?" Dalia asked.

"Well, that's when I'll give him a call. I'll explain that I have a press release ready describing everything that happened and put the blame for withholding the contents of the urns from the public squarely on his shoulders. I think he'll recognize the reaction from the world to that, and he'll change his mind. From there we'll have some negotiations, and I think things will work out."

Dalia left the Director's office with renewed hope. She met the others in her office at nine o'clock; all except Uncle Moshe, who said he had to take care of some important business. They immediately headed for the cafeteria, and found a quiet spot in the corner of the room.

Dalia briefed them on the meeting with her boss, and Ari said, "It sounds like the Prime Minister isn't going to be very happy. Lisa and I were planning to go back to the dig, but now I think we'll wait a few days to see what happens."

Chapter 57

General Yidlan had briefed the Prime Minister on his unsuccessful attempt to demand absolute secrecy. He explained that Andre Braverman was a name given to him by Dalia Herbst, and she told him the documents inside the urns would require translation into Modern Hebrew. The Prime Minister thanked the General, and explained that his staff would now take over the task of finding a translator willing to sign the secrecy agreement.

The task was assigned to the Prime Minister's senior aide. He knew how to twist arms and make things happen. He called Professor Braverman first. The professor was cordial and listened to the aide's request. Braverman then asked, "Will I be able to talk to my colleagues and publish?"

The aide answered no and Braverman said, "Then why would I agree to sign the agreement? These artifacts need to be shared with other scholars. I'm afraid you'll have to get someone else to help you out."

"Can you recommend others who might be willing to help us?"

Braverman gave him a few names and wished the aide good luck. As soon as the aide hung up,

Braverman called his good friend Director Becker and briefed him on his just completed call.

It was late afternoon before the Prime Minister's aide had run through a short list of experts, all of whom refused to sign the agreement. He walked into the Prime Minister's office and gave him the bad news. The Prime Minster said, "It's a damned conspiracy. We'll screw each one of these guys. I'll make sure they'll never get another government grant again."

"Mr. Prime Minister, I think they fear the wrath of their colleagues more than your elimination of any grant money. If I was to guess, I'd say Director Becker at the Antiquities Authority has already talked to each of them, and these guys fear any actions he may take against them more than anything else."

"So what do you suggest?"

"Sir, I recommend you make peace with Director Becker. I'm sure you can both come to a reasonable accommodation."

The Prime Minister dismissed his aide and thought about the situation as he conducted some other pressing business. Late in the afternoon, his aide came into his office; Director Becker was on the phone.

The Prime Minister lifted up his phone. "Good afternoon Director Becker. How may I help you today?"

Becker said, "Let's forget about the pleasantries Mr. Prime Minister. Let me read you a press announcement I'm planning on releasing after this discussion, unless of course we can reach some agreement on what we're going to do about these precious artifacts."

Becker was silent for a few seconds and then continued. "The press release is dated today. *The An-*

tiquities Authority is happy to report a significant archeological find. In the last few days thirty-three ancient urns believed to be from the time of King Zedekiah around 425 BCE were discovered in the Timna Valley. The IDF has taken possession of these urns because of their importance.

The Prime Minister's Office has refused to allow unhampered access to the contents of these urns. Instead, the Prime Minister has insisted that anyone viewing the contents of the urns sign a pledge of secrecy. This demand is against all reason. Scholars throughout the world deserve to be able to analyze these artifacts without restrictions. The world deserves nothing less."

"Well Director Becker, that's quite a press release. What do you hope to accomplish with that message to the world?"

"Mr. Prime Minister, I hope I will not have to release the document. In exchange for not sending out this press release, a few conditions must be met. First, the military may continue to protect the urns and their contents. Second Doctor Dalia Herbst will be allowed to coordinate an examination of the contents of the urns with the experts she chooses to assign to the project. Third, we will work closely with your office to provide any translations of any written documents as soon as they are available, but the Antiquities Authority, as is stated in our charter, will control the release of any findings to the outside world. And finally, we will work with your office to announce the existence of the urns within the next few days."

The Prime Minister was caught between a rock and a hard place, but he didn't want to totally capitulate. He settled on a modest demand. Director Becker, I will agree with one condition; my office will release the announcement."

Becker smiled at the minor request. "Agreed, as long as my office approves the wording. Mr. Prime Minister, should my people continue to work with General Yidlan?"

"Yes Becker, please work with the general."

After cooling off from the conversation, the Prime Minster told his aide to come in. He reviewed the nature of the agreement and asked him to relay the information to General Yidlan. The aide left to call the general.

After talking to the Prime Minister, Becker contacted Dalia who was in her office. He described the deal. "Jacob, you're one hell of a good man. I'll contact Yidlan and begin making arrangements to examine the contents. I'll make sure you're there when we open the first urn."

"Thank you Dalia, I'd consider that a real honor."

Dalia called her friends and gave them the good news. They decided to meet for dinner to celebrate together.

Chapter 58

At first the Grand Mufti sat calmly listening to the news conference, and then he suddenly erupted into a raging fury over what he had just heard. His hopes for ever proving the legitimacy of his people's claims to Palestine and Jerusalem were being pushed into a deep abyss, never to be raised again. His entire life he had been struggling to keep the dream alive in his people; and now everything was lying in ruins, and all because of these ancient artifacts.

His duty to Allah and his people demanded that something be done. He could not allow these urns to be opened. If the scrolls that were certainly inside were ever analyzed by impartial experts, his life's work would have been for naught. He ordered his assistant to immediately summon Kassab to his office. While he waited for his head of security to arrive, he considered his alternatives; but terrorist methods were not his expertise. He concentrated on the big picture. He needed to destroy the urns and as a bonus kill the people who had created this unfortunate situation. These scrolls must never see the light of day.

Kassab arrived with an overriding sense of fear for his own life. He had failed in his mission to capture the urns, and in the process almost fifty of his best men were now either dead or being held prisoner in Egypt. Would the Grand Mufti decide to punish him for his failures? The leader of the Waqf had been stoic when Kassab had summarized the disaster at the bunker in the Sinai Desert. And then the final blow, the Israelis and American had somehow escaped from the cave.

The Grand Mufti, calm now and in full control of his emotions after his raging outburst, directed Kassab to sit down across from his desk. "Did you see the news conference?" he asked.

Kassab knew exactly what news conference the Grand Mufti was talking about. "Yes sir, it's going to be a disaster for our cause."

"No Hakeem, I think not. I just had a vision, no doubt sent to me by Allah himself. On the day of the ceremonial opening, the urns, the scrolls inside the urns, and all of the people in attendance at the ceremony will be destroyed."

The Grand Mufti looked at his head of security with a smile on his face and waited for a response. Kassab considered the foolishness of the Grand Mufti's vision, but was smart enough not to question his statement. Instead he asked, "Sir, did Allah share with you how this might be accomplished?"

"Yes Hakeem, he did. He said you would decide how this would happen. He said it was your last opportunity to demonstrate your worthiness to continue to lead our cause. So let me make this very clear; if you don't succeed in this assignment it will be the last mission you ever lead."

Kassab left his leader's office shaking; sweat was dripping from his face. He had been given a short reprieve, but it would be very short indeed if he could not find a way to destroy the urns.

Back in his office, he sat down at his desk and considered the problem. To destroy those urns during the opening ceremony he needed to have access to the IDF's main military base in Haifa. He considered flying a plane into the building where the ceremony was being held, but he had no way of getting any aircraft or finding a pilot willing to be martyred for the cause.

He did, however, have a lone operator who worked at the military complex in the cleaning crew. The man would probably have clearance to work in the building where the ceremony would be held. How could he use this man to achieve the Grand Mufti's goal?

Kassab did his best thinking in the small park across the street from his office. He left the building, and a few minutes later he was sitting on his favorite bench alongside a soccer field. He was deep in thought, focusing on the development of a plan to destroy the ancient urns and horrible scrolls contained inside.

Having an operative inside the military complex was one thing, but bringing in explosives was a far different matter; and then there was the problem of placing the explosives close enough to the urns. One thing was clear; he needed to talk to the man who worked inside the military base. There was very little time to set up the meeting through the usual intermediaries. He took out his cellphone and found the man's phone number recorded in secret code. "Hello, is this Abdulla?"

The person answering the phone answered no. Kassab apologized and stated the number he was trying to reach. The man answered, "You missed it by one digit. My number ends in a three not a four. Better luck next time."

Better luck next time was a secret code. Kassab replied with, "My eyesight isn't very good."

With the brief exchange, a meeting had been set up for that night at an out of the way café in the Arab Quarter of old Jerusalem.

Chapter 59

Kassab's conversation was picked up by the IDF's National Security Agency, and the information was immediately forwarded to General Yidlan. Yidlan read the transcript of the conversation and considered the message. Kassab had never tried to call the correct phone number. This was obviously a code of some sort, but what was most troubling was the location of the person speaking to Kassab. The location wasn't precise, but it was clearly someplace in the administrative section of the Haifa Military Base.

He immediately called in his aide and asked to speak with his counterpart in Mossad. A minute later, Simon Levy was on the phone. "Hello Simon, listen my friend, I need your help. As you know, our good friend Kassab is the head of Waqf security. We think he just set up a meeting with one of his operatives working out of our Haifa Military Base. The operative was using a pre-paid cellphone, so we don't know who it is. We need your people to follow Kassab when he leaves the office today and listen into the meeting. I'm thinking this has something to do with those ancient urns. We know the Waqf wants to destroy them all before the opening ceremony. Can you set something up quickly?"

Levy answered, "So Kassab is at it again. I'll have him followed. We'll have something set up in the next hour. Is he at Waqf headquarters now?"

"He made the call an hour ago from the park across the street from his office. Thanks for your help. Let me know what you can find out."

Levy immediately called in his head of operations and directed him to set up a surveillance team to eavesdrop on the possible meeting.

An hour later the first member of the Mossad team arrived on the scene, and he positioned himself on a side street with a clear view of the main entrance to Waqf headquarters. Within the next hour three more men and two women arrived at the park. The leader of the team, Ruvain Lieb, sat next to one of the female agents posing as his wife on a park bench facing the front of Waqf headquarters. Lieb had been briefed by Simon Levy. That in itself was unusual. The need for a quick response meant all of the needed assets were not yet in place. That would take at least another two hours.

Lieb thought about the problem as he pretended to read his newspaper. His female partner appeared busy knitting a sweater, but she was really watching for any unusual activity. Lieb knew if the Waqf operative was at the military base in Haifa, he was probably a non-military employee. That meant the meeting, if that's what the code name implied, probably wouldn't take place until after the man's working hours. Hopefully, Kassab himself would be at the meeting, otherwise another person probably would have made the call.

Lieb knew these things were always hit or miss and mostly miss. The code might have nothing to do with a meeting. Maybe it was an authorization code to initiate the operation, and if that was the case, then they were already too late. So now it was the waiting game. One of his men was stationed behind the building in case Kassab decided to leave by the backdoor.

Chapter 60

General Yidlan decided to beef-up security of the urns. He immediately contacted the base commander and briefed him on the problem. Within the hour, two dozen MPs had arrived at the building where the urns were being stored and positioned themselves in highly visible areas. The base's bomb squad arrived a few minutes later and began a search of the building.

Lieutenant Goldman introduced himself to Dalia Herbst who was sitting at a desk near the urns meeting with some people. "I'm sorry to interrupt but I just received a call from the base commander to increase security at this building."

Dalia asked, "Why Lieutenant?"

"I don't know Doctor Herbst. I was only told to inform you that we're tightening security. I'm going to have pictures taken of everyone working with the urns, and other people attempting to gain access will not be permitted inside the building without your permission."

Lieutenant Goldman left the building as the bomb squad began their search, and Dalia immediately called General Yidlan. "Good afternoon General. A Lieutenant Goldman just informed me that security is being tightened around our building. Is there a reason for this?"

"Doctor Herbst, we just intercepted a call from the head of Waqf security to someone on this base. We think the Waqf may still be trying to eliminate the urns, and I'm not taking any chances."

Dalia replied, "I appreciate your concerns. Please let me know if there's anything I can do to help."

After the call, General Yidlan decided to take some additional steps. He contacted Colonel Weiss and asked his team to oversee security of the urns. Yidlan then called the base commander who objected to Weiss's team being in charge. Yidlan listened to the complaint and then pulled rank; Colonel Weiss would be in charge.

Chapter 61

Kassab left his office a little after four o'clock and decided to walk to the meeting place. Parking in the area would be a problem. He was a bit early, and he needed the exercise. The Old City was alive with thousands of vendors interrupting tourists walking along the narrow street. Kassab looked in disgust at the many infidels ruining his city. Once the Waqf took over Jerusalem, he would take steps to eliminate the infidels from this sacred area.

Lieb's agents were following Kassab as he walked along the street. They were experts in surveillance. Every few minutes they changed positions and even changed their outer clothing to avoid detection. It wouldn't have mattered much because Kassab was lost in his own thoughts and was totally unaware of their presence.

The outdoor café was one of those out of the way places frequented only by the local Arab community. Kassab found an empty table under an olive tree and ordered a coffee. Two of Lieb's agents sporting fashionable beards in the local Arab style sat down at a nearby table and ordered tea. They weren't close enough to overhear any conversations, and their sophisticated eavesdropping equipment was in their mini-van parked two blocks away; not close enough to monitor anything at the café.

A little before five o'clock a middle-aged man arrived and greeted Kassab. The man bowed slightly as they shook hands. Kassab motioned for the man to sit down at his table, and then he called a waiter over to take the man's order. One of the agents took several pictures of the man with a smartphone, but unfortunately the man was sitting with his back to the agents. One of the agents walked to the bathroom and tried to get a better picture on his way back to the table, but the best he could manage was a shot of the left side of the man's face.

At first Kassab did most of the talking, and the mysterious man sat across from Kassab with a serious look on his face. Finally the man spoke, and from then on the conversation moved back and forth across the table.

Suddenly, Kassab grinned. It was as if he had finally gotten the information he needed from the man. A few minutes later, the mysterious man stood up from the table and shook Kassab's hand.

One of the agents got up from the table and followed the unknown man while the other stayed at the café to watch Kassab. As soon as the man began walking on the street, he took out his cellphone, and after a short conversation, he continued walking along the narrow streets of the Old City. Lieb and his team knew the man had probably come over from Haifa. That meant he either arrived by car or had taken a train or bus. If he had arrived by car, Lieb's plan was to place a transponder on the man's car before he drove away. That might be tricky, but his team knew exactly how to do it without being discovered. Following the man on a bus or train presented fewer problems.

Everything was going according to plan until a car suddenly pulled up next to the man they were following. He quickly got in, and the car accelerated out into traffic before Lieb's team could plant the transponder. The car's license plate was covered in dirt, probably intentionally, and could not be read.

Lieb called in the mini-van, but it was too late; the car was long gone. All the team had for their day's work were a few incomplete pictures of the unknown person. The team immediately sent the pictures to Simon Levy and then headed back to the office.

Chapter 62

General Yidlan studied the picture of the side of the man's face who had met with Kassab and the dark-blue four door sedan entering traffic. Yidlan didn't recognize the pictures of the man, but with over one-thousand non-military personnel working at the base, that was to be expected. He called in his assistant and explained the situation. "Lieutenant Davis, I want you to go to Human Resources and personally check to see if this man works at the base; I want an answer in a few hours. Call me at home."

Lieutenant Davis started to leave Yidlan's office until the general stopped him. "Oh, also check with base security and see if any employees have an old car like this. Find an expert who can tell us the make and model."

Yidlan considered what was happening. This wasn't a bunch of amateur terrorists. These were well-trained professionals. The question in his mind was what did the Waqf want to accomplish? Of course it was obvious; they wanted the scrolls to disappear. They didn't want the scrolls to ever be seen by historians. To accomplish that goal, the Waqf had two options. They could try to steal the urns before they were opened, or they could destroy the building where the urns were being kept.

Stealing the urn would require a significant force, and the Waqf would have to breach several layers of security. That, the general knew, was not about to happen. The second option seemed the most likely. Yidlan thought about possible ways to effectively blow up the urns, and he considered the same possible scenarios as Kassab. He too abandoned the option of flying an airplane into the building; not because he didn't think the Waqf could find an airplane or a suicide bomber to fly it, but because the Waqf had contacted an operative on the base, and if they were using an airplane, they wouldn't need to risk making that contact. Any visitor on the base could easily determine the building where the urns were being held. It would obviously be the building with all the MPs providing protection.

No, the operative being contacted meant this was going to be an inside job. And that meant the Waqf would be trying to bring explosives onto the military base. If they could do that, then they could drive a truck-full into the building; or worse yet, sneak the explosives into the building itself.

By the time the general arrived home for dinner, he knew he needed to take a few more precautions. He called Colonel Weiss. "Morty, I've been thinking about how the Waqf might destroy the urns, and we need to guard against a suicide bomber driving a truck-full of explosives into the building. I want you to place a series of concrete obstacles all around the perimeter of the building to prevent any penetration by a truck"

Weiss accepted his new orders and wished the general a pleasant evening.

A little before nine o'clock, General Yidlan received a call from Lieutenant Davis. There were no matches to be found in Human Resources' data base. The picture was just too poor to allow for any positive identification. In addition, the 1969 Ford Fairlane used by the Waqf people was not registered on the base's approved car list.

The general went to bed expecting a sleepless night, and his expectations were fulfilled. He spent the entire night pondering the problem.

Chapter 63

Abu Muhammad thought Kassab's idea was sheer lunacy. How would he ever be able to smuggle explosives onto the base without being caught; and even if he was successful in doing that, planting these explosives in the actual auditorium where the urns would be opened was surely impossible. Abu considered himself nothing more than a janitor trying to make a few extra shekels as a spy for the Waqf.

The call from Kassab had shocked him. How had he gotten himself into this mess? Abu's good friend Yassar had recruited him eight years ago, and now he turned to him for help. Not being familiar with Jerusalem, he had asked Yassar to drive him to the meeting place. Abu had listened to his handler's boss respectfully, but with growing apprehension. Everyone working at the base knew about the important archeological find, and Abu even understood why the Waqf wanted to destroy the urns before they were opened. It was just that he knew this was a suicide mission, and somehow he would die trying to fulfill the Grand Mufti's demand.

Abu arrived at work and began his rounds. Kassab had made it very clear to Abu; he needed to come up with a plan by the end of the day. He tackled the easiest problem first. How would he smuggle explosives onto the base?

The answer came to him as he rolled his supply cart down the street. A delivery truck was unloading housekeeping supplies at the janitorial services administrative building. The solution to his problem was obvious because it was so simple. Kassab's people would have to help out, but that was his problem. If the explosives could be hidden inside the chemical supplies, he had access to the warehouse, and he could get to them without a problem. Luckily, he was responsible for cleaning the auditorium where the ceremony was scheduled to be held.

After completing his morning housekeeping rounds and eating lunch in the employee cafeteria, he entered the auditorium by the backdoor and began cleaning the bathrooms on the first floor. Carpenters were busy expanding the stage for the many dignitaries who would be at the ceremony. A large clear-plastic enclosure was also being built to hold the many urns that had been discovered, and technicians were busy attaching a small air-conditioning system onto the ceiling of the plastic enclosure.

After cleaning the toilets, he pushed his large supply cart into the auditorium and down toward the stage. He spent over thirty minutes picking up discarded building supplies and emptying garbage cans. Nobody paid much attention except for a few workers who thanked him for cleaning up the area.

Abu knew the auditorium was used for many theatrical productions, and there were several trap doors and lifts leading to the stage from the basement of the building. He thought about placing the explosives under the stage, but that location seemed too obvious. There were security guards stationed all around the building where the urns were being kept, and a heightened level of security would certainly be present once the urns were moved to the auditorium for the ceremony. Abu had seen enough movies to know the guards would probably be using specially trained dogs to sniff for explosives. The basement was just too obvious a place to hide the material.

The place to hide the explosives came to him in an inspirational moment. He happened to look up at the ceiling above the stage and his eyes moved from the small air-conditioning system being assembled on top of the enclosure to the air duct just above it. The duct was part of the auditorium's air-conditioning system, and it was located just above the enclosure that would house the urns during the ceremony. He doubted anyone would be looking up in the air ducts for explosives, and there were plenty of ladders around he could use to reach the vent. With the right tools he would be able to gain access to the air duct and plant the explosive charge.

Up until now, he had been an inconsequential spy, a nobody making a meager wage from the Waqf for the reporting of monthly activity at the military base. Now he was being asked to be like James Bond, but without the training. He stared again at the vent in the duct and began to think that he just might be able to place the explosives up there without being caught.

There was something distasteful about this whole thing. Over the years he had grown to like many of his Jewish co-workers. These people weren't evil as the imam at the mosque where he prayed had said. They were people just like himself, struggling to pay monthly bills and support their families; and if he was successful, this explosion might very well kill some of these people who he knew and liked.

Yes, the Jews had taken the land of his ancestors away from him, and many Palestinians became refugees after the 1947 war; but his family had decided to stay, and he was an accepted member of Israeli society. So the question circulating through his mind was did he really want to do this? Abu struggled with an answer to that question.

Chapter 64

After picking at his evening meal, Abu wrote a note to Kassab. He described his findings and explained how the explosives could be smuggled onto the base as part of the daily shipment of cleaning supplies from Sabre Supplies. He outlined his plan to place the explosives in the air-conditioning system above the ancient urns.

He rolled up the note and placed it in a small circular metal cigar cylinder, and then placed the cigar tin behind a loose stone next to the garbage can behind his apartment. He used some chalk to place a mark next to his building. His handler Yassar looked for the white mark each night, and if present, he retrieved the note from the dead drop and delivered it to Waqf headquarters. Hopefully Kassab would be reading Abu's message early the next morning.

Killing innocent people bothered Abu, but he was a Muslim, and Islam was at war with the Jewish state. The imam at his mosque had been teaching this for years. It was a Jihad, and as a good Muslim, he had a sacred duty to carry out the wish of Allah.

Abu spent a restless night thinking about the best way to place the explosive charge in the air-conditioning duct. It would have to be at night after the workers had left for the day. Abu worked on the day shift, and that created a problem. Tomorrow morning he would talk to his supervisor and ask to be placed on the nightshift for a week. He would say his relatives were visiting, and he wanted to spend the days showing them around the country. He knew many nightshift workers who would love the opportunity to work the dayshift for a week. He was certain his boss would allow him to make the change.

Chapter 65

Hakeem Kassab received the message from his operative's handler a little after his morning coffee break. Yassar sat outside Kassab's office waiting to see if he would be bringing Abu new instructions.

Kassab considered Abu's proposed plan. The Waqf had access to plenty of C-4 explosive, but to be certain the urns were destroyed, he would probably need at least twenty kilos. How to hide twenty kilos of plastic explosives in a shipment of cleaning supplies? Kassab had no idea what type of supplies were delivered each day. He needed that information before he could determine how best to smuggle the explosives onto the base, and then he needed to figure out how to get those twenty kilos of explosives onto the delivery truck.

He brought Yassar back into his office and ordered him to immediately get back to Abu. Abu's plan was approved, but they needed Abu to take pictures of the types of supplies delivered each day by the supply company.

After Yassar left his office, Kassab called in Mansour Ali, one of his senior men and outlined Abu's plan. He asked the man to visit Sabre Supply Company and figure out how to place explosives onto the truck leaving for the military base.

Chapter 66

Mansour Ali sat in his car watching trucks enter and leave Sabre Supply Company. He had arrived a little after lunch and was getting a sense of how the company operated.

Mansour was certain the delivery truck for the military base would have left early in the morning on its daily run. The afternoons seemed to focus on unloading an endless number of trucks from various manufacturers of cleaning supplies. Names of well-known companies were emblazoned on the sides of these massive delivery trucks.

Toward the end of the day, Sabre's delivery trucks began returning from their daily runs, and the returning empty trucks were being staged in the company's expansive parking lot.

About four o'clock things began to change. Sabre's trucks began moving from the parking lot to the company's eight loading docks, and Mansour could see a surge in activity as trucks were loaded with a variety of supplies for the next day's deliveries. After the trucks were loaded, a clipboard containing what looked like the trucks manifest was placed on the back of each truck with magnetic clips.

The loading process continued until after eight o'clock. By then over sixty trucks had been loaded and were sitting in the parking lot ready to make tomorrow's deliveries. Security at the company was minimal. A lone guard sat in a guardhouse at the entrance to the parking lot, and a second guard seemed to be making periodic rounds inside the office area and warehouse. Security cameras seemed non-existent.

Mansour left for some dinner and returned to Sabre a little after midnight. He was dressed in black and parked his car on a nearby side street. He walked across an open field to the back of the parking lot where he was out of sight of the front entrance and guardhouse. In less than a minute, he had climbed over the fence and was watching for any security guards.

After waiting a few minutes, he walked up to the nearest delivery truck and looked at the manifest with a small penlight. The bill of lading was printed on the company's letterhead. Mansour took a picture of the document. The name and address of the company to be receiving the delivery was just below the company's logo. The back of the truck wasn't locked. Mansour opened the back of the truck and climbed inside. Everything seemed to be loaded on pallets. Mansour inspected a few more trucks and they were all duplicates of the first.

Mansour knew the most difficult part in loading the explosives would be finding the right truck. He climbed back over the fence in the back of the parking lot and was finished for the night.

Chapter 67

Abu checked the dead drop just before he went to sleep, and found the message from Yassar. Kassab had agreed to his plan and now wanted pictures taken. Easy enough Abu thought. The Sabre delivery truck usually arrived a little before noon. He could take an early lunch break and take some pictures with his smartphone as they unloaded the supplies.

The next morning, Abu started out in his boss's office. His supervisor quickly agreed to move Abu onto the nightshift for one week, and after Abu's boss called his counterpart on the nightshift, the man was delighted to make the change beginning tomorrow.

Abu went about his daily work and took an early lunch. He sat down at a picnic table just outside the loading dock and waited for the Sabre truck to make an appearance.

The truck pulled up to the loading dock a little after twelve o'clock, and as they unloaded the truck, Abu took multiple pictures of each of the pallets. He immediately forwarded the pictures to Yassar who would send them to Kassab.

Two hours later dozens of pictures of the pallets being unloaded from the truck were sitting on Kassab's desk. Hakeem studied the pictures and smiled when he saw the picture of the pallet filled with cartons of soap. Kassab recognized the name of the supplier and the master carton was probably filled with bars of soap packaged in individual boxes, and from the size of the master carton, Kassab guessed there were about forty-eight bars of soap in each master carton. Two master cartons should be enough to hold all of the C-4 explosives.

Kassab called in his assistant and told him to purchase several master cartons of the soap. The assistant recognized the popular brand and knew a dozen stores in the area would carry large quantities of the popular soap.

Chapter 68

That night after work a message was waiting in Abu's dead drop. It told him to deplete the inventory of the bars of soap and make sure the person in charge placed an order for more soap to be delivered the day after tomorrow. The explosives and detonation system along with instructions would be delivered to the military base inside the Sabre truck. The two master cartons containing the explosives would be marked with a blue "X" on the top of each carton.

Abu's first nightshift began at midnight. The military base's administrative area was deserted. Abu immediately looked inside the cleaning supply area of the warehouse. Twenty cartons of soap were sitting on a pallet in the usual location. Abu placed four cartons in his cart and left the warehouse. He placed the four cartons in a variety of storage closets inside the large administrative building.

Throughout his late-night shift, he made periodic trips to the warehouse, and by the time his shift had ended at eight o'clock, all of the cartons of soap had been removed from the warehouse.

Abu left a note on the desk of the person responsible for ordering supplies, and explained there was no more soap in the warehouse, and he needed more as soon as possible. He left for home and some much-needed rest knowing that the lady ordering supplies, who he knew very well, would certainly order the soap immediately.

The person in charge of ordering supplies arrived at work at nine o'clock and immediately saw Abu's note. She couldn't understand the need for soap. A shipment had just arrived yesterday. She checked her records, and sure enough, a full shipment was delivered yesterday and placed in Bin 9W in the warehouse. She walked next-door to the warehouse and searched for the shipment. Abu was right; the pallet in Bin 9W was empty. Thinking the shipment might have been misplaced by the warehouse staff, she searched every bin for the missing soap but without success. She sat down at her desk and immediately called Sabre Supply. The order entry clerk receiving the call confirmed the soap would be delivered in the next day's shipment.

Chapter 69

General Yidlan arrived at work in a foul mood. He needed to identify the Waqf's spy as soon as possible. He had been mulling over an idea at breakfast and called a friend of his at Mossad's Technical Services Group. "Jacov, it's Chaim Yidlan. We've got a problem here that you may be able to help us solve. We have a voice recording of a spy who works on our base, but we don't have a picture of him. If I remember right, you have a special voice recognition software program developed by the CIA. If we get you the voice recording of possible suspects, can you get a match with our first recording?"

"Absolutely Chaimy, send over the first recording, and I'll load it into our system. How many possible suspects are you looking at?"

"Hundreds Jacov; probably all the non-military males working at the base."

Jacov whistled at the magnitude of the task but just told his friend to send them over.

General Yidlan called in his entire staff and explained the urgency of the situation. He gave them their orders, and the entire staff left for the Human Resources Department. Yidlan immediately called the head of Human Resources and explained his problem.

Three hours later, Abu was abruptly awakened by the sound of the phone ringing. It was someone at the military base calling to verify his personal benefits information. She explained a computer malfunction had compromised some of the data. After verifying his address and employee number, he hung up the phone and immediately fell back to sleep.

Chapter 70

Waqf technical people had carefully opened the soap master cartons. It took them almost three hours to replace the individual bars of soap with the C4 explosive. They wired a cellphone into a control system in each master carton, and when they were finished, the C4 explosive could be set off by calling either cellphone. Before closing the master cartons, they wrote instructions for detonating the explosives and marked the top of the cartons with a blue "X".

Late in the day Mansur collected the two master cartons, and carefully placed them in his car's trunk. He collected some additional gear from the supply room and left for Sabre Supply Company. By six o'clock he was watching supplies being loaded on trucks for the next-day's delivery. The process was exactly the same as the day before.

He left to grab a leisurely dinner at a nearby shopping mall. He returned four hours later and parked on a street behind the Sabre parking lot. The loading of the trucks had been completed, and only the lone guard stationed at the entrance to the parking lot was providing security.

It took two trips for Mansur to carry the explosives to the back fence. He was straddling the fence in less than a minute. The two cartons of explosives were attached to ropes. He carefully lifted them to the top of the fence and then lowered them to the other side.

Mansur left the explosives by the fence and began searching for the truck scheduled to deliver supplies to the military base the next day. He found it near the back corner of the parking lot, and luckily it was out of sight of the guard. The manifest on the back of the truck indicated a dozen cartons of soap were on the truck. He opened the truck's rear door and quickly found the boxes of soap amongst the many pallets in the truck. He removed two cartons from the truck and carried both to the back fence where the explosives were located.

It took Mansur almost thirty minutes to substitute the cartons of explosives for the real soap. He smiled to himself as he drove away in his car. It had been a relatively simple mission, and now it was up to whoever was on the military base to plant the explosives.

Chapter 71

The Sabre shipment arrived just before noon, and a little after two o'clock, the pallet of soap was placed in Bin 9W. Abu arrived on the late shift and immediately checked the warehouse to see if the explosives had arrived. He wheeled his cart along the rows of storage bins and stopped at Bin 9W. Near the bottom of the pallet, two master cartons with blue "Xs" on the tops of the cartons were clearly visible.

His heart raced as he stared at the deadly packages. He had been hoping the explosives had not arrived, or better yet that the boxes of explosives had been discovered by the security guards. No such luck, however, and now the ball was in his court once again, and he dreaded the next step, because he knew he would probably get caught and then spend the rest of his life in prison.

He carefully placed both cartons in his cart and moved to other bins. He filled his cart with all the supplies he would need for his night's duties. He waved to another nightshift worker who was at the other end of the warehouse loading her supply cart and left the building.

He had been planning his route for the last day. He stopped first in a building that was always deserted after the first shift, and wheeled his cart into the bathroom on the third floor. He placed an *out of order* sign on the bathroom door and opened one of the master cartons. His face broke out in a sweat as he looked down at the C4 explosives disguised as bars of soap. A small electronic circuit board was taped to the top layer of soap, and a cellphone was wired to the circuit board and taped to another soap box.

The second master carton was a duplicate of the first with the addition of a sheet of paper with the necessary instructions for activating the explosive charges. Abu quickly closed the master cartons and read the instructions. After placing the explosives, he only needed to turn on the cellphones to activate the detonation system. The batteries on the circuit board would power the system for a maximum of three days.

The ceremony for opening the urns was scheduled for tomorrow afternoon, so tonight would be his only chance to place the explosives and arm the device. He was shaking as he read the instructions a second and then a third time. He placed the sheet of paper in his pocket and washed his sweating face in the bathroom sink.

He was scheduled to take a long dinner break at two o'clock. That would be the time to place the explosives. He went about his business, trying to remain calm, but it was impossible. He passed one of the other nightshift workers as he wheeled his cart between buildings. The person asked if he was okay, and Abu explained he was coming down with the flu. The man immediately left, not wanting to get infected.

A little after one o'clock, Abu wheeled his cart into the auditorium building. He looked at the stage. It was deserted. He then quickly wheeled his cart through the entire building looking for any people who might be inside the building. It was empty. He decided to change his plans and immediately place the explosives. Some guard might be checking the building later on. Now was his chance.

Back in the auditorium, he wheeled his cart onto the stage. Everything looked ready for the ceremony, but the ladders and boxes of tools were still on the stage. Everything was probably going to be cleaned up as soon as the workers arrived for work in the morning.

He struggled moving a ladder from the back of the stage to the plastic enclosed room where the urns would be held. He leaned the ladder against the newly constructed miniature room's wall and carefully carried each master carton of explosives up the ladder, placing both directly under one of the air ducts in the ceiling.

Abu had brought a variety of screwdrivers with him, and luckily the duct's vent was secured with common Phillips screws. It took him less than a minute to remove the vent and another two minutes to carefully activate each cellphone and slide the cartons of C4 explosives into the duct. He secured the vent and returned the ladder to its previous location.

Abu looked at his watch. The whole thing had taken less than ten minutes. He quickly cleaned all of the bathrooms in the building and wheeled his cart onto the next building on his rounds. After arriving in the first bathroom at the next building, he sat down inside a stall and began to cry. The tears weren't about guilt; they were about the relief at having succeeded in placing the explosives without being caught. His whole body shook as he sat on a toilet.

It took him over ten minutes to regain his composure. He finished his shift without taking any dinner break, thinking he wouldn't be able to keep any food down; and he didn't want to have to explain his stressed out looks to any of his fellow workers. He punched out at the time clock a little after eight o'clock and then drove home. He was still shaking as he arrived at his apartment. He left a note in the dead drop explaining what he had accomplished and then sat at his kitchen table sipping some hot tea. He hoped the drink would settle his stomach.

Chapter 72

Dalia arrived in the auditorium just as the workers were completing the final cleanup of the stage. She talked to the foreman, and after confirming the temperature and humidity of the viewing room were just right, she called Colonel Weiss on his cellphone and gave him permission to transfer the urns to the auditorium.

Weiss had spent several days planning the logistics and security for the move. While the urns were being loaded onto two armored bank trucks, four explosive sniffing dogs with their handlers arrived at the auditorium and began their search for explosives in the building.

It took almost an hour before the dogs arrived on the main floor of the auditorium. Two dogs seemed disturbed as they searched the stage. Their handlers allowed the dogs to spend extra time on the stage, but they finally moved onto the second floor and the remainder of the building.

After they gave the okay to Colonel Weiss, he began moving the urns. The convoy was surrounded by MPs for the short trip to the building where the ceremony would be held. The MPs cordoned off the streets surrounding the building and increased their patrols.

Dalia and her staff managed the transfer of the urns into the specially constructed room. She looked at the stage from out in the auditorium and was pleased with the visual feel for the display of the artifacts. The urns were center stage which was exactly what their status deserved.

The dignitaries would be arriving in just over five hours, and she busied herself by checking out the auditorium's sound system.

Chapter 73

General Yidlan received a call from Jacov just before twelve o'clock. "Chaimy, I've got some good news. We've identified the voice signature with just over a ninety-seven percent probability. The guy's name is Abu Muhammad."

Yidlan asked, "Are there any others with a close match?"

"None Chaimy; I'm certain he's your man."

The head of Human Resources answered Yidlan's call. "General, Abu Muhammad is a janitor working on first shift. He should be on the base right now."

"Call his boss; I'll hold on until you find out where he is."

Yidlan was put on hold, and a minute later he found out that Abu Muhammad was temporarily on late shift and was not on the base. Yidlan thanked the head of Human Resources and called in his senior staff. "Lieutenant Davis, call security and confirm that Abu Muhammad is not on the base. Then send Colonel Weiss and his team out to his apartment. It's in Haifa, 1202 Stephen Wise Street. Hopefully he's sleeping, and we'll be able to pick him up. He's our spy, and I want him caught in the next hour. Make it happen."

Lieutenant Davis left to carry out Yidlan's orders.

Yidlan sat back at his desk and suddenly decided to pay a visit to the auditorium. He wanted to personally check out the security at the building. In a few hours the urns would be opened, and then all this security bullshit would become a thing of the past. Once the cat was out of the bag, the Waqf would have lost its ability to destroy the content of the urns. Pictures of the scrolls, or whatever was inside those urns, would be spread quickly throughout the world via the internet.

Yidlan found Dalia Herbst in the auditorium making final arrangements for the upcoming event. After observing the urns that had caused him such grief in the last few weeks, he approached her as she finished her discussions. "Doctor Herbst, so this is your big moment. You and your people have done a wonderful job preparing for the big event."

Dalia looked at the general with some suspicion. He had been the evil messenger from the Israeli head of state, but he had also been granting her and her people the freedom to do as they wished; and even though his security measures had been somewhat extreme, he was certainly committed to protecting the ancient artifacts. "General Yidlan, how nice to see you; I hope you'll be coming to the ceremony this afternoon?"

"I wouldn't dream of missing the event. I wonder if I might have a word with you in private?"

The general led Dalia out into the street and they found a convenient bench normally used by people waiting to catch a local bus. He spent time bringing her up to speed on the search for the spy. Dalia paid close attention, and her stomach knotted up at the thought of a possible attack on the urns.

"So you think they're planning on attacking today?"

"That's my worry. This guy Abu Muhammad was a janitor. He cleaned the auditorium every day. Then he suddenly requests to move onto night shift for a week. He claims it's because his relatives are in town, and he wants to show them the city. I think that story's bullshit. What he wanted was access to this building in the middle of the night when nobody was around."

"You think he planted an explosive device?"

"Yes that, or something else. Colonel Weiss is on his way to apprehend the man right now. If we're lucky, he'll be there, and we'll make him talk."

Dalia didn't want to think about what *make him talk* meant. Instead she asked, "So what do you want us to do?

"I'm going to order the bomb squad to conduct another search of the building, but as a safety precaution, I want you to prepare to remove the urns quickly. If we can't get this spy to talk, or if the bomb squad can't find a bomb, then I'm going to ask you to postpone the ceremony."

Dalia thought about the request. Postponing the meeting was the conservative call, the right call, but today was going to be the highlight of her career; and although she wouldn't admit it to herself, she desperately wanted to bask in the limelight afforded by the ceremony. "General, that's the right call. We must do everything we can to protect the urns. I'll have the armored trucks wait at the loading dock in case we need them."

Chapter 74

Colonel Weiss knocked on Abu Muhammad's door. With no reply, he knocked a second time, but with greater urgency. "Open up! It's the IDF!"

Still no answer. Weiss was a believer in a citizen's rights. He was certain he would be violating this spy's rights if he broke down the door and entered the man's apartment; but what the hell, people would probably die if a bomb went off; he didn't have to think twice. Weiss motioned to Sammy who charged into the door with his shoulder. The door's lock burst into pieces and the door flew open. Four of Weiss's men hurried through the front door and found an empty apartment.

The Colonel sent his men throughout the apartment building looking for anyone who might know the whereabouts of Abu Muhammad. A half hour later they had interviewed all of the residents and nobody knew anything, or at least they weren't admitting to knowing anything.

He finally called his superior officer. "General Yidlan, Weiss here; he's not at his apartment, and none of the other residents know anything."

"Okay Morty, come on back to the base and help search the building for any explosives, but leave a couple of your people there in case he shows up."

Chapter 75

The bomb squad arrived in the auditorium with over two-dozen men and two explosives sniffing dogs. The general talked to their senior officer and explained the situation. "Lieutenant, I want your men to search everywhere. Don't rely on the dogs, because there might by some sophisticated liquid explosives they won't be able to detect; and when I say everywhere, I mean everywhere: on the roof, in the basement, in every closet, down each toilet bowl in every bathroom. If there's any opening in a wall, floor or ceiling, I want it checked. Do I make myself clear?"

"Yes sir, you do indeed. You can count on my team sir. If there's a bomb in this place, we'll find it."

"That's very commendable Lieutenant Joseph, because if you can't find it and it goes off, you and your men along with the rest of us are going to be dead."

The men and dogs of the bomb squad hurried off, and the general sat down in the first row of seats in the auditorium. To others in the room he appeared to be relaxing, but actually he was doing no such thing. Chaim Yidlan was trying to think like the man who planted the device. The hiding place must have been chosen with care. Certainly the man must have known the place would be searched, and dogs would be helping locate the device.

What was the goal of the explosion? Obviously to destroy the urns. The explosion must destroy the urns, and that meant the device must be hidden near the urns. Also, to be certain to destroy the contents of the urns beyond anything salvageable, they were going to have to use a significant amount of explosives. The Waqf probably didn't have access to the most sophisticated chemical explosives which meant at least a cubic meter of material would be needed. You just don't hide that much material easily. He suddenly had an idea. "Lieutenant Joseph," he screamed, "Over here on the double."

One of Joseph's men relayed the order, and a minute later the out of breath lieutenant ran up to the general. "Lieutenant, if you were the person hiding the device and you wanted the contents of the urns destroyed with no hope of ever finding them again, how would you do it?"

Joseph thought for a moment. "Sir, I'd use about twenty kilos of high explosives and place it either directly below or above the room where the urns were being kept."

"My thoughts exactly Lieutenant. So with that concept in mind, please focus your resources in the basement just below the stage and on the second floor just above the stage. If anything looks suspicious, then take it out of the building. Remember, they have theatrical productions here, so there may be many props in the basement. Maybe the bomb is inside one of those props."

Lieutenant Joseph left to redirect his men, and the general sat back in his chair going over possible locations. Someone had to think while the bomb squad ran around frantically looking for the device.

Dalia Herbst was still directing her staff. She wanted to make sure the spotlights on top of the clear-plastic room were aligned perfectly. She noticed two were not shinning on the urns. She asked one of the workers to get a ladder and adjust the lights.

The general watched as the worker brought a ladder from behind the curtain at the back of the stage and leaned it up against the clear-plastic wall. He began carefully climbing to the top of the enclosure and crawled carefully along the top, and with Dalia guiding him, he adjusted the two spotlights.

General Yidlan, who was observing the activity, suddenly had an idea. "Lieutenant Joseph," he screamed, "Over here on the double."

An out of breath Lieutenant Joseph arrived two minutes later. The general pointed to the air-conditioning duct in the ceiling just above the glass enclosure. "Lieutenant, if your twenty kilos of explosive were placed inside that air-conditioning duct just above the enclosure, would that result in the total destruction of the urns."

The lieutenant smiled, "Yes sir, it would make one hell of an explosion. Not only would the urns be destroyed, but the building would undoubtedly collapse down on any remains and finish the job."

"So why don't you have one of your men get his ass up there and check that vent out, and please be careful. There might be a tripwire attached to the vent to trigger the device if the vent is opened."

Joseph got on his cellphone and began giving orders. Five minutes later one of his men arrived with a bag of tools and a device that looked like the endoscope Yidlan's doctor had used during his last colonoscopy. Joseph climbed the ladder and placed the tip of the video probe inside the vent. "General, you're right sir. I see two cartons up here about one meter away from the vent. There are no apparent triggering devices attached to the vent. I'm going to open the vent."

"Stop right there Lieutenant Joseph. Go no further until we remove all of the urns and evacuate the building. I know you and your men know what needs to be done, but just in case you fuck up, I want the fewest people injured as possible."

Joseph and his lead man stayed on the stage. Everyone else quickly left the building. Most left by the back loading dock where they carefully placed the urns inside the two armored trucks. Within ten minutes, the auditorium building was evacuated and the armored trucks safely moved onto the airfield in one of the secure hangers.

General Yidlan sat quietly on a bench across the street from the auditorium while Dalia paced back and forth in front of him. "Doctor Herbst, please sit down. You're giving me an ulcer."

"General how can you be so calm?"

"Dalia, I learned a long time ago that once you've done everything you can and you've left the actual work to others, staying calm is the best approach. It sends a message to your troops that you're still in control, and that gives them the confidence they need to accomplish great things."

Dalia finally sat down next to Yidlan, but her stomach was churning. The minutes dragged on, but finally Lieutenant Joseph emerged from the front of the building and approached the general. "Sir, we disarmed two cartons of C4 explosives. My men have resumed searching for other devices, but these two are no longer a problem. They were set to be triggered with cellphones."

The general interrupted, "My guess is that my good friend Hakeem Kassab wanted to personally trigger the devices after all of the guests and dignitaries were on the stage. It would have made one hell of a statement don't you think, and it would have been on television all around the world. Lieutenant Joseph, let me have the cellphones. I want to make sure we trace the telephone number of whoever makes the call."

An hour later Joesph's team had completed their extensive search and had found no additional threats. With that announcement, the urns were returned to the auditorium and Dalia continued her preparations for the ceremony that was now only two hours away.

Chapter 76

The auditorium was filled to capacity a full thirty minutes before the beginning of the ceremony. The international press had been invited to the Haifa military base, and they were present in droves. Director Becker stood in front of a microphone in front of the large crowd of journalists and scientists, including representatives from Scientific American, National Geographic, and Archeology Today. He spoke to the guests about how the urns were found. He avoided any mention of the Waqf or how the urns were stolen, and then later recovered. Instead, he focused on the importance of the archeological find.

He then introduced Doctor Dalia Herbst, the scientist who would be coordinating an analysis of the contents of the urns. Dalia in turn introduced Doctor Lisa Green, the person who actually found the hidden scroll in the catacombs describing the location of the thirty-three urns. Lisa showed an overhead projection of the picture of the ancient scroll that had led to the discovery of the artifacts. She then showed a translation of the scroll and explained the meaning of the birthplace of the columns of Solomon and the Finger of God, and finally showed a map of where the urns were found in a hidden cave in the Timna Valley.

She pressed a button and a curtain rose exposing the thirty-three urns lined up in the clear-plastic chamber behind the podium. The crowd gasped at the enormity of the find. Lisa and Professor Braverman then put on protective clothing and entered the isolation chamber. While they were preparing to open the urns, Dalia explained the urns had been numbered and Doctor Green and Professor Braverman were going to open the urn with the lowest number, which was hopefully the urn containing the oldest documents.

Kassab sat at his desk in the Waqf headquarters building. Not only would the urns be destroyed with a simple phone call, but he would be able to witness the whole thing on his television. The world would soon know the true power of his movement. As Doctor Green and Professor Braverman entered the chamber he dialed the number of the first cellphone attached to the explosives. He waited a few tense-filled moments wanting to see the carnage created by the blast, but nothing happened. He quickly dialed the number of the backup cellphone and waited for it to ring. Again nothing was happening on the stage. The explosive charge wasn't going off as intended. What had gone wrong?

Kassab hurried from his office building, his rage building beyond what even he was capable of feeling. He called Abu Muhammad on his cellphone and demanded to know what had happened. Muhammad explained he had placed the explosives in the air duct last night, and he had no idea why the explosives never went off.

Hakeem walked aimlessly in the park across from his office, not really seeing any of the others enjoying a late afternoon walk. Instead he focused on revenge. He knew his own life was lost, but as Allah was his witness, others would pay a price, and as rational thought began to overcome his visible rage, he decided that he must end the life of the one person who had started this terrible affair.

While Kassab plotted his revenge, a video camera inside the isolation chamber allowed the reporters in the room and the world audience to see the actual opening of the first urn. Lisa was very nervous as she picked up a sterile scalpel and cut through the wax seal of the first urn. She then carefully pried open the clay lid protecting the contents of the urn for thousands of years. She looked into the urn with a flashlight and reported the presence of many scrolls filling the urn to capacity. Using sterile gloves, she carefully removed one of the scrolls with a long specially designed forceps. She cautiously lifted the scroll out of the urn and placed it on a white sterile drape. The parchment scroll seemed to be in perfectly preserved condition.

Lisa had been instructed on how to open ancient scrolls without damaging them. She followed the instructions, and after carefully unrolling the scroll, she placed the open scroll on a clear-plastic sheet and covered the open scroll with a second clear-plastic sheet.

Professor Braverman then stood in front of the scroll. He began reading the document and after a few minutes, he began to cry. The audience was silent, not even a cough or sneeze from the people witnessing the historic event. The professor turned to the crowd. "Forgive my tears," he said, "but this is the most extraordinary ancient document I have ever seen. It will take me several days to provide a perfect translation, but I will give you a rough translation."

He turned back to the document and spoke again into the microphone. *"In the sixteenth year of the reign of King David, the King decrees that the land of the Philistines be now and forever protected by General Jaazaniah ben Shaphan the victor in the battle against the Philistines. His land will extend from the Kingdom of Israel south to the lands of the Tribes of Arabu and from the Red Sea west to the Mediterranean Sea."*

The audience began clapping and stood in appreciation at the enormity of the implications of the words on the scroll. Not only was the Kingdom of David, the ruler of Israel, now vetted, but the validation of the land of Israel was confirmed for all time. For many who were there, it was the seminal moment in confirming the history of the Jewish people.

The celebration lasted well into the night. Director Becker bought dinner for everyone. Dalia was happier than she could ever remember, and why not; she would be heading a project more important than the Dead Seas Scrolls, one that might last her entire career.

Lisa on the other hand had mixed feelings. She was certainly excited about the first scroll and wondered what insight the other scrolls might provide into the history of the Jewish people. But she was planning on returning to California. She had just purchased her return ticket, and she dreaded the day when she would be saying good bye to Ari and her other friends.

It was after midnight when Ari and Lisa finally arrived back in his apartment. They both had done too much partying and immediately fell asleep.

Ari's phone rang a little after two o'clock and woke them both from a deep sleep. Ari handed Lisa the phone. "It's for you."

Lisa took the phone. "Hello, this is Lisa Green."

"Lisa, It's Dean Webber at the University. I've been trying to reach you all day. I finally got this telephone number from the Antiquities Authority. I saw the press conference on the television. I can't believe you were the one who discovered the ancient scroll. Listen, I know you're planning on coming back, but I've just talked to the Board of Regents, and I have an offer to make. We would like to fund a new position in the Department of History. The tenured position of Professor reports directly into me and funds a ten year Sabbatical for the study of the urns. On behalf of the university, I would like to offer you the position, on the condition that you agree to write a book on the findings of the ancient scrolls. What do you think?"

Lisa couldn't believe what she was hearing. "I'm sorry Dean Webber, did I hear you correctly; you want me to stay in Israel for ten years to write a book on the scrolls."

"Yes, that's right Lisa. I've seen your writing, and I know you have the skills to write an excellent manuscript. I'm sure it will become the definitive text on the meaning of the scrolls. So will you accept the position?"

"Yes, absolutely Dean Webber. I will accept the offer and work at writing the best historical text imaginable."

Dean Webber said, "I'll send the written offer to the Antiquities Authority. I'm sure you'll be pleased with the terms."

Lisa sat up against a pillow in shock. Ari looked at her after hearing only one side of the conversation. "What was that about?"

Lisa looked at him and began to cry. With tears flowing down her face, she said, "I'm staying here. The University wants me to stay and write a book about the scrolls. I can't believe it; they're going to fund a new position for ten years. I think he mentioned tenure. Oh Ari, I'm going to stay."

Ari, who was now wide awake, held Lisa in his arms. Now they were both crying; shedding tears of joy. Their lives had been changed forever. Suddenly, Ari got up from the bed and returned a minute later with a chilled bottle of Champagne and two glasses. He popped the cork and the beverage spilled onto the bed. They both laughed as Ari poured two full glasses. He looked his love in the eyes and said, "Here's to us and a new life together."

They clinked their glasses, and both downed the champagne in one long drink.

Chapter 77

Hakeem Kassab had been thinking irrationally for several hours. His rage had focused on Lisa Green. She had started all of this, and she would now pay the ultimate price. He knew she had moved in with the Israeli. He had been waiting outside Air's apartment and had seen them arrive a little after midnight. They had both looked in a festive mood, and that only increased his anger beyond his ability to think clearly. He was now operating on pure emotion.

He waited a few hours until he was certain both were asleep. The street was deserted, and he quickly gained entrance to the apartment's lobby. He found a back stairway and walked up to the third floor.

He looked down the hallway, and as expected, it was empty. He found Ari's apartment and placed his gun down on the hallway carpet. After checking for any residents in both directions, he began picking the lock on Ari's front door.

Lisa lay in bed trying to fall back to sleep. The day had been too much, and now this, the ability to stay in Israel and be with Ari, and to continue to work with the scrolls. It was all too good to be true.

Lisa heard the muffled scratching sound coming from outside Ari's apartment. As her senses, now fully heightened, focused on the strange sound, she realized that someone was trying to break into the apartment. She shook Ari awake and whispered to him.

He was up and alert in an instant. He ran to the front door just as the door swung slowly inward. Kassab was holding a pistol in his right hand and was surprised when his arm was suddenly grabbed.

Ari pulled Kassab into the center of the living room, trying to keep the man's pistol pointed away from his own body. Both men struggling for survival slammed into the living room couch. With both of Ari's hands trying to keep the pistol pointed safely away, Kassab's left hand was free to pummel Ari, and repeated blows struck Ari in the head. A strong blow bloodied Ari's nose, and blood ran down his face onto the floor. Ari kicked out with his right leg, and Kassab fell to the floor with Ari on top. The pistol was pressed between them as they rolled over and over, both men trying to gain an advantage.

Lisa was horrified at the fight unfolding before her. She had never seen this man before, but he was intent on killing Ari, and Lisa was not about to stand by and let it happen. She looked around the room for something to use to stop this assassin. Her eyes focused on the commando knife on the nightstand next to the bed. With no time to think of the consequences, she ran to the table and grabbed the knife. She rushed into the living room and carefully approached the two men who were rolling on the floor. She wasn't thinking; she was just reacting to the scene playing out on the floor before her. The two men rolled up against the living room wall with Kassab on top of Ari.

They were still struggling to achieve an advantage when Lisa decided to strike. She dropped down onto her knees and wedged Kassab up against the wall. She raised the military blade above her head and brought it downward into the center of Kassab's back. She pulled it out and then thrust the blade into his back a second and then a third time.

The muffled sound of the gun overwhelmed what had been a silent struggle. Lisa's brain had somehow forgotten about the gun in Kassab's hand, and now both men lay still on the floor. "My God, what have I done?" she screamed.

She stood up and looked on in horror at the two men. Finally there was movement, and Ari pushed Kassab's lifeless body off of him. Lisa rushed to his side and held him in her arms. They remained in that position for several minutes just demanding the comfort of each other's embrace.

They both finally stood up and backed away from Kassab's body. Ari, now fully recovered from the struggle, called Moshe Stern. Lisa, her body still shaking and her hands and feet covered in blood, sat down at the kitchen table. She looked at the body now dead on the floor. She had actually killed another person, and she realized she had no regrets. The man had been trying to kill her love, and she knew she would do anything to save him. She would do it again if she had to.

Ari pulled up a chair next to her and kissed her tenderly on the cheek. "Thank you, you saved my life."

Lisa started to cry. She was in emotional overload, and her body now shook uncontrollably. Ari's arms enveloped her body, and he held her in his arms. They remained in that position until the police arrived.

Two officers, with their guns drawn, entered the apartment and quickly concluded the threat had ended. Ari spoke to the officers and explained what had happened while Lisa sat motionless at the kitchen table, her eyes transfixed on the body lying on the floor. She was certain the Waqf would not stop until she and Ari had been killed. This was never going to end. How could she go on like this? She and Ari would be looking over their shoulders for the rest of their lives, never knowing when the next attack would occur.

Moshe Stern arrived a little after four o'clock. He took one look at the body lying on the floor and whistled. "Do you know who this is?"

Lisa and Ari both answered no.

"This, my friends, is Hakeem Kassab, the head of Waqf security. He and the Grand Mufti are the ones who've been giving all of these orders. His failed plot to destroy the urns at the ceremony must have been the last straw, and he decided to try to kill both of you as a final act of revenge."

Lisa asked, "Does his death mean they're going to stop trying to kill us?"

Stern answered, "Probably not; but it's time we put an end to the Waqf's activities. There's only one person standing in the way of your safety, and that's the Grand Mufti. It's time for our government to stop him once and for all. Lisa, I promise I'll take care of this. One way or the other, I'll take care of this."

Lisa was skeptical. Her life had been threatened too many times for her to believe there was any hope at all.

Stern continued, "By the way, the guy who planted the explosive device in the auditorium was picked up today. It seems Kassab called him after the bomb failed to go off. The IDF traced the call to an apartment in Haifa where they picked the guy up. He's agreed to cooperate, and he's singing like a bird."

Ari fixed a fresh pot of coffee, and as Forensics completed their work in the living room, he and Lisa sat out on the balcony. Lisa's body had stopped shaking and now as she looked out toward the Rock of the Dome and the West Bank, her mind finally returned to her recent promotion and her future studying of the scrolls.

"What are you thinking my love?"

"I'm tired of living in fear of the next attack on our lives. I refuse to keep looking over my shoulder."

Ari looked at the woman he loved with a tear in his eye. He pulled her toward him and kissed her passionately on the lips. "You know," he said, "I'm in love with one great lady."

Chapter 78

Moshe Stern called General Yidlan later that morning. "Chaimy, it's Moshe Stern."

"Moshe, it's good to talk to you again. I just want you to know, your niece is one hell of a woman."

"I agree Chaimy, but I'm slightly biased. I called to let you know that there was an incident at Ari's apartment early this morning. Hakeem Kassab tried to enter his place and kill Lisa and Ari. Luckily, they killed Kassab instead.

"I still have the matter of Professor Bornstein's murder to resolve. Here's my dilemma. We have more than enough evidence to bring the Grand Mufti to trial and probably get a conviction; but I hesitate in doing that. I think his arrest could create some serious political consequences for the Government. I think the Waqf will rally their supporters, and we could have some riots over this, perhaps even another intifada. The country doesn't need that right now."

"So what do you propose Moshe?"

"I think this might be a job for Mossad. Perhaps if the Grand Mufti has an accident, something that doesn't implicate Israel, it might allow justice to be served."

General Yidlan thought about Stern's proposal and laughed. "Moshe, since when does the legal justice system condone an assassination?"

"Chaimy, I'm a pragmatic detective. We don't need another intifada to break out over this; I just want justice to be served. What do you think?"

"I'll talk to the Prime Minister. Knowing him, I think he'll be in the mood to have the Mossad take care of this. I'll get back to you as soon as I know something definitive."

"Thanks Chaimy, I'll await your call.

Epilogue

The Mossad agents had been following the Grand Mufti for almost a month. Certainly killing the head of the Waqf wasn't a problem, but doing it in a way that wasn't perceived as an assassination was a big issue. They had only one chance to do it right.

The Grand Mufti was a creature of habit; he had lunch every Friday with Imam Wadi. The plan developed by the strike team involved taking advantage of this weekly meeting. One of the agents, posing as an Arab, took a job as a busboy at the restaurant where they dined. For three weeks he was one of the better employees at the restaurant.

Friday finally arrived, and the Grand Mufti sat at the same table as he always did. The Mossad agent delivered the bottled water to the table and slipped the liquid drug into the man's glass. The drug was well known in the Mossad. When placed in a drink, it resulted in an apparent heart attack and was very difficult to trace.

The Grand Mufti was eating his couscous with eggplant when he felt a sharp pain shooting up his left arm. He turned suddenly white and tried to stand up. He told his friend he was having a heart attack, and he collapsed onto the restaurant floor. The restaurant immediately called an ambulance, but the call was routed to another Mossad agent. The ambulance that arrived five minutes later took the Grand Mufti to a nearby hospital where a doctor used by the Mossad pronounced him dead on arrival.

The Grand Mufti's luncheon guest reported the heart attack back to the people inside Waqf headquarters, and after a quick review, the Waqf concluded the Grand Mufti's death was from natural causes.

¤ ¤ ¤

It took Dalia Herbst a few weeks to arrange a meeting with the Minister of the Interior. Her reputation as the woman in charge of the ancient scrolls now afforded her special privileges. Over the two hour meeting, Dalia retold the true unvarnished story of their quest for the ancient urns. She spent a great deal of time telling the minister about their rescue by Saladin and Malik. She then concluded by explaining to the minister about the inability of the Bedouins to lay any legal claim to the land of their ancestors.

"So what shall we do?" the minister asked.

Dalia answered, "Minister, I've been thinking about this problem for some time. I know there are major political problems here, and I understand the Government is always slow to act, but I think a good start would be to appoint a Special Commission to come up with a recommendation. I think the commission would be perceived as important if it was headed by a person everyone trusts, and I think the retired head of the Supreme Court would be the ideal person. I would also like to see Saladin Abdul-Hamid on the commission representing the Bedouins."

The minister agreed to consider Dalia's proposal. That was all that Dalia could do. She had no authority; she could only try to convince those in power about the fairness of the Bedouin's claims.

◘ ◘ ◘

Lisa had settled into her new life in Jerusalem. Dalia had arranged for her to get an office in her building, and she was spending most of her days at the military base in Haifa talking to the experts who were carefully removing, translating, and preserving the many scrolls in the thirty-three urns.

After dinner one night, Lisa and Ari walked in a park near his apartment enjoying the beautiful evening. She held him close and said, "I'm thinking I'm the luckiest woman in the world. I'm alive standing next to the man I love. I've just received a promotion and the assignment of a lifetime, and I'm overlooking the birthplace of modern religions. Both of us have lived a lifetime of excitement packed into just a few weeks, and none of us, not you or me or Dalia or Uri will ever be the same. I refuse to keep on looking over my shoulder in fear of the next attack on our lives. I'm going to put the fear of attack out of my mind and take each day as it comes."

Ari reached into his pocket and removed a small black-velvet bag. She opened the bag and out popped something that looked very familiar. It was the same statue of Ishtar she had found at the dig many weeks ago. Ari said, "I convinced Professor Bornstein's office to give it to you as a gift for your services at the dig."

Lisa put the bronze goddess with its new gold chain around her neck and kissed Ari on the cheek. "Wait," he said, "there's something else in the bag."

Lisa unfolded the second bit of tissue and a diamond engagement ring fell into her hand. She looked at her man. "Does this mean?"

Ari didn't let her finish. He kissed her deeply on her lips and said, "Yes it does!"

Made in the USA
Charleston, SC
20 April 2015